horizon

alyson noël

st. martin's griffin ☙ new york

HORIZON. Copyright © 2013 by Alyson Noël, LLC. All rights reserved. Printed in the United States of America. For information, address St. Martin's Press, 175 Fifth Avenue, New York, N.Y. 10010.

www.stmartins.com

Design by Anna Gorovoy

The Library of Congress Cataloging-in-Publication Data is available upon request.

ISBN 978-0-312-66489-3 (trade paperback)
ISBN 978-0-312-57717-9 (hardcover)
ISBN 978-1-250-02077-2 (e-book)

St. Martin's Griffin books may be purchased for educational, business, or promotional use. For information on bulk purchases, please contact Macmillan Corporate and Premium Sales Department at 1-800-221-7945, extension 5442, or write specialmarkets@macmillan.com.

First Edition: November 2013

10 9 8 7 6 5 4 3 2 1

Praise for *Fated* by Alyson Noël

"Alyson Noël paints a magical New Mexican landscape."

—*New Mexico Style*

"Noël does a terrific job of slowly unspooling secrets and motivations with writing that is both charismatic and spunky."

—*Los Angeles Times*

"A rush of romance will sweep you away in this hauntingly mystical read. I'm already as addicted to Daire and Dace as I was to Ever and Damen. Next book, please!"   —*Justine* magazine

"With fantastic characters and an amazing plot, *Fated* will suck you in and leave you breathless. Noël is a master with words . . . with passion and thrills around each corner, this book is a must-read."   —*RT Book Reviews* (Top Pick!)

"Atmospheric and enjoyable . . . Noël's many fans will be eager to find out what happens next."   —*Publishers Weekly*

"Readers will feel the pull of Daire's quest just as forcefully as Daire herself does, and will count the days until the release of *Echo*."

—*Shelf Awareness, Maximum Shelf*

"A fast and enjoyable read . . . with some very unique plot twists and balance among the romance, conflict, and family relationships."   —*Deseret News*

"Two boys, one light and one dark, factor heavily into the intriguing, twisting story line, which is sure to draw Noël's numerous fans."   —*Booklist*

can create a world filled with fast-paced, heartbreaking plots along with awesome characters and such a magical world."

—Cover Analysis

"I loved this book. All the characters were beautifully developed including some of the minor characters. . . . I, for one, had high expectations of this book because of *Evermore,* and *Fated* definitely met those standards."

—Flamingnet

"The world-building in *Fated* is fantastic. . . . The plot is amazing and the rich Native American history along with the supernatural elements of the book, just made it even better. . . . *Fated* is a story of *pure* magic—breathtaking and wonderful, *all at once.*"

—Kindle & Me

"*Fated* was absolutely original in its own way! From the vivid descriptions to the spiritual world the author, Alyson Noël, has cleverly created, I was so intrigued and stunned by this book that I can't wait to see where Noël takes this series because she sure as hell has a winner right here!"   —*Tales of the Inner Book Fanatic*

"This novel is something different from anything I've ever encountered. *Fated* has a rich mythology, full of spirit animals, spirit journeys, fate, soul-seeking, and of course, good and evil."

—Thirteen Days Later

also by alyson noël

In memory of Matthew Shear: A large-hearted soul with a booming laugh and a ready smile who took a chance on me eight years ago when he published my first novel. My life is forever changed for having known him.

Animal Spirit Guides

Rabbit

Rabbit represents creativity, fertility, and new life. Rabbit teaches us how to plan and how to set plans in motion. Commonly hunted, Rabbit creates tunnels in the earth, open in front and back, which it can use to escape, reminding us never to allow ourselves to be boxed into a corner. With its ability to move from a statuesque pose to great speed, and to turn rapidly and double back, Rabbit encourages us to take advantage of fleeting opportunities. Active at dawn and dusk, Rabbits are guides to the mystical world, showing us how to recognize hidden teachings, intuitive messages, and signs in the universe around us.

Ram

Ram represents new beginnings, balance, and imagination. Ram teaches us to trust our ability to land safely as we take advantage of new opportunities and pursue new endeavors. Able to gain a foothold on a tiny piece of rock, the spirit of the Ram is one of courage and balance as we move through life and along our spiritual path. Its spiral horn a symbol of creativity and imagination, Ram empowers us to be spontaneous and to seek out great adventures.

Bison

Bison represents abundance, gratitude, and the sacred life. Bison teaches us to work with the natural rhythm, to follow the easiest path, and not force our way through life. With its massive head and humped shoulders being symbolic of stored-up power and abundance, the spirit of the Bison reminds us that by combining our own efforts with that of the divine we can enjoy the abundance of the universe. Bison's enormous size cautions us to stay grounded to the earth and walk a sacred path, to always be humble and grateful for the gifts that come our way, and to honor ourselves and others.

Turtle

Turtle represents perseverance, determination, and longevity. Turtle teaches us self-protection through nonviolent defenses. A shore creature relying on both land and water, Turtle prompts us to protect the earth so that she can continue to nurture us and provide abundance. One of the oldest reptiles on our planet, the spirit of the Turtle instructs us to get in touch with our primal essence, to retreat inward, slow down, and express our ideas only when they are ready. With its keen ability to sense vibration through its skin and shell, Turtle encourages us to awaken our senses, both physically and spiritually.

Bobcat

Bobcat represents patience, insight, and solitude. Bobcat teaches us to be alone with ourselves without being lonely. An accomplished hunter that relies on strategy, stealth, and patience, Bobcat reminds us that to achieve our desires we must plan well, be agile, and above all be patient. With its sensitive tufted ears and acute eyesight, the spirit of the Bobcat encourages us to tap into the unseen world and seek out hidden meanings to better understand the spiritual path we are traveling. Its short bobbed tail, black on the tip and white underneath, is symbolic of Bobcat's power to turn the creative forces of life on and off as needed.

Our deepest fear is not that we are inadequate. Our deepest fear is that we are powerful beyond measure. It is our light, not our darkness that most frightens us.
—Marianne Williamson

spirit
horse

one

Daire

It's been months since I last had the dream.

Months since I was trapped in its unyielding grip.

And though I try to resist, try to force my way back to the safety of consciousness, I continue to slip.

I'm aware but not lucid.

The dream is not mine to control.

As always, it begins in the forest. A forest that exists in the Lowerworld—that unseen dimension yawning beneath this world, the Middleworld, with the Upperworld sprawling above.

It's a place I've visited many times, in both waking and dream states. A place that consists primarily of compassion, love, and light.

Primarily.

But not entirely.

Or at least not tonight.

It's Raven who leads me. Soaring above an unchanging landscape of crisp cool air and wide verdant lawns with lush bouncy blades that spring underfoot. His purple eyes glimmer, rushing me past a tall grove of trees cloaked with leaves so thick, only the faintest trace of light filters in.

Raven's driven by purpose.

I'm driven by need.

Along with an irrepressible longing to reunite with the boy who awaits me.

A boy who is no longer a stranger. No longer faceless and nameless.

Now that we've watched each other die, now that we've been intimate, there are no secrets between us.

In the dream, Dace bears the same glossy dark hair and gleaming brown skin he does in real life. The same astonishing icy-blue eyes banded by gold that reflect my image thousands of times.

Kaleidoscope eyes.

He's my fated one, as surely as I am his.

And yet, with so many answers secured, the question remains: *In this particular dream—which one of us will die?*

Raven lures me through a valley of boulders—past a swiftly moving stream teeming with vivid, blue fish—only to vanish the moment we've reached the clearing. Leaving me to stand on my own, running an anxious hand over the front of my dress. A dress that once seemed inexplicable, but that I now recognize as the one I wore on my return from the Upperworld.

Finally, the pieces of this strange, surreal puzzle begin to fall into place.

Though how this will end is anyone's guess.

"Daire."

He speaks my name from a place just behind me, and for one sweet moment, I shutter my eyes and inhale his deep, earthy sent. Stretching time for as long as I can, knowing all too well how brief this moment will be.

He places a hand on my shoulder and turns me to face him. And although I've played this role countless times, there's no suppressing the sharp intake of breath when my gaze meets the immaculate angles and curves of his face. The strong, smooth brow that can signal anger, amusement, or desire with only the slightest shift—the high, elegant cheekbones—the square chin and strong jaw—the sure, straight nose—the enticing, full lips. He stands before me in offering, his torso lean and bare. Displaying wide, strong shoulders, and finely drawn abs that narrow into slinky, trim hips where a pair of faded, old jeans dip precariously low.

He reaches toward me, lifts a hand to my face. Brushing his fingers around the curve of my jaw, he bestows on me a look that's meant to assure me that he's in on it too. Wise to the potential for danger ahead but determined to enjoy this scene until another one shifts into its place, we head for the other side of the forest and wade into the misty, swirling waters of the Enchanted Spring. Both of us all too aware this is where the dream takes a turn, yet, pawns that we are, we merge toward each other, unable to veer from the script.

Dace's fingers glide over my flesh, leaving ripples of warmth in their path, as his lips press urgently against mine. His kiss so bewitching, it renders me breathless, drunk with his touch, yearning for more.

He works the slim straps of my dress, pushing the fabric down past my shoulders, my waist, until I stand bared before him. Then he dips his head low and brings his mouth to my breasts. The feel of his tongue teasing my flesh, causing my legs to grow weak, my spine to yield. The two of us caught in the grips of the sweet, glorious pleasure of being together, until he lifts his chin and says, "It is time." His eyes are burning, deep, and fixed right on mine.

Quick to agree, I nod in reply. Sensing the truth behind the words, though I've no idea what they mean.

"There is no going back. You are meant to be mine."

Going back?

Why would I want to do that?

I was born to find him—of that I am sure.

I move past my thoughts and pull him back to me. My lips swelling, pressing, only to find Dace is no longer before me—someone else has taken his place.

Someone who bears the same strong, lean body—the same

sculpted face. And while the eyes share the same color, flecked by brilliant bands of gold, the similarity ends there.

These eyes are cold.

Cruel.

And instead of reflecting, they absorb like the void I sense them to be.

Cade.

My sworn enemy.

Dace's identical twin.

The one I was born to kill.

If he doesn't get to me first.

I yank hard at my dress in a desperate bid to cover myself, as I shove a hand to his chest and struggle to push him away. But he's unfeasibly strong and remains right in place.

"Where'd he go? What'd you do?" My gaze darts all around.

My question met with a tilt of his head, a quirk of his brow, and an absurdly muttered, "Who?"

"Dace! Where is he? What have you done?" The words ring high-pitched and shrieky, though they're no match for the frantic pounding of blood rushing my ears, my heart pummeling my rib cage.

"I am Dace." He smiles. "And Dace is me. We are one and the same. I thought you knew that by now?" He grins, and I watch in horror as his face morphs to resemble Dace's before returning to his own sinister visage. Transmuting back and forth, over and over as I slam a fist against his shoulder, fight to break free.

This is not how the dream goes.

I don't like this new ending.

"The light and the dark. The yin and the yang. The negative and the positive. We are connected, bound in mystical ways. One cannot exist without the other. As you already know."

"You may be connected, but you're *not* the same. Dace is *nothing* like you! You're a demon—a trickster—a—" His face morphs back to Cade, and I finally break free. Desperate to find my way to dry land, only to discover the landscape has changed.

The Enchanted Spring has morphed into a steep, narrow mesa jutting out of the earth.

Before me lies an endless abyss.

Behind me stands Cade.

Preferring to die on my own terms, my own way, I inch forward until my toes clear the edge.

"Daire, please. No more games. No more running away," he pleads.

I gather my dress in my hands, only to find it changed too. No longer the white gown I wore in the Upperworld, this gown is a deep, sunset red, with swirling skirts, an open back, and a deeply plunging neckline.

Without hesitation, I lift my arms to either side and teeter precariously. Allowing the wind to catch me, render me floaty and weightless as I drift through the ether as light as a Raven feather.

A glorious sensation I desperately try to prolong—though the effect is short lived when Cade grasps the back of my gown and hauls me back to him.

Circling an arm at my waist, he clutches me tightly, and says, "Stop fighting me. Like it or not, this is your destiny. It's time we finally do this."

I try to respond, but my voice is on mute.

Try to shirk from his touch, but I'm frozen in place.

Caught in the endless abyss of his gaze, I am helpless, his to command.

Watching as he lifts my hand before me and slides a brilliant blue tourmaline ring onto my finger.

two

Dace

I wake to the sound of screaming.

The sound of screaming and someone pounding hard on my chest.

I bolt upright, flip on the bedside lamp, and catch Daire by the wrist before she can wale on me again.

"Daire—" I whisper her name, fight to still her body, her breath. Ease her away from the darkness of nightmares and back to the light of consciousness again.

Her lids snap open, and when she sees me, she starts swinging with renewed ferocity.

"Daire—it's me! Stop. Stop it—you're safe—you're okay."

She rears back, yanks her hands from mine, and flicks on her lamp. Her breath hectic, pulse racing, she pulls her knees to her chin and watches me with a deep wary gaze.

I remain on my side. Try to give her some space. Time to wrestle her way out of whatever twisted dream has left her in such a scared state.

"How can I know for sure it's you with your hair like that?" She glares, pulls a grim face, causing me to run a self-conscious hand through my newly shorn locks. "How can I be sure you're not Cade?"

"You serious?" I flinch at her words. Scold myself not to feel hurt. It's a mistake a lot of people have made since I got my new look. Still, I never expected that from her. Right from the start, she was able to determine what only few could see—it's the eyes that define the real difference between Cade and me.

I inch toward her slowly, taking great pains not to alarm her. I angle my face toward the light so she can better see my face, my eyes. Allowing a few beats to pass before she heaves a deep sigh and relaxes her stance.

"Care to talk about it?" I risk a quick glance at the clock and stifle a yawn. Noting the small hand on the two, the big on the five. No wonder it's still dark out.

"No." She slips down the mattress, props her head on a pillow, and sprawls her bare legs before her. "I mean, maybe. Yeah." She sneaks a look at me. "You sure you're not too tired?"

I shake my head, rub a hand over my chin in place of the white lie I choose not to verbalize.

"Well, in a nutshell, I had the dream." Her shoulders sink when she says it, as though releasing a very great burden.

I nod, having figured as much. No stranger to the dream, I know firsthand how disturbing it is to watch my brother kill Daire while I helplessly look on. That dreadful image has a way of lingering well into the waking state—haunting me for days.

Only in Daire's dream, she watches me die at Cade's hand.

Though from everything she's told me, the effect is the same.

Either way, there's no denying the overall message screams loud and clear:

Daire and I may be fated—but we're fated to end.

Still, no matter how insistent, I refuse to believe it.

Refuse to give it any real weight.

Whether it's some kind of prophecy—or Cade's twisted machinations invading our sleep—I can't say for sure.

What I do know is that the things we most fiercely believe in have a way of coming true.

And so I choose to believe in us.

Believe in a future that is ours for the making.

After losing my soul, and nearly losing Daire as well, just six months earlier, I know how empty my world is without her. Never again will I allow myself to doubt the rightness of the two of us together.

I will do anything to be with this girl.

I rest a hand on her shoulder, gather a lock of her soft, silky hair between two of my fingers. Quick to remind her that we already lived the dream last Christmas Eve when we watched it play out in real time. Cade killed her, and having discovered that Cade and I are connected—that if he goes, I go—if he lives, I live—I slammed the athame into my gut in an attempt to set things right once again.

Only it didn't quite go as planned . . .

"But this dream had a new ending." She averts her gaze, pulls her shoulders in, causing my hand to drop to my side as I brace for what's next. "He . . ." She makes a face, licks her lips, and starts again. "His face switched between yours and his, and then, when it settled on his, he forced a ring onto my finger."

I flinch, unsure what to say. So I stare at the peeling, bubbled paint on the far wall and opt for silence instead.

But when she huffs under her breath, when her gaze bores into my cheek, I know she's waiting for me to respond. To say something reassuring. Convince her it's not as bad as she thinks.

Being a guy who works better with details and facts, I blurt out the first thing that springs into my head. "Are you saying he proposed? Like—down on his knees asking for your hand?" Instantly aware that I said the wrong thing when I see the look that she shoots me.

Her jaw set, arms crossed in defiance over her chest, she tilts her chin and says, "No knees. Just a ring. A big, shiny, blue tourmaline practically the size of a boulder." She lifts her hand, glares hard at her ring finger, as though half-expecting to find the ring still there.

"So he wanted to marry you or claim your soul?"

"Where Cade's concerned, I'm sure it's one and the same."

I nod. Allowing a few beats to pass before I say, "Okay, so where do I fit in?"

She slews her gaze toward me.

"Well, from the way you've pretty much staked your claim on your side of the bed, I'm guessing the dream version of me did something bad. And, well, whatever it was, I apologize. Had I actually been there, I would've reacted differently, I assure you."

She shakes her head, pushes her hair from her eyes. "It's just— well, first you and I were kissing, you know, like the dream goes . . . but then, the next thing I knew, Cade had taken your place, and—"

"Sounds like the usual script to me," I cut in, but again I've said the wrong thing.

"Hardly." She mumbles a few unintelligible words under her breath. And while she doesn't quite roll her eyes, by the way her cheeks tense, I know that she wants to. "Anyway—" She sighs, forces herself to move on. "When I asked what happened to you—he said you were one and the same. That there was no distinction, no difference, no divide. That you are bound—couldn't exist apart from each other—"

I lean against the pillows, go back to staring at the ugly far wall. Trying to keep the edge from my voice but coming nowhere close to succeeding. "And since no one's seen Cade since the Rabbit Hole blew up six months ago on New Year's Eve—and since not long after that climactic event I decided to chop off my hair, which is still much longer than his, but hey, a minor detail we shouldn't get caught up in, you actually think I might be Cade pretending to be me." I shake my head but, like Daire, stop short of rolling my eyes.

My brother is despicable.

Evil.

My brother is solely responsible for killing her grandmother. And yet she's confusing me with him?

"You honestly think I got some crazy, mirrored contact lenses so my eyes would reflect in the way you've come to expect? You honestly can't tell that when I say *I love you* I am speaking from the very deepest part of me? You honestly can't tell by the way I touch you, look at you, that you are absolutely everything to me?"

"Dace—" She rolls toward me, places her hand over mine, and looks at me with those astonishing emerald-green eyes. "I'm sorry I said it. Truly, I am. It was stupid, and paranoid, and completely nonsensical, and pretty much the opposite of how a good, responsible Seeker is supposed to react in times of great stress. It's just that . . ." She swallows, lifts her shoulders, and goes on to add, "Sometimes, I can't help but think that I'm missing something. Some terribly obvious clue that's staring right at me. And then, when I had the dream and I woke up next to you . . . well, for that split second I thought—"

"You thought I might be the clue. You thought you were sleeping with the enemy." The moment I take in her face, the fight seeps right out of me. She's scared. Uncertain. Her burdens are great. And ever since Paloma passed, she's felt alone in the world. It's my job to love and support her. It's my job to provide strength when she needs it. I wrap my arms around her, encouraging her to inch closer as she closes her eyes and buries her face in my chest. "You haven't missed anything." I whisper the words into her soft silky hair. Drop a long string of kisses along the top of her head.

She pulls away ever so slightly and gazes at me with eyes that betray the depths of her anxiety. "But I have." She nods fervently. "I'm absolutely sure of it. No way can things truly be as peaceful as they might seem on the surface."

"Don't we deserve a little peace?" I pull her back to me, deluding myself into thinking that if I can just hug her enough, love her enough, I can vanquish her fears.

"This is Enchantment." The sound that follows is the closest thing to a laugh that I've heard from her in a while. "Since when does anyone get what they deserve?" She mumbles that last part into my chest, peering up at me to see how I react.

I crack a smile, hoping she'll crack one too. But the moment is lost, and in the span of a breath she's off and running again.

"I've gone over it countless times." She pushes into a sitting position. "And I've absolutely no doubt Cade killed Paloma via that cursed tourmaline I unwittingly gave her. I've researched it a good bit, and it's not nearly as whacked as it seems. Crystals and gems emit energy. Everything, at its very essence is comprised of energy. And while energy never dies, it can be altered, transformed, and in the wrong hands, a gem can be cursed with a hook that connects the recipient to the giver. Allowing them to either control the receiver's soul, claim the receiver's soul, or end the receiver's soul—depending on the intention."

The words leave me as cold as they did the first time I heard them. Though I'm not sure why she sees fit to repeat them, unless she's in search of reassurance, which I'm more than happy to provide. "I don't doubt you, Daire. Heck, Leftfoot, Chepi, and Chay have already confirmed it."

She lowers her gaze to her legs and flexes her calves, causing the long, taut muscles lining the front of her thighs, the result of daily six-mile runs, to lift and swell in a way so enticing, I'm forced to steer my gaze elsewhere.

"Thing is—if the elders are right, then how come everyone who attended the Rabbit Hole New Year's Eve party left with a swag bag containing a tourmaline, and yet not one of them is showing even the slightest sign of any ill effects?" She lifts her gaze to me, draws the sheet to her waist. "People are living like they've always lived. If anything, they're living a little better. I don't know if you've noticed, but Enchantment doesn't seem quite as depressed and gray as it once did. The citizens aren't as downcast. They step lighter, laugh more often and easily—"

"Maybe they're just happy to live in a Richter-free town? Maybe they're thrilled that for the last six months, there hasn't been a single sighting of Cade, Leandro, or Gabe. Don't forget, you and I both watched Cade run into that smoldering building—maybe El Coyote is finally dead? Maybe Phyre and her crazy, snake-wrangling, doomsayer dad, Suriel, did us a favor?"

Though I wasn't entirely convinced of what I just said, Daire is even quicker to dismiss it. "They're not dead. Not even close." She gives a firm shake of her head. "Don't forget, Cade was in human form when he ran into that burning building. He was unable to shift into his demon self. Which means if he went, you'd be gone too."

"But I'm still here, and I cut my hair, and now you're suspicious." I drop my chin to my chest, hardly able to believe I brought the conversation full circle again. Still, now that it's out there, we may as well clear this thing up so we'll never have to revisit it.

It never once occurred to me that a haircut could cause such a fuss. Had I known, had I even the slightest inkling of the kind of upset it would cause, I would've left it alone. Truth is, I'm not even sure what compelled me. I guess, ever since last New Year's Eve, when I found myself overcome by a strange, all-consuming force that never quite made itself known (but that's definitely responsible for saving my life), I've felt changed.

Altered at the deepest part of my core.

Like I was on my way to becoming someone else.

Something else.

And ever since, the old me no longer rests quite as easily in my skin.

Since most transformations begin with the physical, I decided to start with my hair.

Hoping to surprise Daire, I went to Lita for help. And by the way Lita reacted, jumping up and down while squealing and clapping her hands, you would've thought I'd given her the winning lottery ticket. Turns out, the girl loves a makeover.

I'd barely broached the idea before she was dragging me into her car and racing toward her salon.

"We're gonna lop off this crazy mop!" she announced, dragging me inside by the shirtsleeve and pushing me in front of her stylist, but not before adding, *"Finally!"*

Soon after, they threw a robe on me, plunked me down in a chair for a wash and condition, and then into another chair for the cut. With Lita hovering nearby the whole time, shouting a list of detailed directions, as though she'd been planning this moment since the first day we met.

"You'll need to cut at least five inches off the back," she told the stylist. "Maybe even six." She scrunched her nose at my offending looks, clucking her tongue against the inside of her cheek and shaking her head in disgust. "Then add some layers around the face. And make sure you keep them long and soft and kind of messy looking, so it appears like it's meant to look tousled and natural since we both know he probably won't ever brush it." She chased that last part with a little laugh to soften the blow, leaving me to wonder once again what my former spirit guide, Axel, could possibly see in this girl.

"Oh—but not too short!" Lita squealed the second the stylist lifted her shears. "Whatever you do—do *not* make him look like his twin!"

I'm guessing the stylist was used to Lita's demands, because she just smiled and nodded and went about the business of cutting my hair. And by the time she set down her scissors and I looked in the mirror, I couldn't do anything but stare, as the stylist smiled, and Lita clapped her hands and cried, "Well, congratulations, Dace Whitefeather—you just took your first step toward cool."

Though, unfortunately, Daire's reaction wasn't quite as appreciative. And while she didn't quite mistake me for Cade (or at least not back then anyway), it took her some time to come around. Though from the way this is going, I guess she's still not entirely onboard.

"Dace—" Daire squirms toward me again and cups her palm to either side of my face. "I'm sorry. Truly. I didn't mean it like that. Or, maybe I did—I don't know. I just—I feel so off-kilter. I can't shake this sense of foreboding. This deep certainty that things aren't quite what they seem. I'm convinced El Coyote is still out there, and Leandro and Cade are just biding their time, licking a few minor wounds, and lying low in an attempt to lure me into a state of complacency . . ."

"Only they'll never succeed." I place my hands over hers and fold them between us. "Because you're way ahead of them, Santos. Your guard is up, you're alert to the signs, and if it turns out you're right, when they come out swinging, you'll be ready."

"Will I?" She tilts her head, studying me with eyes gone red and glittery, while her bottom lip displays the tiniest hint of a quiver.

"Of course you will." I pull her into my arms. Holding her tightly until her body begins to slacken and yield, and my breath rises and falls in tandem with hers.

With her daily runs and punishing workouts, her strict healthy diet that allows no room for even the smallest indulgence—with her incessant focus on learning Paloma's craft and becoming the very best Seeker she can—I sometimes forget just how vulnerable she really is. But here, in my arms, with her skin so soft and her heart beating gently next to mine, I'm awash in shame over what a fool I've just been.

None of this was ever about me. This entire discussion may have been triggered by the dream, and the certainly hideous memory of my brother forcing a ring onto her finger, but it was never about my hair.

Never about her mistaking me for Cade.

That was all just a smoke screen for what's really bothering her.

She misses her grandmother.

She's wracked with a mountain of grief she insists on keeping tightly in check.

And until she's able to confront it head-on—it's my job to provide comfort, along with a safe place to land in the middle of chaos.

I pull her closer until the matching gold keys we wear at our necks as a symbol of our love clink lightly together, as I whisper soft words in her ear. Reminding her that she's not alone—we're in this together. I will never, ever leave her.

"If Paloma was here, she could help me see what I'm missing. She was tuned in to everything, never missed a sign. If my *abuela* was here, she would . . ." Daire chokes back a sob, shuts her eyes tightly against the deluge of tears she refuses to shed.

I bring my palms to her face and press my lips against hers. Whispering, "Hey there, green eyes, it's going to be okay. Really, I'm here. I'll always be here. We'll get through this together. I promise . . ." Hushing her fears with my kiss, I go about distracting her the best way I can.

three

Daire

This time when I wake, it's in the nest of Dace's arms cradled snugly around me. His soft, even breath pushing at the side of my cheek.

I turn my head slowly and fill my eyes with the beautiful slumbering sight of him. My gaze trailing over the taut muscles of his chest, the valley of his abdomen, to the soft trail of hair that leads from the edge of his navel to parts now obscured by the sheet.

He's so loving, so loyal, so decent and *good*, I can hardly conceive how I could ever, even in one dream-dazed, delusional moment, mistake him for Cade.

They may be identical on the surface, Dace may have a piece of Cade's dark soul lodged inside, but that's where the resemblance ends.

They are nothing alike.

He stirs. Awakened by the weight of my look, he curls his arm tighter and pulls me so close there's no denying his need is once again matched by my own.

No matter how many times we're together, no matter how many mornings we wake up like this, it always seems there's more to discover.

Sometimes I feel like I'll never uncover the full extent of his mysteries.

The thought makes me smile.

I allow my mind to project into a faraway future. Imagining how we might look with wizened faces and graying hair. Still loving, still laughing, still adoring, still discovering . . .

Though no sooner have the pictures begun to unfold than I force myself to shake free of the thought.

Dreaming of the future is a frivolous indulgence I cannot afford. Paloma warned me from the start that Seekers are not known for their longevity—and their romantic relationships always end tragically.

The memory of her words causing an involuntary flinch that prompts Dace to say, "What is it?" He lifts his lids slowly, displaying icy-blue eyes glazed with sleep and desire.

I shake my head and press my lips to his, trailing my fingertips along the column of his throat where I pause on his pulse. Shirking all thoughts of the past, along with all wishes for the future, I settle into the present—the only moment I can ever truly claim for my own.

Dace meets my kiss with warm urgent lips, as my hands grip his shoulders and pull him so close our bodies become a tangle of tongues and limbs pushed urgently together in a desperate bid to be joined. Until he maneuvers me beneath him in one seamless move and eases himself inside.

We mold and cling, separating for a few excruciatingly delicious moments, only to rejoin so completely there's no boundary between us. No way to tell where Dace leaves off and I begin. Our hearts as bound as our flesh, we soar in tandem—pausing for one deliriously heady moment, before falling into a sated, spent heap.

When I open my eyes, Dace is propped on his elbow, his gaze freely roaming my face. "I never get tired of looking at you."

I bite my lip and grin. Trying not to think about the mascara smudges under my eyes, the sheet creases marking my cheek, my hair lying limp against my forehead. I just smile like I believe him, and return his adoring look with one of my own. "You know, I think I'm actually beginning to like your new look." I bring my fingers to his brow, brush the tips against his long sweep of bangs. "Who knew Lita had such vision?"

He catches my hand in his and looks at me as though he's about to reply, but instead clamps his lips shut as though he thought better of it.

"I know what you're thinking." I rise onto my elbow, fluff my pillow a bit, and lean back against it. "It took me a while to come around, but I truly do mean it. This new look really highlights your face. And you know how I feel about your face . . ."

He shakes his head. Shoots me a look that invites further elaboration.

So I drop a few kisses onto his forehead, his chin, his lips to better illustrate. And just like that, I'm lured right back into the magick of him.

But with a full day of training and appointments ahead, I force myself to push away from the bed and follow the haphazard trail of clothes I left on the floor late last night in my rush to be with him.

"That's it?" Dace inches his way up the headboard to watch me get dressed. "You just love me and leave me? Is that how this is?"

"Yep." I retrieve my shorts from the crumpled heap on the floor and sneak a leg in, followed by the other. Performing an exaggerated shimmy as I ease them up over my hips in a move that is admittedly performed purely for his own viewing pleasure.

"Tease." He retrieves my bra from under his pillow and flings it at me, chasing the word with a grin.

"You're the tease." I catch the bra in my fist and struggle to get the clasp and straps properly situated.

"How do you figure?" He rubs his chin, shoots me a playful look.

"You're the one who won't move in with me."

"Oh. That." In one fluid move, he's off the bed and searching for a clean pair of jeans from the folded-up pile in the plastic laundry basket that stands in for a closet. An attempt to evade a conversation I'm determined to have.

"I really don't get your resistance," I say, and not for the first time. "I mean, we're together pretty much all the time anyway. And if we lived together, I wouldn't have to leave here every morning, and you wouldn't have to work so hard to keep this place going. You know, two birds, one stone."

His fingers freeze on his zipper as his gaze lifts to meet mine. "How can you say stuff like that?"

"Like what?"

"Two birds, one stone. Sheesh, Daire, you're guided by Raven. How do you think he'd feel to hear you say that?"

"You changing the subject?"

"Did it work?" He cracks a mischievous grin.

"Not even close." I frown and pull on my tank top, then sit on the old wooden trunk shoved in one corner, and slide my feet into my sneakers.

"Okay, I admit, I'm old-fashioned. There are worse crimes, you know."

"Old-fashioned?" I make a sound between a snort and a laugh. "Please." I roll my eyes, scrape my long, tangled hair back into a ponytail. "Nothing old-fashioned about what we just did." I nod toward the bed, hoping to glimpse a blush at his cheeks. It's not often I get to see such a thing.

"I'm old-fashioned when it counts. Which means we're not going to live together because it's convenient, or saves money, or whatever other reason you want to drum up. When we do live together, and I fully intend that we will, it'll be because we're properly wed."

"*Properly wed?*" I shake my head. Make a face of distaste. Go about adjusting the soft buckskin pouch Paloma gave me, the one that holds the collection of magickal talismans I earned during my Seeker training, along with the beautiful turquoise heart Dace gave me. "Don't you think we should maybe graduate from high school first? And then, oh, I don't know, go to college, then on to grad school. Rack up a whole slew of impressive degrees, score the job of our dreams, win a ton of promotions, and then, when there are no more summits to scale, we settle into the fiction that is the happily ever after of holy matrimony?"

Dace shoots me an appraising look, whistles softly under his breath. "Wow, someone has marriage issues."

"I grew up on movie sets." I shrug at the memory. "Surrounded by celebrities who were either falling in and out of marriages every ten seconds or cheating on the spouses they had with anyone who was willing to bed them. All of which may have left me a tiny bit jaded."

"A tiny bit?" Dace quirks a brow, pulls a worn, gray V-neck T-shirt over his head. The one that molds to his chest, clings to his abs, and accentuates his biceps, leaving me no choice but to force my eyes away if I've any hope of getting on with my day. "It's not like I plan on proposing tomorrow, or even next year. Just . . . someday."

"Fine," I say. "We'll deal with your *someday* when we get there. *If* we get there. But I'm warning you—no public displays. No stadium jumbotron half-time proposal. No hiding the ring at the bottom of my champagne glass. Nothing you'd ever see in a movie or some cheesy reality TV show."

"So, these are the rules for the proposal you don't actually want?"

"That's the starter list. There's more. Believe me, much more. But until then, I'm afraid you'll just have to put up with Love 'Em and Leave 'Em Santos, all because you won't accept *my proposal* to come live with me, rent free." I keep my tone light, jokey. Refusing to betray the deeply rooted fear that our future is so uncertain, we probably shouldn't tempt it with conversations like this.

Before Paloma died, she gave me a lineage transmission that allowed me to see the kind of things it would've taken her many years to teach. Including the tragic story of her past—how her husband, my grandfather, Alejandro (a Brazilian Jaguar shaman of the highest order), was killed at the hands of the Richters—along with her only child, my dad, Django, when he was still just a teen. Bestowing me with the breadth of her knowledge and insights in no more than a flash.

I also saw the story of every Seeker who walked before me.

Watched as they all—every last one of them—fell at the hands of Coyote.

So why should I be any different?

Why do I deserve the kind of happily ever after denied to my ancestors?

"Don't doubt the future, Daire."

I return to Dace. Surprised to find him standing before me, displaying his uncanny ability to read every shift in my mood. I ease my face into a tight grin, quickly turn away, and riffle through my bag, mumbling, "How can I not?"

"Because I know something you don't."

Just as intended, the words lure me in, coaxing me to face him again. "Oh yeah, and what's that? Care to share this great wisdom of yours?"

Without the slightest trace of mirth, he places a hand on each of my shoulders, and fixes his gaze intently on mine. "There's only one force more powerful than evil—"

I blink a few times, drawing a blank on what that might be. Clearly, he's not referring to me. No Seeker has ever successfully kept evil at bay—or at least not for very long.

"Love."

I can feel the word as he says it.

Can actually feel the force of it shooting toward me as it rolls off his tongue—emanates from the tips of his fingers. Its ferocity—

its urgency—its absolute, undeniable truth leaving me so startled, I can't think of a single thing to say in reply.

"Love, Daire. Love is stronger than evil. Love is the answer. Love is all there is. Love conquers. Love heals. Love unites. All you need is love. Love makes the world go round . . ."

The energy continues to swirl all around me, causing my head to spin, my heart to flutter—lasting only as long as Dace maintains his grip on my shoulders. The moment he drops his hands and steps back, the illusion is gone. Leaving me sad, deflated, and more disappointed than I care to let on that, while the sentiment sounds nice on the surface, it can't be that easy.

As much as I long to believe him, it's wishful thinking at best, and I can't afford to fall into that trap. I've spent the last few months preparing to avenge my *abuela*'s death and rid the world of Richters once and for all. I can't risk going soft.

"Mmm . . . I'm pretty sure it's money that makes the world go round. I'm pretty positive that's how the song goes." I guard my heart by deflecting his words with a sarcastic reply, but as soon as it's out, I flinch with embarrassment. The words ring unnatural and forced—stinging like a betrayal after all we've been through.

I bite my lip hard and return to the search through my backpack, but when Dace grasps my hand, urging me to look at him, I can't help but give in.

His tone as serious as his face, he says, "Not our song. Not this song. Not the song of you and me."

He speaks with such conviction, I'm just about to yield, when I remember the lineage transmission Paloma gave me and the undeniable truth she revealed.

There's no disputing the facts that unfolded before me that day.

Still, it doesn't stop me from melting just a little when Dace pulls me toward him and presses his lips to the tip of my nose.

"All you have to do is believe. Have a little faith. That's really all that's required. Miracles aren't nearly as uncommon as people like to think. Leftfoot says they're manifested by love, and we've got that in spades. No reason we can't work a few miracles of our own."

I soften my stance. Willing to concede that he just might be right. That it really might be as simple as that. Paloma always said that intent is magick's most important ingredient. Maybe if I just allow myself to believe hard enough . . .

I shake my head and force myself to pull away. Force myself to say, "You work on believing, while I go work out."

"Skeptic." He grins.

"Optimist." I playfully stick out my tongue.

"You got time for coffee?"

I shake my head.

"Want a ride?" He swipes his keys off the dresser, jangles them before me.

"Nah, I think I'll run."

He lifts a brow.

"May as well squeeze in a workout before the temperature has a chance to shoot into the triple digits again."

"You know it's okay to take a break now and then?"

I choose to ignore that. I can't afford breaks. Can't afford to let down my guard.

"Fine. Then at least wear this to keep the sun off your face." He tosses me a baseball cap advertising a surf brand. "And say hey to Axel." He follows me out the front door and down the rickety steps that lead to the parking lot.

"At least *he* agreed to live with me." I glance over my shoulder, wait for Dace to catch up.

"The way I remember it, he had nowhere else to go." He squeezes my hand, gives a good-natured grin.

"And you're not even the least bit jealous?" I angle my face toward his, catching the amused glint in his eyes.

"You serious?" He shakes his head. "Jealous of Axel?"

"Yeah, of Axel," I say, feeling inexplicably defensive, but then my emotions are all over the place. "A single guy who's actually pretty good-looking if you like tall, strong, angelic types with lots of muscles and lavender eyes. He was practically moved into my old room before I could even finish making the offer."

Dace stops beside his truck. "Daire, I'm not jealous of Axel. For one thing—he was my spirit guide since I was a baby, and he still feels the need to look after me even though he's officially been stripped of the title. For another—I trust you. I trust in our love. After all, I am the optimist, remember?"

"And third?" I place a hand on my hips. "I can see it in your eyes, there's a third."

"And third—do I even need to mention Lita?" He laughs, causing his irises to glimmer in a way that's mesmerizing. "You may be the Seeker, but are you seriously willing to get between Lita Winslow and the professed love of her life?"

I dip my head and sigh, chasing it with a groan for good measure. Since the moment school ended, Lita has devoted her entire summer to being with Axel. Which means she's been a permanent fixture in my den—when they're not holed up in his room.

Yet another star-crossed romance that was doomed before it could properly start.

Or at least according to Paloma, who warned me it would never amount to anything good.

Paloma was pragmatic. A realist, like me. And while it's really quite refreshing to be around a true believer like Dace, I can't quite convince myself to join him in that eternally happy place.

"Lita's pretty territorial where Axel's concerned. I'm not sure even someone as powerful as the Seeker could forge a wedge between them," Dace says, breaking me out of my reverie and proving, once again, just how tuned in he is to my moods.

"Speaking of powerful . . ." I leave the question to dangle, there's no need to finish. We both know I'm referring to last New Year's Eve when all hell broke loose and Dace found himself in the grips of an incredible shift he couldn't quite shake, didn't want to shake, as he tells it.

Though despite his optimism, I know he's concerned it might've been the result of the dark bit of soul he stole from his brother that's still lodged inside. And I can't say I've ruled it out either.

"No sign of the beast." He opens the door of his truck and tosses his bag onto the seat. "Must be lying dormant." He turns back to me and tilts his face toward the sun, shielding his eyes with his hand. "Sure you don't want a ride? Looks like it's gonna be another scorcher."

I shake my head, shake out my limbs. Try to loosen them up for the long run ahead.

"Okay, then." He climbs into his truck. "See you tonight?"

I nod.

"Your place, my place, or the Enchanted Spring?" He closes the door between us and leans out the driver's side window.

"My place." I make a face when I say it. Still feels weird to refer to it as mine and not Paloma's, but I'm quick to push the thought from my head. "Xotichl and Auden are stopping by. And of course, Lita and Axel will be there."

Dace gives me a swift kiss good-bye and revs up his truck, as I take a deep breath, adjust my cap, and break into a run.

four

Lita

I pop the oven door open and frown. Although I followed Paloma's recipe to the letter, my blue-corn muffins don't smell like Paloma's, don't look like Paloma's, and how come they're all sunken in the middle instead of fat and fluffy like hers always were?

"How long have you been awake?"

Axel pads into the kitchen, raking a hand through his platinum-blond, sleep-tousled curls as I slam the oven door closed, and hope that between now and the next five minutes when the timer goes off, some of Paloma's kitchen magick will begin to kick in.

Though deep down inside I know the truth—Paloma is the missing ingredient. There's just no replacing her. Most likely we'll be having stale bagels for breakfast again.

I toss an oven mitt onto the counter and sigh. "Couldn't sleep. And I didn't want to wake you, so I thought I'd make us some breakfast. But from the looks of things, that's going to require a miracle, so don't get your hopes up." I allow my gaze to roam the expanse of his smooth, well-muscled chest, down the length of his finely chiseled abs, all the way to the elastic waistband of his new gray sweatpants.

"As a Mystic, I've worked plenty of miracles." He crosses the kitchen until he's standing before me, lowering his head to drop a kiss onto my lips. "How bad is it?" He glances toward the oven. "Should I perform a healing?" He wraps his arms around me, holds me tight at the waist, and centers his deep purple gaze on mine.

"I'm pretty sure it's well beyond that. But you could fix your sweatpants." I jerk the tag at his waist. "They're on backward."

He casts a sheepish glance down the length of him and laughs. "Thought they felt a bit off. Loose in some places, snug in others. Guess I'm still not used to these things."

"You mean, pants?" I stifle a giggle. Enjoying the spectacle of watching him drop them to the floor and getting 'em turned right around without a hint of embarrassment, as I sneak an anxious glance toward the door. The last thing I need is for Daire to walk in and catch Axel standing naked in her kitchen. "Guess it takes some getting used to." I cock my head to the side, feigning a look of deep thought. "After all, the separate leg holes do require an entirely different skill set from wearing a dress."

"Tunic." Axel smiles, grasps me about the waist once again. "In the Upperworld, I wore a tunic. The females wore dresses."

"An important distinction." My gaze makes a greedy feast of his face, wondering if I'll ever grow tired of looking at him.

"Glad to clear that up." He grins. "But what I don't understand is why I'm required to wear anything at all when, according to you anyway, you prefer to see me in my most natural state."

"Axel!" I press a hand to my lips, swallow a self-conscious giggle. All too aware of my cheeks turning the full spectrum of red. Normally I wouldn't be embarrassed by a statement like that. Normally I would volley right back with something equally flirtatious. But the way Axel delivers it with such sincerity, such guileless honesty, the best I can ever do is blush in response.

While he's certainly manly in all the ways that count, sometimes he seems almost childlike in the way he's so uncorrupted by the world. Unlike most people, he's not driven by the usual things—vanity, pride, and ego hold no importance for him. He's straightforward, always impeccable with his word. And his belief in me is so absolute, sometimes I find myself cowering under the weight of it, wondering if I even deserve it.

I guess because it's so unlike the way it was with Cade, where everything was a manipulation, a game. And while I don't miss those days in the least, while I mostly wish I could banish them from my storehouse of memories, the truth is, I'm not always sure how to take Axel's brand of earnest, wide-open love.

While it's clear he's nothing like Cade, I'm not always sure just what he is. No longer a Mystic—having broken one of his most sacred vows when he decided to spare Daire's life last Christmas Eve—he's since been denied admittance to the Upperworld—the place he called home.

Though he's not entirely human either.

Which means our ways are still new to him.

And once, when he accidentally nicked his finger while trying to cut a tomato, I watched him bleed gold.

"How about Radiant Being?" He grins, proving, once again, his uncanny (and highly annoying) ability to read my mind. Catching my frown, he pulls back and says, "Sorry, was I eavesdropping?"

"Clearly." I return to the oven, if only to confirm I've committed yet another case of muffin-murder. Stale bagels it is. I flip off the heat, set the pan on the stovetop to cool, and head for the fridge in search of cream cheese and jam.

"Lita, have I upset you?" He stands beside me, a scolded-puppy expression marring his beautiful face. Having failed at something he doesn't quite understand—his intent is always to please. "I'm sorry," he says. "I'm trying to learn your ways, truly I am. Being in love is all new to me. I thought the whole point was to share everything?"

He cocks his head, sending a tumble of white-blond curls to fall enticingly into those alluring lavender eyes.

"I'm new at love too." I frown at the empty jam jar, place the container in the sink, and chuck the tub of cream cheese onto the counter. "And while people may claim that they want to share everything, they don't really mean it." I fold my arms across my chest and face him. "Thoughts are meant to be private, okay? It's not okay to listen in."

He nods intently, as though committing my words to memory, and I can't help but grin in response. I don't remember anyone ever taking me quite so seriously.

"It may please you to know that the ability is fading where all others are concerned. Though for some reason with you, it remains strong as ever."

"Lucky me."

He moves toward me, unfolds my hands, and rests them on the top of his shoulders. "I take it as proof of the deep connection we share. Proof that coming here was the right thing to do."

The words hit me hard, and I take a moment to absorb them while I study his expression. The last six months we've been together have been such a whirlwind, such an exhilarating head rush, I guess I never once stopped to consider all he gave up to enter my world.

"Axel—do you ever . . . regret that you're here?"

When his reply doesn't come quickly, my shoulders sink in relief. Glad to see him taking time to consider, knowing that when he does answer, he'll do so truthfully. Being impeccable with his word means he's not always quick to reassure.

"Sometimes I get homesick." His face assumes a thoughtful expression. "But then, I look at you, and suddenly I get to experience all of the wonderful emotions that were denied me before. Before you, everything I knew about falling in love was confined to theory. And while I'll eventually grow used to living without magick and tunics, now that I've found you, I could never consider a life without you."

I choke back a sob, start to look away. But then he catches me by the chin, tilts my face toward his, and says, "I'm willing to skip breakfast, if you are?"

All I can do is nod in return.

And the next thing I know, he lifts me into his arms as though I weigh nothing at all, and carries me down the hall toward his room.

five

Dace

Since I have some time before I need to show up for work at the gas station, I drive into town and park the old, white heap just outside of Gifford's, aiming to enjoy a cup of that freshly brewed coffee advertised in the window, and maybe read a bit from the stack of books I've been lugging around.

I wave to old man Gifford and head for a table in back. Only to hear my name being called from the far side of the room, as Leftfoot and Chay gesture impatiently toward the steaming cup of coffee they have waiting for me.

How they knew I'd show up when I only decided myself just a few moments ago is beyond me.

Then again, the elders are pretty much tuned in to everything. They probably willed me here without my even realizing.

I grab the chair next to Chay and drop my books before me. Lifting my cup to my lips, I watch as Leftfoot swipes a title from the top of the stack, glances at the front and back covers, heaves a disapproving grunt, and drops it right back.

"Where'd you get those?" Chay glances between the spines and me. "Lucio's back room?"

"Santa Fe."

He narrows his gaze, takes a sip of his coffee. "When'd you start smuggling contraband? Those sort of books have been banned from Enchantment for years." He speaks the words lightly, but his face remains as stoic as ever.

"What can you learn about the mystical arts from a book that you can't learn from us?" Leftfoot chimes in, sounding miffed and offended.

I shrug, lower my cup, and decide to answer honestly. "So far, nothing."

Leftfoot grunts in reply, but this time it's of the satisfied variety.

After covering all of the usual small talk—the stifling summer heat; hottest year on record; Chepi's general health and well-being and her continued suspicion of Daire, which seems to be softening since Paloma's passing—we move onto the whole point of their luring me here. And of course, it has to do with the Richters. Three in particular: Gabe, Leandro, and Cade. Otherwise known as my cousin, my father, and my twin. Though I prefer not to think of them that way.

Gabe is a creep.

Leandro is a dark sorcerer and rapist, who used my mother to wield his black magick to conjure a son even darker than he.

And as for Cade, well, next time I see him, I plan to kill him.

I guess you could say there's no real sentiment where the Richter side of my family is concerned.

And while it's clear that no one has seen any of them, like Daire, they're not convinced that's necessarily a good thing.

"Work continues at the Rabbit Hole. Which means someone must be in charge of rebuilding, and if not Leandro, then who?" Chay looks from Leftfoot to me.

"It's a big family." I dip my head for another sip of coffee. "There's no shortage of cousins. Any one of them could've taken the helm."

"You really believe that?" Leftfoot's narrowed eyes meet mine, practically daring me to disappoint him and insist that I do.

I shake my head. Should've known better than to be so glib. As a longtime student of Leftfoot's, I know better than most that he requires absolute seriousness in matters like this. "No," I say. "I don't believe it for a second. Guess I'm just trying to enjoy the break while it lasts."

"Really?" Leftfoot leans toward me, as Chay busies himself with his soft-boiled egg and fruit plate.

Gone are the days of the covert cheese Danish. Now that Paloma's no longer around to lecture him about the evils of sugar, seems he's finally decided to heed her word. Just one more way he chooses to honor her memory. The other is the woven leather bracelet he wears at his wrist bearing a carved silver Wolf's head.

Paloma was guided by Wolf. And I can't imagine how he gets through each day without her. If I was in his place . . .

I shake free of the thought and return to Leftfoot, who's still waiting for my response.

"Is this how you enjoy the break? By reading books on shape-shifting?" He flicks the stack with his index finger and thumb.

"Looks like you've already decided the answer." I meet his look square-on. Even though he's technically my uncle, Leftfoot's always been like a father to me. Although he struggled to raise his son, Lucio, on his own, he never hesitated to look after me. And I've never thought of him as anything less than a dad. Because of it, we argue as much as any father and son.

He shoots me a look that manages to convey his extreme annoyance while still managing to be supportive and fatherly. Tossing a wad of bills on the table, he rises impatiently and motions for me to follow.

"Where we going?" I glance from him to Chay, but Chay just

pushes away from the table and shrugs, even though I'm convinced he's informed. The two of them are thick as thieves. Always in cahoots. There's no dividing them.

"Your honeymoon is over." Leftfoot slips an arm around my shoulders and pushes me into the daylight. "We've got work to do. Serious work. Make no mistake, the worst is yet to come."

six

Daire

Having spent the first sixteen years of my life studiously avoiding pretty much all forms of physical activity that don't involve lounging and/or reading, I'm amazed by how much I've come to love running. How quickly I've taken to it. How fast I've progressed.

Turns out there's nothing like a good, brisk run to clear away the cobwebs and relieve a little of the tension crowding my head. Not to mention how it's a useful way to get home after a night spent at Dace's. Or at least until I get around to getting my driver's license. And though there are quicker routes from which to choose, none allow for as good a view of the Rabbit Hole.

I slow when I reach the far corner, cast a quick glance each way, then dart across the street and edge toward the alleyway. Where I take a quick detour and cruise by the chain-link fence where I secured the padlock as a symbol of Dace's and my love, if only to ensure it's still there. With so many forces working against us, there was no guarantee. Then I move toward the clamor of hammering and workers shouting from the other side of the barrier. The clouds of dust and noise providing ample proof that the rebuild continues. Though the barrier fronting it is so solid, tall, and imposing, it's impossible to get a sneak peek—one thing is sure: El Coyote is alive and well and planning on making one hell of a comeback.

And I've no doubt Dace knows it too.

No way does he truly believe that they're dead.

Dace is too smart to ever believe such a thing.

Like me, he's prepping for what's next—whatever that may turn out to be.

I've caught him doing push-ups, crunches, and lunges when he thinks I'm not looking. I've even caught him shadowboxing, but I just slipped back into bed without saying a word. If he wanted me to know, he'd tell me. Besides, I'm sure his secrecy is less about keeping things from me and more about quelling my fears. And while I've no doubt his aim is well intentioned and sweet, truth is, it's not really working.

Great clouds of dust waft over the partition, as a chorus of jack-hammers and drills drone on without ceasing. About two months after the explosion, the construction began. And now, after four months of their working in earnest, I have to think it'll be ready soon.

And then what?

The doors spring open and it's back to business as usual?

With large crowds of people lining up for overpriced drinks, loud music, and mediocre food?

I duck my head low and place a hand on each knee, forcing deep exaggerated breaths as though I need a break from the run, but really using the moment to take a good look around. Searching for at least one familiar face—something to clue me in to exactly what's going on.

My wish seemingly granted when a big, black truck pulls into the lot that, at first glance, I mistake for Cade's. It's only when I see the red-and-orange flames licking the sides, and Marliz behind the wheel, that I realize it belongs to her fiancé, Gabe.

While she's not exactly the person I was hoping to see, I can't help but wonder why she's still here, driving his truck, if Gabe's supposedly dead.

I lower my cap, tuck my chin to my chest, and crouch to one knee. Fumbling with my laces as though retying my shoe, I track Marliz as she slips free of the cab, takes a quick nervous glance all around, and darts for the barrier, leaving me only a handful of seconds to decide what to do.

Our relationship, if you can call it that, has always been troubled. She's the first person I met in Enchantment (other than Paloma and Chay), and to her credit, she did try to warn me away. But aside from that—and the brief period I managed to release her from the Richters' curse when she fled to L.A. with a little help from my mom—she's pretty much been working against me. Last time we spoke she made good on her threat to thwart me. And with the Richters holding her spellbound again, there's no reason to believe she'd be up for a chat.

Still, I shout her name as loudly as I can in an effort to be heard over the din. Watching as she pauses and turns, her yellow-blond hair swirling around her slim, suntanned shoulders—her heavily made-up eyes widening when she finds me waving from a few feet away.

She stands frozen before me, her tattooed arm, with the snake slithering around her bicep, clutching hard at her purse, as her long, skinny legs teeter atop a pair of impossibly high wedged heels.

With both hands raised in surrender, wanting her to know I mean no harm, I slowly approach. All too aware that the slightest misstep will only serve to scare her off.

"Marliz—it's me. Please don't run. We need to talk . . ."

Her gaze darts wildly. She lifts a hand to her hair. Then the next thing I know, she's spinning on her heels and racing for the barrier. Her left hand raised before her, she aims her bright blue tourmaline ring toward the wall, causing a blinding flash of bright light and a glimmering veil of dust that seems to swallow her whole. One moment she's there, and the next I'm left staring at the empty space where she stood. Wondering if I somehow imagined it, until I see the trampled mound of glittering powder she left in her wake.

After a quick look around to ensure no one's looking, I drop to my knees and skim a tentative hand over the top. Coating my fingers with a strange, dark, sparkling substance with razor-sharp edges that looks nothing like the usual construction dust.

I quickly fill my palms with the stuff, pull my hat from my head, and drop it into my cap. While I may not know what it is, one thing's for sure: This is not your average rebuild.

The Rabbit Hole is getting a mystical makeover.

The building's enchanted—protected by some kind of spell—and the Richters are at the helm of it all.

Just as I suspected, they're not dead—they haven't gone anywhere. They may be lying low for now, but they're in there—somewhere—I feel it in my bones.

They're plotting.

Planning.

Biding their time.

Just as I'm biding mine.

seven

Dace

"How long is this gonna take? I have to be at work in an hour." I cast an agitated glance at Leftfoot, but he purposely ignores me and hurries me along toward my truck.

Settling beside me, he thrusts an impatient finger toward the window and says, "Make a left at the corner."

"Care to tell me where we're headed?" I crank the key in the ignition, once, twice, until the engine roars to life.

"Do you always need to know your destination?" His eyes dart toward mine, the question as wry as his look.

"As the driver, I find it comes in handy, yeah." I clench my jaw and ignore the stop sign at the corner, hardly bothering to slow as I barrel into the turn.

"Who taught you how to drive?" Leftfoot squints. His eyes so hooded it's impossible to tell if he's joking or serious.

"You did." I shrug. Aware of the tension draining from my shoulders, my spine, when his delighted laugh bellows between us.

"But I'm serious about needing to get to work," I say, thinking maybe this time he'll listen. "I can't be late. That sort of thing doesn't go over well."

"This is more important than work." Leftfoot bobs his head as he takes in a string of broken-down adobes lining the street.

"Easy for you to say." I shake my head, rub a hand over my chin.

"You want to work at that gas station forever?" His gaze veers toward me.

"Forever?" I turn to face him. "No thanks. For the duration of the summer? Well, yes, that's what I was hoping. I need money to live on, Leftfoot. I live in the real world, you know."

"You live in the Middleworld." Leftfoot grins, slapping his knee as he laughs hard at his joke.

"And you don't?"

He shakes his head, eyes glinting at the turn this conversation is taking. "As medicine man, I have one foot in this world, and one foot in the spirit worlds. And today, if you'll stop resisting my efforts, I'm going to teach you how to bridge those worlds too."

"Seriously?" I quirk a brow. "And we can accomplish all of that in the span of an hour? Because that's all I've got, as I've already mentioned."

"Don't kid yourself." His grin fades. His voice takes a sharp turn. "This day should come as no surprise. I've been leading you to this moment since you were a kid. You're finally deemed ready."

"I'm finally deemed ready? Or the El Coyote situation has become so dire my shelf date got bumped?"

"Does it matter what prompted it?"

"You're in charge, you tell me."

He laughs again, even though I was entirely serious and not trying to be funny. He grabs his belly and howls like the madman I'm suspecting he is. Finally calming himself enough to lead me through a series of turns that takes us straight to the reservation where I was born and raised.

"Why didn't you just tell me we were headed here?" I make no attempt to hide my annoyance.

"Because you would've taken a route of your choosing, which would most likely involve a shortcut or two."

"In the interest of saving time and fuel, yeah, you're right, I would have."

"And what purpose could that possibly serve when I need you to get used to following directions?" He looks at me like he wants me to reply, but before I can, he's off and running again. "Make no mistake, since the moment you inhaled your first breath, your life has been a test that you are always on the verge of failing. If you want to pass, and you're ambitious to the degree that I'm sure that you do, then you need to listen. You need to pay attention. You need to let go of your attachment to things that hold no real importance. And you need to learn to embrace the importance of taking the necessary steps to do a job properly."

"What does it matter, if the end result is the same—or, in my case, even better?"

"You think that just because you shave ten minutes off the clock and save an extra gallon or two of fuel you would've been better off?"

I look at him dumbfounded—sure that the question must be rhetorical.

"Then I'm afraid this is going to take even longer than I thought." He shakes his head sadly and motions for me to drive on.

Instead of directing me to his house, like I thought, Leftfoot leads me to Chay's where he and Leftfoot's apprentice, Cree, are busy getting four of Chay's vast stable of horses saddled up and ready to ride.

"All set?" Leftfoot glances between the two men.

Chay nods, Cree grunts, as I resist the urge to look at my watch.

Thing is, as nervous as I am about being late for work—or, more likely, losing my job—I know better than to doubt Leftfoot for long. Around these parts, he's honored, revered. And though he's taken me under his wing since the day I was born, I try not to take his teachings for granted. It's taken me years of hard work, over a decade spent earning his trust and respect, to even get to this point.

From what I've seen over the last sixteen years, many have knocked on his door, but only a few are allowed entry.

Whatever he insists on revealing today must be important—possibly sacred. He knows what a struggle money's always been for Chepi and me. He would never risk a job I sorely need if he wasn't convinced it was of the utmost importance.

He turns to me with a knowing gaze, leaving me to suspect that he spent the last few minutes eavesdropping on my innermost thoughts. Then he nods toward the smallest horse in the group—the one that's barely bigger than a small Shetland pony—and motions for me to hop on.

I stand before the horse, refusing to budge. Sure this is yet another one of his tests I'm destined to fail, but no way am I riding that thing. I'll look ridiculous. He's smaller than the pony I learned to ride on.

Leftfoot shakes his head, working his jaw as he says, "Do yourself a favor and rid yourself of your vanities and the foolish assumptions they cause you to make. You've never ridden Big Thunder. I guarantee he'll surprise you."

"Big Thunder?" I shake my head. Shuffle my feet uncertainly. But after a few prolonged moments under the elders' impatient glare, I climb on. And just as I suspected, they waste no time indulging a long, hearty laugh at my expense.

Chay and Cree take the lead, talking mostly among themselves, as Leftfoot occasionally calls out to various animals and birds. Many of which are considered to be dangerous and predatory—but who, in the thrall of Leftfoot's calm, peaceful energy, merely follow along for a bit, before moving on. While I mostly fight to keep pace and stay on my steed, whose power and strength defy his small stature. Studiously making a point to observe all I can, remembering what Leftfoot said about my life being a test, and knowing this particular lesson began the moment I ran into him at Gifford's. Leaving no doubt he'll call upon me to access these observations later.

The ride drags on much longer than expected, consuming the better part of the day. Finally ending when Leftfoot dismounts by a small grove of trees where we tether our mounts in the shade and continue on foot up a long, steep trail ending at the mouth of a cave.

Same cave I visited when my vision quest collided with Daire's.

She was scared. Hungry, thirsty, tired, and desperate to end it. Caught in a sort of netherworld between delusions and reality, she was just about to slip past the border and wave a white flag in surrender, when I appeared before her and urged her to stay. To see her initiation through to its end.

I told her we were different. Not like the others. That our paths were chosen for us and it was our job to follow them and live up to the task. Something that I become more convinced of each day.

Then I gave her a glimpse of her future.

Showed her the radiant, magnificent being she could someday be if she could just stay the course.

Luckily, it worked.

Still, being here now somehow feels wrong. This cave belongs to the Santoses. Without Daire, I have no right to enter.

The elders move around me, as though I'm some annoying obstacle they're forced to tolerate. Chay sprinkles a fresh layer of salt along the front entrance that's meant to keep it free from predators and intruders—including, possibly, us? As Leftfoot looks at me and says, "You recognize it?" Accurately reading my expression.

I nod. "It's sacred ground for Seekers." I meet his gaze. "I'm not sure we have any right to intrude. We have our own sacred places— why force ourselves on theirs?"

"Since when have I ever forced myself anywhere?" Leftfoot makes an exasperated face and pushes ahead of me until he joins Cree and Chay inside the cave, while I remain stubbornly fixed outside. Trying not to cringe under the weight of Leftfoot's scrutinizing glare when he says, "You questioning me?"

I shift my weight from foot to foot, knowing I shouldn't question him, that I have no cause to doubt his wisdom, yet there's no denying the truth.

I rub a hand over my chin, shoot him an apologetic look.

Only to see him grin as he says, "Good. You passed. Never trudge onto sacred land without a proper invitation. But now that you've been summoned, you have a handful of seconds to join us, before the offer will close and you'll be shut out for the duration."

eight

Daire

I enter the house to the sound of shrieks and giggles drifting from under the door of my old room that can only mean one thing: Lita and Axel are at it *again*.

I head for the sink, drop my cap on the counter, flip on the faucet, and stick my head under the spray. Looking to cool off after a long run in the scorching heat, and hopefully drown out the blare of the love-fest down the hall.

With my ponytail clinging to my neck, and water streaming down the back of my tank top, I pour a tall glass of iced ginger tea and position myself before the fan I've propped on the counter. Surveying the pile of dirty bowls in the sink, the mixer stand speckled with crud, the baking pan left to cool on the stove—all the usual remnants of yet another failed breakfast experiment.

I'm annoyed by the mess.

Annoyed to always return home to this.

But mostly, I'm annoyed by the sheer force of their happiness—and my inability to warn them of their ill-fated future.

We're doomed.

Every last one of us.

Making me feel like a virus—infecting everyone around me.

The only ones who stand half a chance are Auden and Xotichl. And yet, there's no denying that things between them aren't quite as intense as they were. Ever since he left Epitaph to work on a solo act, he's off playing gigs in other faraway cities. And while I know it's been hard on Xotichl, she's mostly really proud of him. She knows how hard he's worked for this, and how much it means to him.

I turn back to the sink and flip on the faucet again. This time filling the basin with warm sudsy water, preparing to clean up Lita's mess, when she enters the kitchen with gleaming brown eyes, cheeks flushed light pink, and a tumble of dark waves cascading messily over her shoulders, the newly bleached ends nearly meeting her waist.

"Didn't hear you come home." She grins happily as Axel comes to stand beside her in a pair of dark denim jeans and a white V-neck tee that Lita picked out for him. And though he looks undeniably good, it's still weird seeing him in anything other than the white tunic he wore in the Upperworld.

"You were busy." The words come out gruffer than I intended, or maybe not. My mood is unstable, my nerves are jangled, and while I'm tempted to blame the heat, I know better. This is about the dream. No matter how hard I pushed myself during my run, I just couldn't ditch it.

"Sorry." Lita's tone is as sheepish as the look on her face. "Sorry for the noise, the mess, and the overall intrusion on your life." She sneaks a peek at Axel, motioning for him to grab the dish towel as she edges me back toward the fan and takes over the washing. "To be honest, Daire, I'm not quite sure how to be around you anymore."

I lean against the counter, unsure how to take that. Catching the cautionary look Axel shoots her as he whispers, "Lita—"

But Lita's not one to be shushed, and so she hands him a bowl to dry as she looks at me and says, "Truth is, when you're not outwardly irritated, you're so cut off and withdrawn it makes me miss the annoyed sighs and frowny faces you make."

My gaze drops to my feet. Her words cut to the bone, yet there's no denying their truth.

"And even though everyone tells me to back off and give you the space that you need—thing is, it's been six months, and—"

"Six months, and *what*? What's that supposed to mean? Is that the timeline you've placed on my grief?" I'm seething, glaring, ready to explode, but to her credit she continues washing and rinsing, keeping her cool.

"That's not fair and you know it. I miss Paloma too. Not a day goes by that I don't think about her. What I meant was, it's been six months of watching you shut us all out, acting like we're in the way. And while I'm aware that, technically speaking, we probably are, we're not the enemy here, okay? We're your friends. And we're here to help. We're *dying* to help. We're *begging* to help. And we feel like we're left to idle on the sidelines, just passing the time. Looking for ways to relieve some of your burden, only you won't let us."

My shoulders sag in surrender. While there's no denying I needed to hear it, that doesn't mean it didn't sting. "But that's the thing—you can't help." My eyes find hers.

"How do you know we can't help if you don't let us try?" She hands the last bowl to Axel, wipes her hands on her shorts, and heads for the stove, where she retrieves the baking pan and unceremoniously dumps the muffin remains into the trash.

"You can't help because I refuse to endanger you any more than I already have."

She dunks the pan in the sink, leaving it to soak, as she squares off on me. "Well, I hate to break it to you Daire, but just living in this godforsaken town puts us in danger. At least with you, we're fighting on the side of good. At least with you, we're protected by knowledge and awareness. C'mon, Daire, let us in. Let us help. You don't have to go this alone."

I look to Axel for support. He more than anyone should know what it's like for people like me. But he remains focused on returning bowls to their cupboards, spoons to their drawers, as I stand before the whirring fan blades and say, "But that's the thing—I *do* have to go this alone. That's pretty much the nature of being a Seeker. We train with a mentor, maybe enjoy a brief, ill-fated love affair that usually results in a child, only to end up alone and dooming those poor children to the same lonely fate. It's what happened to Paloma, and all those who came before her. It's a well-documented fact. I can prove it, if you want."

"No need, I believe you." She shakes her head, scrunches her forehead. "Though I can't help but think you've successfully beaten the odds too many times to surrender so easily."

I push away from the counter and turn to gaze out the window toward Paloma's garden and the collection of strange, hybrid plants I've struggled to take over. While they continue to thrive and bloom, it's not with the same intensity as when they were under my grandmother's care. She's a hard act to follow. And while I'm doing my best, I can't help but feel like I'm falling remarkably short.

While I've no doubt Lita's feelings are echoed by the rest of my friends, while she's merely acting as a spokesperson, it's not nearly as easy as they think. And the irony is that her all-consuming love for Axel is as doomed as my own love for Dace.

That's just the way it's always been. And history has an uncanny way of repeating itself.

"Intent is magick's most important ingredient," Axel says from behind me. "And belief is the spine of intent."

I whirl around to face him, having almost forgotten about his talent for eavesdropping on thoughts. "I thought that was fading?"

"It comes and goes." He shrugs. "The point is, I'm not giving in without a fight. So why have you given up long before the fight's even had a chance to begin?" His voice is even, his expression determined. His deep lavender eyes shifting from the deepest violet to the softest lilac.

"So you know." My tone is resigned, my gaze appraising.

He returns the look with one of his own.

"You're not buying into their silence. You know they'll resurface."

Lita shifts between us, waiting for someone to clue her in to the truth behind our veiled conversation.

"I'm sure this is the calm before the storm. And I'm committed to enjoying a quiet respite for as long as it lasts." Axel arcs an arm toward Lita, and she's quick to scurry to his side. "I'm prepping, Daire, just like you are. But I'm also indulging in a chance to rest, refuel, and yes, even enjoy myself." He hugs Lita tightly, kisses the top of her head. "Maybe you should try it sometime. Might do you some good."

I glance between them. So flushed and satisfied—so caught in the grips of their heady swirl of happiness—who am I to deny them? Besides, I'm pretty sure Axel already knows the grim possibility of things actually working between them. After all he forfeited—first to save me, then to be here with Lita—they deserve every smidgen of joy they can manage. Won't be long before such things are much harder to come by.

I hook a thumb in the general direction of their bedroom and say, "You call that a *quiet* respite?" Enjoying the sight of Axel's pale face flushing red as Lita shoots me a worried look that fades the moment I grin. "Go." I wave them away and head for my room. "Frolic. Be free. We'll catch up tonight. For now, I need to go change. My first client is due any minute."

nine

Dace

Cree builds a small fire as Leftfoot gestures for me to sit beside it.

I swipe a hand across my brow and shoot him a skeptical look. "Is this really necessary?" I point toward the flames. "It's triple digits outside. I was enjoying the relief."

"Sit." Leftfoot scowls. Chay frowns. And I'm quick to obey. "This is not about your enjoyment," he says.

"Clearly." I flash a quick grin, but Leftfoot's not having it.

"Tell me what you see." He kneels beside me, ducks his head toward the flames.

"I see a fire, burning logs, wisps of smoke." I shrug, knowing better than to pretend to see more when I don't.

"Look deeper. Meditate on the flames for as long as it takes."

"As long as it takes to *what*, exactly?"

"You'll know it when you see it."

He settles beside me, humming a familiar childhood tune, as Chay lingers behind, and Cree leans against the far wall.

I stare into the flames. Forcing my breath to slow, my gaze to relax, as I work on ridding myself of all expectation. Despite Leftfoot's constant reminders that there are no right and wrong images when it comes to scrying, it's tough to overcome my innate need to please him.

I've spent the last six months preparing myself both mentally and physically. Pushing my body to the edge of exhaustion with punishing workouts—pushing my magick to surpass the usual skills—pushing my mind to see more, intuit more, to embrace the absolute oneness of everything in the universe. And though I've been on the lookout for signs of transformation, a stirring of the beast that made itself known last New Year's Eve, there's been no sign of him.

Until now.

The wood cracks and sizzles.

The flames swirl and dance.

As great whiffs of smoke rise and bend, shrink and expand. Morphing into a replica of the beast that dwells deep within.

I recognize it the instant I see it.

He's glorious.

Breathtaking.

Fierce and strong.

A creature of stature and grace, with long sharp talons and a crown of white feathers encircling his head—capable of so much more than I'd ever be on my own.

"Talk to me," Leftfoot says, sensing the shift in my mood.

After I give a detailed description of the beast, Leftfoot nods his approval and motions for Chay to bring me the large, cotton sack he hauled all the way here. The contents rattling as he deposits the bag beside me, I take a moment to give silent thanks for the magick to come, then yank on the drawstring and snake a hand toward the bottom. My fingers butting against a smooth, long object with identical holes on either side, I ease it free of the opening and raise it before me.

Although I know I shouldn't be surprised by what I see—after all, Chay's a vet, which gives him plenty of access to such things—

that doesn't stop me from gazing upon it in wonder. Up until now, I'd never seen an actual horse skull before.

I flip it over in my hand, as Leftfoot says, "You are guided by Horse—a symbol of freedom, power, and enlightenment. His is a commanding presence. A powerful spirit animal. Teaching us the benefits of patience, kindness, and cooperation. The spirit of the Horse encourages us to awaken our power to endure and reach our full potential. Now it's time for you to reach yours."

I lift my gaze to the flames, watching as the image of the beast continues to undulate before me. The sound of Leftfoot's voice filling the cave. "Set the skull before you, then place your palm over the top of the bag and use your magick to summon the other bones to you."

I'm quick to obey, first palming a rib bone, then what looks to be the cervical vertebrae.

"After arranging the bones from smallest to largest, place your hands on your knees, palms facing the ceiling, then project the bones into the fire using only your will. And whatever you do, whatever occurs, do not flinch. Do not resist. Stay steady, strong, and unwavering in your focus. Don't try to control the ceremony. Allow it to unfold as it will."

I concentrate on the bones, sending them soaring into the flames, where, one by one, they explode on contact. The resulting resonance so jarring, so deafening, it takes all of my will not to take cover and bolt for the exit.

The bones splinter and crack. Dissolving into hundreds of jagged pieces that swirl above our heads in three distinct clouds of disparate particles that eventually find their way to the ground, where they fall in perfect formation as a heavy silence settles around us.

I look to Leftfoot for guidance. Unsure how to interpret the event. Watching as the old medicine man continues to stare into the flames. "That day at the sweat lodge, you claim to have made your choice based on what you saw during your soul jump. In case you've been wondering, I showed you that message for a reason."

I nod in assent, knowing exactly which message he refers to. Although Leftfoot showed me a lot of things that day, invited me in for an all-access pass into his soul code, there was one message that stood out amongst all the rest.

One that I had to delve deep to see.

One that changed everything.

And though I know the reveal was no accident (nothing Leftfoot does ever is), later, when the plan turned against me—when the darkness inside lodged itself deep and resisted all attempts to expel it—when my eyes turned like Cade's—when Daire grew first concerned, then afraid—I couldn't help but wonder *why*.

Why did he show it to me when he knew all along what I'd choose?

"Sometimes you must venture into the dark to bring forth the light." I repeat the message he shared with me. Having adopted it as my mantra from the moment it was revealed, the words come easily.

"While the statement is true, you used the line as proof that you should make the choice you were determined to make all along." His tone is sharp, though it's not meant to sting. Leftfoot is merely stating the truth.

"And every action yields a reaction." I frown, the words coming from a place that allows for perfect recall of that day.

"The moment those dueling curls of smoke rose up before you, your choice was made. Maybe even before." Leftfoot's face grows dark, hooded, as he returns his focus to me. The absolute veracity of his words leaving me no choice but to duck my head in shame.

I'd decided long before I entered that sweat lodge which path I'd choose, and I used the events as an excuse to proceed. I was sure that choosing darkness over light would strengthen me—allow me the necessary edge to defeat the Richters and protect Daire.

Now I know better.

After a long bout of silence, I lift my chin and regard him with smoke-stung eyes and a profound sense of unease. "Did I make the wrong choice—or was I merely following my destiny?"

"Destiny is inevitable." Leftfoot's gaze centers on mine, though his thoughts grow distant, drifting to a faraway place. "In the end, all roads lead to the end."

"You once said that the bit of darkness I ingested is the very thing that makes me human, maybe even normal."

"The darkness inside you allows for a more human experience. Giving you the very thing you lacked before: an insider's knowledge of the two faces of man—the constant struggle between darkness and light. But make no mistake, you're not entirely human, Dace. Your inherent nature is something much greater."

I close my eyes and sigh.

My birth. Of course. What else could it be?

I'm the product of violence.

Black magick.

Dark interference.

Sorcery at its worst.

Wrought from the bleakest, purest form of evil, my creation was aided by demons, beasts, the restless undead, and other dark, fetid things dredged up from the depths.

"There's a reason you survived. A reason Leandro couldn't extinguish your light, no matter how hard he tried. And it's not for the reason you think. Seems you have a big role to play."

I lift my gaze to meet his, hoping he'll choose to elaborate on what that role might be. But he just motions for me to get up and stand beside him.

"Time to read the bones." He arcs a finger toward the scattering of skeleton bits now spread across the dirt in patterns that at first look don't make any sense. "Describe what you see."

My gaze moves over them until three very distinct shapes begin to form.

I inhale a sharp breath. Swing my head between the startling array of bones and the old medicine man beside me.

It can't be.

There's no way.

After everything that's happened, how could it amount to this?

Leftfoot motions toward that rising curl of smoke that once represented the glorious beast within, now transformed into the dreaded monster I'm in the midst of becoming.

"The bones never lie." His voice is a match for the remorse that I feel. "This is one of the oldest forms of divination. And, in your case, it's appropriate to say it came straight from the Horse's mouth." He cracks a smile, offering a welcome bit of levity in a room gone heavy with dread.

Though my own expression is bereft when I say, "Now that I know, what do I do?"

"That's always the question, isn't it?" His gaze grows so hooded, so shadowed, it's impossible to read. "I'm afraid my guidance ends here. The next move is yours."

I balk. Sure he can't be serious. Despite the absolute finality of his expression, his word. "You're abandoning me? Now? Just when I need you the most?"

"I've taught you as well as I was able. Instilled within you the necessity of rooting yourself firmly in your own truth."

I stare at him incredulously. "And what kind of truth is that?" I motion toward the bones. "I never wanted this! Everything you taught me brought me closer to the light. And now . . ." I rake a hand through my hair, press my fists to my eyes. Hardly able to believe the horrible turn destiny has decided to make.

"Know this." Leftfoot rests a comforting hand on my shoulder. "It's never enough to just accumulate knowledge and skills. It's what a person does with what he knows that defines who he is."

"Every man must decide the kind of path he'll walk." I return my focus to the bones, reciting yet another of Leftfoot's many lessons. "Turns out it's not true at all. I never wanted this path. Never asked for any of this."

"Didn't you?" Leftfoot moves away, all the while watching me intently. But I can't meet his look. Can't bear the truth in his gaze. "You made your choice that day in the sweat lodge. And now it seems it's taken on a life of its own."

I clutch at my stomach, feeling sick, drunk, as though I might vomit. I stoop toward the dirt. Duck my head low until the key that swings forward, slaps at my chin, serves as a sobering reminder that no matter how dire the prophecy, I can't afford to give in.

Daire.

Everything I did was for her—for us—and now look.

"Only one way to vanquish the dark . . ."

I shake my head, struggle to pull myself up. My eyes finding his as I say, "Turn on the light?"

"The question is, will you? Can you? Or is it too late?"

I turn to see Chay and Cree, watching intently, their faces etched with deep lines of worry. Then I return my focus to the bone fragments before me. Shifting my focus from image to image until the message is sealed on my brain, hardwired into my soul. And when it's done, it seems I know just what to do.

I raise both hands before me, like a maestro conducting a symphony, and send the bones whirling back into the fire. Only, this time, instead of exploding, they snuff out the flames.

The cave grows dark.

The temperature drops.

And without so much as a single word between us, we gather our belongings and find our way back. The elders maintaining a wide berth around me now that my truth is revealed.

They fear me.

No doubt they should.

Still, it's nothing compared to the fear I feel toward myself.

ten

Daire

After a busy day of performing healings and determining the spirit animals of newborns (always my favorite), I head for Kachina's stall in search of some fresh air and the clarity that often comes from a nice long ride. Needing to slip away for a bit before my house fills with friends and I'll be forced to make good on Lita's request that I start accepting their offers to help.

Kachina bobs her head up and down and whinnies in greeting, as Cat crouches and glares from the corner of the stall. Though he doesn't scram the second he sees me, as he usually does, and I consider that progress.

I toss a bridle onto Kachina and lead her from the yard. Allowing my horse to wander aimlessly as my mind does the same.

Usually I try hard to guide it, stay focused, on track. But today my fatigue overrules me, and it's not long before I'm immersed in the memory of the day we lowered my *abuela*'s body into the earth. The ripe scent of freshly churned soil—the plaintive call of the lone raven soaring overhead—so immediate, so accessible, it's as though I'm transported in time.

It's been six full months since she passed.

Six full months since Cade Richter's last heinous act.

Still, the pain of losing her is so raw, so real, it's like a festering wound that refuses to heal.

I can't imagine ever not feeling this way.

Can't imagine how I'll ever learn to live with the big, gaping void that remains in her place.

As always, Kachina displays an uncanny ability to tune in to my moods, if not my needs, when she leads me straight to the small, humble graveyard that rests off the side of the road.

The first time I came here, I instantly pegged it as shabby, random, and tragically run-down. But once I took the time to settle in and appreciate the abundance of handmade crosses and markers—the fat handfuls of blooms lovingly gathered in honor of loved ones; the helium-heavy balloons tethered to rocks, commemorating those who've passed on—I was quick to change my tune.

It's a place of love, honor, and reverence.

It's a place I've come to think of as sacred.

And it's been far too long since my last visit.

I slide off Kachina's back and give her a light slap on the rear. Urging her to wander and graze, as my feet instinctively carry me to the simple, rectangular plaques marking the place where the bodies of my father and grandmother rest.

Paloma once warned me to never mistake the gravesite as the soul's final resting place. Assuring me that communion is possible anywhere. Still, at this particular moment, this is the place I most need to be. And I'm grateful for my horse having realized the truth that eluded me.

The patchy, parched grass pricks at my knees as I drop to the ground and take a good look around. Relieved to confirm that the magick wrought by the elders has stuck, and any attempt by the Richters to desecrate the place has been successfully thwarted. The grounds remain as untouched as the day Paloma brought me here to reveal the tragic truth of my father's brief life.

The son of a powerful Seeker and revered Jaguar shaman, Django was destined to wield formidable power. But he turned his back on his destiny and ran off to L.A. at sixteen, only to fall madly in love with my mom, then die just a few months later in a motorcycle crash Paloma claims was no accident.

It was the work of the Richters.

Only they acted just a few days too late.

The seed was already planted.

Jennika was pregnant with me.

Yet, despite my vow to not repeat Django's mistakes—to live up to my legacy and accept the destiny I was born to claim—sometimes I fear that I'm failing.

Missing the signs.

Falling remarkably short.

Though I'm not here to plead for the guidance and help of the dead. I'm on my own now. Something made all too clear the day the lone raven circled Paloma's grave. I'm merely in search of the calming encouragement only they can provide.

I need a father's protective embrace.

I need a grandmother's wisdom.

I need the reassurance that I really am equipped to deal with the Richters, now that I'm sure they're preparing a comeback.

And while Jennika would be here in a heartbeat—all I have to do is call and she'll come running—I'm reluctant to do so when it was hard enough to convince her to leave.

Besides, Jennika's finally settling into a life that's good for her. She finally has a shot at forming a real and lasting relationship with Harlan. One where she's not up and running the second things start to progress. I need to leave her to it. Give her the room she needs to make it work without my interference.

Like me, Jennika's been running too long.

It's time for us to lay down some roots.

I settle between the graves and ease onto my back. Reveling in the coolness of the earth, the fading wisps of clouds overhead, I stretch my arms to rest on each mound, and try to divine what to do next.

As Paloma once taught me, everything is made of energy, which means everything is alive. According to her, it's as easy to scry from fire and tea leaves as it is to receive messages from the face of a rock. All that's required is a willingness to believe, an ear tuned toward one's inner voice, and a bit of focused concentration.

Only this time, despite my intent, despite my desire to *see,* the clouds remain an unreadable, stringy, white blur. Until a sudden stir of wind brushes past, lifting the strands of my hair and riffling the frayed hem of my faded denim cutoffs—and I take it as a sign.

As a daughter of the wind, this is no accident.

Rather it's a timely reminder that I'm not as alone as I feared.

Never have been.

As Paloma once said: *To become powerful is to allow a great power to work through you. No one walks alone.*

While I know she was referring to the ultimate power, at the moment I take great comfort knowing she and Django are included.

The sun continues to drop. Wind swirls and skips. And I rise to my feet and brush myself off.

Soon, it'll be time to head back and confront the night still to come, but well before then, I have something important to do.

Though I didn't realize it until now, as it turns out, it's the reason I'm here.

I heave a deep breath and face the glorious, sun-shadowed peaks of the Sangre de Cristo Mountains. Finally willing to admit that until I confront my grief, I won't be able to confront anything else.

For the last six months I've buried my sorrow in a punishing regimen of grueling workouts and daily six-mile runs. Then, after tending to the never-ending stream of Paloma's former clients that I've taken on, I drop by Dace's apartment in a state of exhaustion, looking to numb myself in his arms.

Yet in the wee hours of the morning, when the streets grow

hushed and Dace is slumbering beside me, there's nowhere to hide. And that's when the pageant of *things I should've done differently* parades through my mind. The most glaring among them: allowing Cade to get the best of me—the best of us—when I gave that cursed tourmaline to Paloma.

Still, no matter how many times I reframe it, it's not like I can change it. The outcome is final.

What's done is truly done.

In the end, life amounts to little more than a series of choices. Some big, some small, but every action causes a reaction—and there's no doubt it's my own actions that landed me here.

Just as Paloma and Django's actions landed them six feet below.

Despite Paloma's warnings, Django chose to run from his destiny and it ended tragically.

Although she suspected the tourmaline was cursed from the moment she laid eyes on it, Paloma chose to keep it.

Tormenting myself won't change what's been done. The only purpose it serves is to punish myself for things that were never mine to control.

Besides, what if there's a chance Dace is right?

What if love really can overcome evil?

What if it's as simple as that?

My thoughts toward myself are pretty much the opposite of loving. I've been ruled by self-hate and fear, and maybe it's time I do better.

After all, Paloma trusted me, believed in me.

Maybe it's time I trust and believe in myself.

With the sun quickly descending, glazing the mountains in a glorious sheen of purples and reds, I take a deep breath, steeple my hands to my chest, and make a true and solemn pledge to do better than I have.

To stop denying my grief.

Stop torturing myself by reliving a past I can't change.

To let my friends in.

Lita was right. We're all in this together. For a short while I knew that, yet ever since Paloma's death I've been driven by fear, and so I've pushed them away in a misguided attempt to spare them from the kind of things that aren't mine to control.

But no more.

With Kachina off grazing—with Wind tickling my skin—with the low guttural cry of a lone Raven soaring circles over my head—I bow in reverence toward the mountain and rededicate myself to my legacy.

To the destiny I was born to claim.

No matter what may become of me—I won't go down easily.

The Richters will pay for the heinous acts that they've wrought on this town—on my loved ones—on the Lower, Upper, and Middleworlds, which are mine to keep balanced.

Then I lift my face to the heavens, drop to my knees, and cave in to my grief. Letting loose the deluge of tears I've held back for too long—allowing myself to fully experience the deep-seated pain of losing my grandmother, my mentor, my friend, a woman I truly loved and deeply admired.

I cry until my vision grows so blurry it's impossible to see even a few feet before me.

I cry until my body grows exhausted and empty.

I cry until I'm suddenly silenced, suddenly strengthened, by an unexpected infusion of the purest, most buoyant stream of joy, beauty, and love flowing through me.

My ancestors are here.

I'm not alone.

Never was.

Although they don't materialize before me, their presence is made known in the glorious chorus that fills up the sky.

Instinctively, I sway from side to side, gripped by a celestial melody I'm sure only I can hear. But when Kachina snorts and whinnies, when she tips her nose and perks her ears, I know she hears it just as clearly as I do.

It's a symphony of leaves chimed by Wind, accompanied by Raven's sweet song. And if I'm not mistaken, I can even detect the low vibrato of Paloma's treasured drum.

A sacred instrument, she referred to as a Spirit Horse. Its music akin to a heartbeat, its tempo said to open the portals that lead to the otherworlds.

There is nothing to fear, she told me then, just as she's telling me now.

This symphony of nature is a message from my *abuela.* Of that, I am sure. A sort of opus from the natural world, telling me it's time to rid myself of doubt. Time to trust in the wisdom of my ancestral bloodline. And I'm not one bit surprised Paloma chose to communicate in this way.

With that glorious chorus swirling within me, I leap onto Kachina's back and race toward home. Only to find a large white box tied with a ribbon as bright and crimson as freshly drawn blood, waiting for me on the stoop.

Dace! He must've left a present to distract me from the dream.

I rush toward it, drop to my knees, and go about removing the ribbon and tipping the lid. Only to release a deluge of bright red squares of packing confetti that spill at my feet.

I plunge my hands in, fingers digging deep. Until they butt up against something silky and cold, unyielding and stiff, that I ease free of the box and hold up before me.

A raven.

A dead raven, to be exact.

Its unseeing eyes marred with precisely placed globs of purple paint intended to mimic those of the raven who guides me.

His neck snapped cleanly in half.

His head crudely twisted so that it points the wrong way.

With a square of creamy white paper crammed in his beak.

I take a cursory look all around, checking for signs of Cade's presence, but other than the coyote tracks left in the finely milled gravel lining the walkway, it seems he's long gone.

Grasping the paper with the tips of my fingers, I look past the masked coyote with blazing red eyes embossed on the front, and unfold the card to find an invite to the Rabbit Hole's Masquerade Ball.

moon shadow

A single event can awaken within us a stranger totally unknown to us.
To live is to be slowly born. —Antoine de Saint-Exupéry

eleven

Daire

"Well, Cade's never been known for his subtlety, that's for sure." Lita leans back against the couch cushions and scowls. "Or his originality, for that matter. A masquerade black-and-white ball? Please."

"I thought calling it the Resurrection Ball was kind of clever," Xotichl says. "You know, the building's resurrecting, they're resurrecting . . ."

"How can you be sure it's from Cade?" Axel cuts in, his gaze moving among us. "No one's seen him in months."

"Well, if not Cade, then it's definitely from one of the other Richters." I glare at the invitation propped on the table before me, and curl my feet up under my legs. "Doesn't matter who delivered it, Coyote was here, and he left a direct challenge to me, to Dace, to all of us. But the worst part is . . ." I focus on my fingers twisting in my lap. Struggling to find the right way to tell my friends that the house is no longer a sanctuary, no longer a safe place to hide, in a way that doesn't leave them terrified.

"There's a worse part?" Lita gathers her hair off her neck and fans herself with her hand. "Well, go on then, let's hear it."

Deciding to just tell it like it is, I say, "Finding that dead raven on the stoop means the protection spell is no longer working."

Lita's eyes bulge. Axel squints. Auden pulls Xotichl closer, while Xotichl's expression turns to dread.

"Not long after I arrived in Enchantment, Paloma assured me the property was protected. Claimed I had nothing to fear as long as I stayed within the surrounding walls. But now, after this"—I jab a thumb toward the invite—"it's clear that no longer holds."

"But we've been so good!" Lita cries. "We've maintained the salt border by pouring a fresh coat every day. And just last week, Axel fixed a weak spot on the coyote fence when he saw one of its supports was coming loose, causing it to sag against the adobe wall."

Axel nods to confirm it, as Xotichl adds, "And every time I come over, which is pretty much every day, I reinforce the protection spell in the way Paloma showed me."

"And yet, despite all our efforts, Coyote still managed to breach." I shrug. Determined to state the facts with as little drama as possible. "It's no longer safe for you here. What you choose to do about that is for you to decide."

"What's that supposed to mean?" Lita lets go of her hair, allowing it to spill over her shoulders in gorgeous, white-tipped waves.

"It means that things are about to get serious. Things are about to escalate. And while I'll do my best to protect you, I think the Richters have just taken the first step toward showing me the extent of my limitations."

I return my focus to my friends. Watching as Xotichl keeps a wary gaze on the box, while seeking comfort in Auden's nearness. What a shame that after all the time they've spent apart, he returns to Enchantment just in time for another round of Coyote versus Raven.

"Everyone has limits," Xotichl says. "We just have to discover theirs." She prods her new glasses up the delicate bridge of her nose. And when her eyes meet mine, I can't help but grin. Despite the dire circumstance we find ourselves in, I'm grateful that her sight has returned. Gives us one positive thing to cling to in the midst of a heaping pile of awful.

I glance at Dace beside me, wondering what he's thinking behind that clenched jaw and narrowed gaze. But he remains as he is, quiet and somber with his focus turned inward, lost in thoughts I can't even fathom.

"Okay, so here's what we know for sure." Lita moves from the couch to the fan, seeking relief from the unbearable heat. "The Richters are back in business, both literally and figuratively. Question is, what are we going to do about it?"

"We're going to rise to the challenge." I look upon my small group of friends, my voice as determined as my gaze.

"Meaning?" Axel looks at me; he's the only one in the room who isn't wilting in the heat, and I can't help but feel envious.

"It's like Xotichl said, everyone has limits, no one's invincible. Heck, even Superman had kryptonite. We just have to discover the Richters' weakness."

They all look at me. Well, everyone but Dace, who continues to dwell in a faraway place.

"We need to be on high alert. We can't afford to slack off or get lazy. If nothing else, this invite is a clear warning that the honeymoon is officially over. It's a direct challenge if I've ever seen one."

"And so what do we do about it? Other than being on high alert and all?"

"You can start by not blocking the fan." Auden motions impatiently. "C'mon, Lita, share the breeze. Flower and I are dying over here."

Lita slinks back to Axel's side, as I say, "For starters, we're going to the masquerade." I lift my glass of iced ginger tea and press it to my forehead and cheeks, transferring the sweat from the glass to mix with the sweat on my skin.

"That's it? We just fix our hair, change our clothes, slap on a mask, and head out—or do we have some kind of plan?" Lita's voice is less sarcastic than her words might imply.

"I don't have a plan. Or, at least not yet." I sink deeper into the cushions, ashamed to admit I'm as clueless as they are. Still, lying won't do any good.

"Okay, so let's put our heads together and come up with a plan," Lita says. "You don't have to go this alone, you know. We may not be Seekers, but I'm sure we can help." She echoes her earlier lecture. "For starters, who's the entertainment? Auden, are you playing the event?"

Auden looks up from his cell. His face shading with embarrassment at being caught texting again. "Sorry," he says. "Just trying to arrange a meeting with Luther to sign some contracts."

"Well, while you have him, ask if he can try to squeeze you into the lineup," Lita says.

Auden looks uncertain. "I think Epitaph's scheduled to play."

"So, make it a reunion, then." Lita makes an impatient face.

"They were pretty pissed when I left. I doubt they'll want to see me . . ." Auden flips the phone in his hand.

"Don't be so sure." Xotichl sneaks closer, whispers into his ear. And he's unable to resist her; it's only a second later when Auden starts thumb typing again.

A few moments later, he says, "Well, Luther's not happy, but he said he'll do what he can."

"Good." Lita nods. "So hopefully we'll have someone to cover the stage. Dace—what about getting your old job back? Any chance of that?"

I turn to Dace, wondering what's going on with him. He got here much later than anticipated, and he's barely said a word ever since.

"Leandro offered." He shrugs, rubs a hand over his chin. "But that was before Phyre blew up the place. For all I know, he blames me."

"Doubtful. Didn't you pull Cade to safety? I'm sure Leandro's aware of that."

"We didn't do it to save Cade." I'm quick to defend our actions, even though there's no need. My friends are well aware of the mystical connection that binds the twins' lives.

"The reason doesn't matter. Fact is, Cade's alive because of you."

"Yeah, and he left a dead raven as a thank you." I shake my head.

"Kind of like when a cat leaves a dead mouse as a gift for its owner," Xotichl says, prompting us to laugh, though the moment's short-lived.

"Still, might be worth a try," Auden says. "Maybe you can head over. Grovel a bit. Appeal to his ego. It would be good to have someone on the inside."

I study Dace's expression, but he keeps it so carefully guarded it's impossible to read.

"What the hell." Dace's gaze briefly meets mine. "The gas station's no longer an option. Not after today." I lean closer, willing him to elaborate, but he just breezes right past it. "And there's no doubt I could use the money. Maybe he'll even give me an advance so I can cover my rent. That is, if I grovel enough." He exchanges a quick look with Auden. "So yeah. Fine. Worth a try, right?"

"Okay," Xotichl says. "So now that we've got two possible insiders, what about the rest of us? Do we pose as normal, clueless partygoers? Or do we go in with an agenda? Or both?"

"Too bad Axel's not still invisible," Auden says. "That might've helped."

"Doubtful," I say. "For some inexplicable reason, Cade was able to see Axel that night just after he stabbed me and Axel appeared to take me to the Upperworld."

"That was a glitch I still can't explain." Axel looks truly perplexed. "I used to be quite adept at light-bending." Fielding Auden's blank look, he explains, "I could will myself to be unseen even by those meant to see me. I was one of the few who could do such a thing. Though it was highly frowned upon."

"Rebel." Lita grins, nudges his side. Causing Axel to beam.

"Anyway," I say, hoping to get this conversation back on track. "While we may not have the details just yet, I think we need to be ready for anything, since clearly they're up to something more than just a reopening." I go on to tell them about seeing Marliz vanish inside and the pile of glimmering dust she left in her wake.

"Glimmering dust?" Axel looks at me, brows drawn tightly together.

I nod toward the hat I left on the counter. So much has happened, I forgot all about it until now. Within a matter of seconds Axel has glided seamlessly from the couch to the kitchen, then back to Lita's side, where he peers into the cap, dips a single finger inside, then looks at me and says, "Onyx. Black onyx to be exact."

"Okay . . . anyone mind cluing me in? I'm a little lost here." Lita looks from me to him.

"They must be using it to enhance the building. It's impossible to get a good look at it what with all the barriers they've set up around it. But that"—I nod toward the cap now placed on Axel's lap—"it's definitely not your usual construction material, which means they're building a bigger, better, more powerful Rabbit Hole."

"By using black onyx they'll add immense power and strength," Axel says. "Not only will onyx provide support and staying power, it'll increase the energetic vibration as well as retain the memory of all that went before."

"So . . . what you're really saying is that we're doomed to bad food and watered-down drinks forever?" Lita grins, trying to add a bit of levity to a room gone suddenly somber. But it's only a moment later when her smile fades and she settles into the grim reality that awaits us.

"They're ensuring that the memory and strength of the Rich-ter ancestry, along with the legacy of their magick and power stays forever retained in those walls," Axel says, and when his eyes meet mine, he looks as worried as I am.

The Richters have found a way to harness the power of their ancestry and the countless acts of evil they've wrought.

In other words: We are greatly outmatched.

Though it may prove worse still. They may have found a way to turn the entire town against us.

I look among my friends and say, "And let's not forget the tourmalines they included in the New Year's Eve swag bags. I'm sure it's just a matter of time until they come into play. There's no way the Richters would ever waste such a valuable resource."

"But why do you think they waited so long to exploit them?" Lita looks at me. "I mean, nothing out of the ordinary has happened for months."

"That's the million-dollar question," Xotichl says, fiddling with the glasses she's still not used to wearing. "Though try as I might, I can't get a read on the energy."

Despite the heat, I'm left chilled by her words. She's been saying things like that so often, I wonder if she has any idea just how frequently she's come to repeat herself where her failing abilities are concerned. Then again, I'm probably overreacting. Maybe she's so excited by the novelty of seeing, it's distracted her from her more mystical gifts.

I return my attention to my friends. "Okay, so the bottom line is, from this moment on, until we come up with an actual plan, we need to be on high alert for signs of anything out of the ordinary."

"And I have to go buy a new party dress," Lita says. "Which definitely calls for a trip to Albuquerque, since it's not like I'll find anything in this fashion-challenged town. Xotichl—you in?"

Xotichl nods eagerly, as Auden says, "I don't know about you, but that sounds like a wrap. Anyone up for a pizza run?"

"I was thinking maybe we could hang in the Lowerworld instead," Lita says. "It's gotta be cooler there than here."

"Maybe so, but last I checked, there was no pizza to be had in those parts."

"True . . ." Lita purses her lips, trying to decide which holds greater appeal.

"Was there pizza in the Upperworld?" Xotichl looks at Axel, but Axel just laughs and shakes his head.

"Poor baby." Lita leans in, ruffles his hair. "You've got a lot of catching up to do. Which means we shouldn't waste a single pizza-ordering opportunity." She pulls her phone from her pocket and scrolls through her speed-dial list as Auden grabs his keys.

"You'll need to pick up some drinks too." I head into the kitchen and peer into the fridge, if only to confirm that other than a nearly empty tub of cream cheese and a package of week-old bagels, it truly is empty. "I'm way overdue on food shopping."

"No worries, we're on it." Lita grabs her purse with one hand and Axel with the other. "We'll take supermarket duty. Xotichl and Auden, you're responsible for fetching the pizza, and Daire and Dace . . ." She looks over her shoulder and centers her gaze on mine. "Whatever's brewing between you, get it settled before we return. This may prove to be our last fun Friday night for a while. So I'd rather not waste it on relationship drama."

twelve

Daire

"Since when did Lita get so insightful?" I tip onto my toes and reach into an overhead cupboard. Glancing over my shoulder, waiting for Dace to react, but he remains frustratingly silent. "Hello? Anyone home?" I drop onto my heels and unload an armful of glasses onto the counter. Poking his shoulder, I say, "Dace. Hey. You in there?"

He squints. Shakes his head. Requiring a handful of seconds to travel from his private world of faraway thoughts to the tiny kitchen in Enchantment, New Mexico, where we both stand.

"Sorry. Guess I'm a little preoccupied." He swipes a hand through his hair, pushes his bangs from his eyes.

"A little?" I quirk a brow, make a face. But when he fails to react, I say, "Anything you want to talk about?"

He meets my question with a conflicted look.

"Did something happen at work?"

He rubs a hand over his chin, purposely avoiding my gaze. "Didn't make it to work today. Spent the day with Leftfoot instead."

He returns his focus to me, but the move comes too late. His words were clearly veiled, and I can't even fathom what sort of secret he's so determined to keep.

I study his face, relieved to find my image reflected in his eyes. Last time he acted like this, that wasn't the case. "Why would spending the day with Leftfoot leave you like this?"

"Like what?"

"Cold. Distant. Remote. Geographically close, but emotionally unavailable."

He looks at me as though he's just awakened from a very long sleep.

"God, I'm so sorry. Is that what I've done?"

I bite my lip and nod.

"C'mere." He reaches for me, clasping me at the waist as he pulls me into his arms. "I'm not trying to push you away, really." But when his mouth tips at the side, I'm not sure I believe him. Dace's inability to lie without giving himself away is just one of the many things I love about him.

"Dace—what's going on? What happened today?"

He shakes his head, returns his focus to me as though willing himself to try harder. The fact that he has to *will* such a thing only deepens my concern. What happened to my *love-trumps-evil* optimist from this morning?

"It's been a long day. A long and tiring day. You know how Leftfoot is . . ."

His breezy attitude clashes with the fine lines forming around his eyes, the grim downward tilt of his lips. Unwilling to partake of his charade, I move to untangle myself from his arms. To my surprise, he lets me.

I move about the kitchen, busying myself with gathering the correct amount of plates, napkins, and drinking glasses. Loading it all onto a tray I carry into the den, where we'll gorge on pizza and watch loads of movies, where Lita will grill me about which actors I knew (and which actors I kissed) back in my former life as a Hollywood makeup artist's jet-setting daughter. The usual plan when we don't head for the Lowerworld.

I place the tray on the table, start to arrange all the settings, when I realize I forgot to include the red-pepper flakes Xotichl loves, and I turn so quickly I smack into Dace.

"For the last time, what is going on with you?" I cry, frustrated to find him pulling away just when I need him the most.

"Daire—when was the last time you checked the prophecy?" His eyes glitter so strangely a chill slips over my skin.

I pause. Struggle to remember. Finally admitting it's been a while. "Maybe a month—quite possibly more." I shrug. "Why? Why is this relevant? What have you learned?"

Without a word, he grasps my hand in his and leads me out of the den, through the kitchen, and up the ramp to the office where the Codex is kept.

thirteen

Dace

When the worst is confirmed, when we've exhausted the subject between us, all we can do is sit quietly and wait for our friends to return.

Bodies stiff, thoughts mired deep in our own private hell, when a blare of chatter and laughter bursts through the door, only to halt a few seconds later when our friends find us sitting silent and stricken, with the Codex propped open before us.

Lita's the first to react. Centering it before her, she reads the words that are branded on my brain no matter how much I've tried to deny them.

> *When air sears and water fades*
> *When tempest winds ravage fire-scorched plains*
> *When Shadow eclipses Sun—the Seer shall fall*
> *Causing three worlds to descend into darkness eternal*

"Okay, so what we have here is another quatrain." Lita shrugs, pushes away from the book as though it's not to be taken seriously. Try as she might to appear unaffected, her spooked expression betrays her. Yet it doesn't stop her from adding, "We averted the last prophecy, so why should this one be any different?" Her gaze searches Axel's, seeking reassurance.

"The last prophecy was thwarted in part because of me." Axel's expression turns guarded as his eyes glow dark violet. "I broke one of my most sacred vows. I interfered in that which is considered strictly forbidden."

A solemn hush descends on the room as everyone takes a moment to consider his words. But I'm focused on the words he failed to speak.

He's one of us now.

His celestial pass, along with his celestial powers, have been revoked.

Which means there's no one left to guide me.

No one left to step in and save us.

And from what I've seen, no one should so much as attempt to spare me.

The Codex mimics the exact same story I read in the bones.

The glorious feather-crowned beast that dwells deep inside is morphing into something else entirely.

Something wicked and foul.

Something capable of dark, malevolent deeds.

Everything I professed to believe just twelve hours ago has been flipped upside down.

Turns out, I'm not the man I thought I was destined to be.

Rather than a creature of light, the savior I imagined—I'm well on my way to becoming the very worst enemy mankind has yet seen.

When Shadow eclipses Sun—the Seer shall fall

It's the takeaway line that says it all.

Somewhere within me stirs the darkness men fear. And it's that very darkness that will eclipse the light of the world and cause Daire to fall.

The girl I've sworn to protect—the girl I'd give my very life for—I'm now destined to destroy.

The countdown has started.

It's just a matter of time before my darkness is unleashed on the world.

Funny, how the last time I saw Cade he was unable to shift, yet now I'm destined to transform into something so heinous it'll make his two-headed, snake-tongued beast resemble the punch line to a really bad joke.

Is it possible the beast that once lived inside him has found a new home in me?

One where it could flourish and grow and turn my light against me—against all of us?

"So what do we do now?" Auden asks. Those six simple words heralding the moment I've tried hard to avoid. Hoped I could delay just a few minutes more.

It's the reason I've been acting so sketchy and distant. I know exactly what comes next and I can't bear to face it.

It may be inevitable, unavoidable, but it's shredding my insides—pulverizing my heart. And worse, it's turned me into the worst kind of liar.

Just this morning I swore to Daire that I would always be with her, would never leave her, that we'd get through this together—and now I'm about to break every vow.

Daire deserves better.

Better than me.

Turns out, we're fated—she was right all along.

Only instead of being fated to love her—to forge a life together—I'm fated to kill her.

And yet, while a part of me still manages to thrive, I owe it to Daire to pull myself together and handle this better. From the moment I arrived, I've been shutting her out. Immersed in the inner turmoil of trying to figure out the best way to say good-bye to the one person I can't imagine ever living without.

Instead of being up-front, finding the right words to tell her myself, I let the prophecy do the job for me, state what I couldn't. A cowardly act I need to redeem.

I take a moment to gather my courage, my thoughts, then I rise to my feet and address my friends first. "Just to be clear, the Shadow the prophecy speaks of is me. I witnessed the same prediction in a bone-reading ritual earlier today. Despite my normal appearance, it won't be much longer before the beast completely takes over. And from what I've seen, there will be no way to stop it, much less control it. So, for your safety and well-being, I'm leaving now and I won't be returning."

Lita gasps, clasps a hand to her mouth.

As Xotichl seeks comfort in Auden.

Only Axel nods his consent. Only Axel truly understands.

While Daire looks a lot like she did when she came to me in the dreams—a beautiful girl trusting me to do the right thing.

I try to say more—want to say more—but the words just won't come. So like the condemned man I am, I lumber toward the front door, aware of Daire racing behind.

I reach for the handle, step onto the stoop. Wanting so badly to pull her into my arms, press my lips to hers, though no longer sure if I should. "When you first discovered I'd stolen a piece of Cade's darkness, you wondered if it wasn't a mistake—that maybe the darkness within was part of my fate. Looks like you were right." My gaze roams over her beautiful features now blunted with pain. "I wish things were different. I wish I'd never—" Before I can finish, she presses a finger to my lips, halting the words.

"Don't waste your wishes on a past we can't change." Her green eyes meet mine. "What matters now is what we do next."

The hope in her voice is like an arrow to my chest, piercing my heart. There's no room for hope—not for someone like me. The beast inside negates all the good I once owned, and I need to convince her of that if it's the last thing I do.

"Daire—you don't know what I saw. It's worse than you think. Worse than you could ever imagine."

"Oh, don't be so sure. I've had the dreams too. I've also had my heart slashed nearly in half by your twin. And what I haven't experienced firsthand, well, my morbid imagination can fill in the rest." She cracks a brave smile, and I hold the image in my mind long after it fades. Wanting it to be the picture I'll carry forever. After all that she's been through, all that she faces ahead, it's incredible the way her radiant spirit still manages to shine.

I will do whatever it takes to keep this girl safe.

Even if it means keeping her safe from me.

"Despite all evidence to the contrary—despite what the bones and the Codex claim—they will not succeed. I plan to win, and I plan to win big. I won't go down easily, and I certainly won't go down alone. I will drag Cade Richter right along with me if it comes to that." Her chin is determined, her gaze resolute. But her voice trembles ever so slightly, betraying the deeply rooted uncertainty that lurks behind every word.

Though I know I shouldn't do it—though I know I should go quickly, quietly—I can't resist reaching toward her one final time. My fingers thrumming with warmth the moment they meet her sweet flesh and I cup her face in my hands.

It was only this morning when I reveled in the surety of being lucky enough to love her forever. And now, the future I'd dreamed of is gone, just like *that*.

Once again, fate gets the last laugh.

"I meant what I said earlier."

She tilts her head, shoots me a curious look. The weight of her gaze meeting mine sparking a small flicker inside the abyss where my soul used to shine.

Won't be long before the beast eclipses that too.

"You said a lot of things this morning," she says. "Things it seems you no longer believe." Her face darkens, as though she can already see the shift occurring within me.

And I can't leave her like that. Can't end us this way. So I go on to say, "When I said that someday we'd live together. Build a future together. Live a normal life together—I meant it. I still want that."

She places her hand over mine, entwining our fingers until they're laced nice and tight. "I'm not sure I was ever meant for a normal life." She blinks. Rubs her lips together. The usual signs of my girl refusing to cry. "But that doesn't stop me from dreaming of one with you. Just the two of us growing old together, enjoying the kind of ordinary moments normal people are lucky enough to take for granted. We can have that, Dace. We *will* have that. I won't give up on us. I won't let you go."

"Daire—" I'm shocked by her words. I thought I made myself clear. I thought she understood. With me she's in danger. Without me, she's . . . well, while not exactly safe, she stands a much better chance of surviving.

"Yes, I read the prophecy." Her voice is hurried, her face tense. "And yes, I heard everything you relayed about reading the bones. But I also know this—you were right this morning when you said that evil is no match for love. I could literally feel the truth in your words. I admit, at the time, I did what I could to deflect them, but only because I thought I needed to remain in warrior mode in order to win. I was sure that my arsenal of tricks had no room for such soft, fuzzy sentiments. But once I had a chance to really stop and reflect, I realized there's not a Seeker in the Santos family tree that didn't act from the heart. And while they may have failed at keeping the Richters permanently contained, that doesn't mean I can't succeed where they failed. It doesn't mean I can't honor my heart, keep you by my side, and take the Richters down once and for all, because that's exactly what I plan to do. I have every intention of winning, and I plan to do so with you. There's no reason that with the two of us working together, we can't fight this thing. Maybe you can even use the beast to help me defeat them."

Her brilliant green eyes blaze with conviction, clearly she believes every word. The sarcasm and cynicism from the morning eclipsed by her love for me.

I press my thumbs to her cheekbones, smooth them across her soft, smooth skin. The feel of her causing an unbearable ache to stream through my body, as the beast thrums and pulsates within. His constant hum a bitter reminder of how after tonight, I'll never be this close to her again.

"Turns out I was wrong," I say, my voice tight, choked, on the verge of breaking. "There is something stronger than love, something that's ready, able, and all too willing to conquer us both—and it lives inside me. Try as I might, I can't control it, Daire. The beast has its own life force, its own agenda, and it won't be long until it completely overwhelms me. I need you to believe me when I say that you will all be better off without me."

Despite my warnings, she remains undeterred. "Fine. I hear you," she says. "But that doesn't mean I have to go along with your plan. You can say good-bye to our friends, but you can't say good-bye to me. I won't give up on us, Dace. Not now, not ever."

Her eyes find mine and we hold the look much longer than we should. Reluctant to relinquish the cache of dreams that, thanks to fate, we'll never get a chance to experience.

She's made her vow, and I've made mine—both of us lead by our hearts. When I swore I would do whatever it took to save her, I meant every word. And as hard as this moment is, the saving starts now. The longer I stay, the more I risk putting her in harm's way.

I fold her hands in mine, pressing for one, sweet, brief moment before I release her for good and my arms fall cold and alien to my sides. "I left a bag by my place on the couch. I purposely left it there because I want you to have what's inside. I also want you to show Axel, Lita, Auden, and Xotichl how to use it. I want you to train them until they're proficient. And when the time comes, I want you to give them firm instructions to use it on me." She starts to protest, but this time it's my turn to hush her. "No hesitations.

No second guesses. From what I've seen, that time *will* come, and I want you all to be ready when it does."

We've come to an impasse, with me determined to leave and her determined to save me. And as hard as it is, it's my job to see this thing through.

Without another word, I lower my head and press my lips gently to hers. Hoping the kiss will convey what words can't—my undying love—my deepest regrets. Then I pull away just as quickly and hurry down the path, resisting the urge to look back.

fourteen

Daire

I press my back against the door, relying on it for support as I watch Dace cross the stone-and-gravel path, make his way through the gate, and disappear from my life. And despite a house full of friends, the truth is, I've never felt so alone.

First my *abuela*. Now Dace.

I'm not sure how much more I can take.

That's the thing about loss—no matter how often one experiences it, it never gets any easier.

And yet, this is nothing like losing my *abuela*. While my grandmother has left the physical world, Dace is still firmly entrenched right here within it. As long as he remains among the living, I won't relinquish the dream of a future together.

Where there's life, there's hope. And despite what he says, I'm determined to get through this.

It's just like I told him, Seekers have always worked from the heart—and I see no reason to change that.

I take a moment to compose myself, run a hand through my hair, and dry my tears with the back of my hand. Then I head inside and face my friends, and hoping to hide the pain of what I've just gone through, I keep it nonchalant when I say, "While I'm still up for pizza, I think the movies might have to wait."

Collectively, they stare at me, until Axel is the first to speak. "Daire, is Dace okay?"

I nod. Feign a brighter look than I thought I was capable of.

"And you? You okay too?" Xotichl leans forward, studies me intently.

I take a moment to look at each of them, making sure I have their full attention. "I am. I'm better than okay. And you know why?"

Lita groans loudly, paces before the giant rock jutting boldly from the middle of the wall. "Daire—you don't have to pretend to be strong on our account." She shoots me a knowing look. "We know perfectly well what just happened out there. After saying good-bye to us, Dace proceeded to say good-bye to you and break your heart. You gotta be dying inside, and it's okay to show it. We're your friends, you don't ever have to hide your feelings from us."

I shake my head and dismiss the thought with an impatient wave of my hand. There's no point in indulging my heartbreak. Not when I have every intention of getting Dace back.

"Don't blame Dace," I say. "He did what he thought was right. He's only trying to protect us."

"Protect us from himself?" Auden cuts in, clearly struggling to grow used to the idea of Dace being dangerous. "Because deep down inside he's not what he appears to be?"

I avert my gaze, reach for the fresh glass of iced tea they poured for me. Hoping they don't notice the way my hand trembles as I bring the glass to my lips.

"Daire, what's going on here?" Lita settles against the rock with her arms folded defiantly across her chest. "You're taking this way too calmly. Is there something you're not telling us? Because in my admittedly limited experience, prophecies are rarely wrong, and this particular prophecy is about as bad as they come."

I place my glass on the table, indulging in a moment's delay before I say, "You're right, prophecies are rarely wrong." Lita nods, seemingly satisfied to see we're in agreement. "But that doesn't mean they're infallible." Her eyes narrow, her lips tighten. "Destiny really can be shaped by free will, and that's exactly what I intend to do."

"Meaning?" Xotichl shoots me a concerned look.

"Meaning that Dace's absence is temporary." An uncomfortable hush falls over the room as my gaze moves among them. Lita is the first to react.

She jabs a thumb toward the Codex, not one bit convinced. "Did you not read what I read? You're doomed. And because of that, the rest of us are doomed too. Yeah, I tried to put on a happy face earlier, tried to pretend it wasn't true, but facts are facts, Daire. And the fact is that Dace is destined to destroy us all, starting with you. As much as I've grown to like him, now that I know what I know, I'm really not up for sharing a pizza with him. And if you insist on bringing him around, then . . ."

She shifts uncomfortably, unwilling to finish the thought, though it's not like she needs to. The silence that follows when no one jumps in to defend Dace, tells me they're all in agreement.

While Dace may have succeeded in scaring them, he hasn't scared me. I know I can help him exorcise the beast. At the very least, I have to try.

"So that's it? We just turn our backs on him? We just run away the moment he needs us the most?"

"Daire—he's beyond our help! He's—" Before Lita can continue, Axel moves to her side, his presence enough to silence her. Still, I can't help but notice how he fails to come to Dace's defense, seemingly content to add no dissent.

"Listen," I say, exerting great effort to remain calm and on point. Getting upset will only give them further reason to doubt me, and with the way things are going, I can't take the risk. "I understand how you feel. Really, I do. But here's the thing, here's what you don't know: We can and will win this. But not if we continue arguing, taking sides, and accepting defeat before we've had a chance to get started. The only way we can win is by *intending* to win." *And possibly with another idea that I'm not quite ready to share . . .*

"Is it really that easy?" Auden strives to keep his tone light, but his skeptical expression betrays him. "I'm sorry to say it, Daire, but I'm with Lita. Dace is dangerous, and what you're offering sounds a little too woo-woo to effectively go against the beast he described."

"I don't expect any of this to be easy, but when has that ever stopped us from trying?" They all look at one another, yet I can't help but notice how they avoid looking at me.

"Daire, you need to understand that you make it nearly impossible for us to trust that you care about our safety when you insist that Dace can be rehabilitated. He told us point-blank that it was too late. That it wasn't his to control. And since it's happening to him, I think he just might be the authority on the topic."

I look from Xotichl to Axel, willing him to chime in. I can understand my friends' unease, but I thought for sure Axel would be on my side.

"You too, Axel?" I fix my gaze on his. "Just this morning you said intent was magick's most important ingredient—that belief was the spine of intent. Did you believe what you said, or were you just humoring me?" His eyes meet mine, but his mood is impossible to read. "Are you willing to stand behind your words, or have you changed your mind? And Lita—" I switch my focus to her. "What about when you said that I didn't have to go it alone? That you were all willing to help? Is that no longer true? Because it's really starting to feel like you're all standing on the sidelines shouting for the kill, when I'm the one in the arena—I'm the one fighting the fight—which means I just might have a better perspective than you."

Lita flinches, drops her gaze to her feet, as Axel pushes away from the wall and swipes a hand through his halo of curls. Looking from Lita, to Xotichl, to Auden, then finally to me, he says,

"I'm here for you, Daire. But I guess there are limits. If it comes down to it, I won't hesitate to save all of you over Dace, and I think we're all hoping we could get that same assurance from you."

They nod in unison, and I take a moment before I reply. "I assure you that if it comes down to making that choice, your safety will be my first priority. But it's really a moot point, since it will never come to that."

"Not exactly the reassurance I was hoping for." Lita scowls.

"Well, it's the best I can do. Which means we'll just have to call a truce on this one and agree to disagree because I'm not going to lie to you. So, that said, I was hoping we could put this behind us and move on. We have a battle ahead and we need to prepare." I turn my attention to Axel, motioning for him to follow when I say, "I need your help in the bedroom."

"Uh—should I be worried?" Lita feigns a look of mock concern that soon shifts to curiosity when we return with a beautifully carved, hand-painted wooden trunk balanced between us. "What is that?" She leans in to get a better look.

"Think of it as my tool chest." I crack a smile. "Paloma gave it to me, along with all the tools I keep locked inside."

"Tools of the Light Worker trade?" Auden says. He's the least initiated among us, but that's about to change.

"Something like that." I spin the wheel of the combination lock I placed there shortly after Paloma passed on. How silly it seems now in light of all that's just happened. Like this simple, metal lock could ever keep a Richter at bay.

Then again, a Richter would never have the slightest interest in the tools I've stashed here.

And that just may turn out to be one of my biggest strengths.

In every encounter with Cade, every time he seemed to get the upper hand, he always made sure to mock the wisdom of my ancestors—my collection of magickal talismans. The pouch I wear at my neck—the small double-edged knife imbued with Valentina's essence—it's all a big joke to him.

Cade relies solely on his devious mind, his abyss of a soul, and the snake-tongued monster residing within. Though last I saw, the beast had abandoned him. Unlike my tools which have never once failed me.

Where failure's concerned, I've only failed myself.

But no more.

I kneel before the trunk and raise the lid. Aware of my friends gathering closer, as I remove the soft, hand-woven blanket I placed on top, then set the tools upon it, one by one.

"Oh," Lita murmurs, her voice, like her face, betraying her disappointment. "I thought there'd be cool stuff. I thought you'd hidden an arsenal in there."

"Make no mistake, in the right hands, this is an arsenal." I shove the bag Dace left well out of the way. I don't have to look to know what's inside. It's his blowgun and darts, but there's no way I'll use it on them. And with my friends all too willing to turn on him, they don't need to know it exists. Then after arranging the pieces so the rawhide rattle on the long wooden stick lies beside the large drum bearing the face of a purple-eyed raven, I place the three feathers that came from a swan, a raven, and an eagle all in a row, and finish by adding the pendulum with the small chunk of amethyst attached to its end.

"Grab some pizza," I say. "Refill your drinks, and get comfortable. I'm going to teach you how to use everything here. And it's probably going to take the better part of the night."

fifteen

Lita

"I feel so guilty." I bite my lip and frown at the overcrowded rack of dresses before me.

"Why? What'd you do now?"

I slew my gaze toward Xotichl. "What do you mean, *'what did I do now?'*"

"Well, I figure if you're feeling guilty, there must be a reason."

"Sheesh." I roll my eyes, shake my head, but it's really more for dramatic effect, my heart isn't in it. "Will I ever live down my diva past?"

"Not likely." Xotichl inches her purple glasses up the bridge of her nose with the tip of her finger.

"Anyway, I didn't exactly *do* anything. The reason I feel guilty is because everything around us is either falling apart, on the verge of falling apart, or, according to the Codex, destined to fall apart. And yet, despite the forecast of gloom and doom with a ninety-nine percent chance of complete world annihilation, deep down inside I'm still bursting with the absolute euphoria of unbounded happiness, and I know it's not right."

"That's what love does." Xotichl bobs her head as though listening to a song only she can hear. Choosing a dress from the rack, she scrutinizes it for a few seconds, only to exchange it for another, and then reject that as well. "Love is irrational. Nonsensical. Makes you feel things that seem wildly inappropriate when you consider the surrounding circumstances. And yet you shouldn't ever question it, shouldn't ever doubt it. You should just accept it for the gift that it is." She pushes away from the rack and scans the rest of the shop.

"I guess . . ." I sigh, unwilling to concede quite so easily. "Still, it just seems so wrong to feel so good when everything around me is going to hell. It's like, champagne corks popping in here." I thump my hand against my chest. "And the raging river of Hades out there." I jab my thumb toward the general direction of the green exit sign. "Not to mention how I'm pretty sure we're starting to grate on Daire's nerves."

"Starting?" Xotichl throws her head back and laughs like it's the funniest joke I've told all year. "I'm pretty sure her nerves were grated from the first night you and Axel laid eyes on each other."

"I knew it!" Feeling suddenly vindicated to confirm what I suspected all along, I lean toward her, grab her by the arm, and say, "You felt it too?" We've never had this discussion, and I'm eager to dissect it down to the smallest bit of minutiae.

"Felt it? I *saw* it." She chooses another dress and holds it against her. But it's way too much fabric and color for her petite frame, and she rejects it well before I can open my mouth to dissuade her.

"But why? Why do you think she's so against us?" I may be pressing it, but I'm determined to continue this topic until it's exhausted. "After all Axel's done for her—whisking her off to the Upperworld and saving her life—after all I've been through—being traumatized by having my perception altered by the Richters for the better part of my life—why can't she just be happy for us? Why can't she support us like we support her and Dace?"

"Because it's unnatural."

The voice comes from behind, and we turn to find Cade Richter looking as smug, slick, and self-assured as ever. Dressed in a pair of faded jeans, a white V-neck tee that clings to his shoulders, chest, and six-pack abs, displaying them to maximum impact, and brown leather flip-flops gracing his feet. Appearing as though he didn't run into a burning building with big, gaping knife wounds in his arm and his side just six months earlier.

No matter how many times I rehearsed this moment in my head, always envisioning me playing it cool while Cade cowered under the glare of my complete and total authority, in real life it plays just the opposite. With me gasping and jerking so spasmodically, I nearly knock Xotichl over.

"Not to mention it's bound to fail." Cade's icy-blue eyes bore deep into mine, and try as I might, I can't break the look. "Guy like Axel has no place here. He doesn't belong in our world. Sorry to be the one to break it to you, Lita, but it seems Santos doesn't have the guts to tell you what we both know is true. Your relationship was dead long before it began."

I stand there stupidly, unable to move, unable to speak. And though I'm waiting for Xotichl to step in and speak for me, turns out, she's as frozen as I am.

"Is that supposed to be a threat?" I finally manage. Unfortunately, it's the best I can manage. Still, I reach for Xotichl's arm and take a step back, pulling her along with me.

"Nope." Cade lifts his shoulders, swipes a hand through his hair. Holding it for a moment before he releases it and his bangs swoop into his eyes. One of his many signature moves. "Not a threat. Not even a warning. Just a fact, plain and true."

I roll my eyes. Huff under my breath. But the effort is forced, and he knows it as well as I do. "And I suppose next you'll be offering to console me when this so-called dead end occurs?" I fold my arms across my chest in an attempt to fend off the strange pull of his energy. Disgusted to find that after all he's put me through, after everything I know about him, I still find myself drawn to him.

"Wrong again." He raises a grin, reaches into his pocket, and lights a cigarette, despite the strictly enforced no-smoking policy. "You may be surprised to hear this, but I've moved on. A lot's changed in the last six months. And as irresistible as you think you are, turns out, I'm no longer into you."

I narrow my gaze, try to read between the words. Telling myself I should be relieved, happy to be released from the burden of his interest. And while part of me is indeed happy, there's another part that feels just the opposite. Sort of deflated, bereft.

"About your little glowing man, you need to know—"

"Axel. His name is Axel. And he doesn't glow." I scowl. But more at myself than him. I have no idea why I continue to engage him. We should've walked away the second we saw him. And yet, here I am, blabbering like a fool, while Xotichl stands gaping beside me.

"He lost his glow?" Cade quirks a brow, takes a deep drag on his cigarette. Then turns his head to the side to give us a better view of his perfect profile as he blows a series of smoke rings. "That's too bad. Only thing he had going for him so far as I could see."

"Whatever. We're done here." I start to push away, but he reaches toward me, binds my arm with his fist.

"Just remember this, Lita—when you and Axel go up in flames—and make no mistake, you will—don't forget you heard it here first. It's a warning you need to take seriously. Consider it my last gift to you."

"And why would you give me a gift if you're so *over* me, like you claim?"

"What can I say? I'm a sentimental guy." He lifts his shoulders, discards his cigarette on the floor where it burns a hole in the carpet. "We share a good bit of history. Had some fun times. I figure it's the least I can do."

"What're you really doing here? What do you want?" Xotichl speaks for the first time since he arrived.

"Same thing you want." The words are mumbled as he divides

his attention between us and his chiming cell phone. "Something to wear to the Rabbit Hole bash. I'm assuming you received the invite?" He returns to his phone with a sardonic grin.

"Oh yeah, we got it." Xotichl scowls. "The dead raven was a really nice touch." She places her hand on her hips and glares, but the effect is wasted on him. "So, I get that it's a ball, but are you really planning on wearing a dress?"

He lifts his chin, shoots her a blank look.

"In case you haven't noticed, you're shopping in the women's department. Men's is on the ground floor. Or perhaps you're not even shopping? Perhaps you're just doing a really bad job of stalking?"

He makes a face at his phone, then returns his focus to us. "Don't flatter yourself, flower. I have no interest in your pedestrian activities. If you must know, I'm shopping for my date. But as it turns out, this place isn't nearly classy enough. A special girl deserves a special dress, no?"

"How special could she be, if she's dating you?" Xotichl says, momentarily forgetting that I dated Cade off and on since elementary school. But I'm quick to forgive her the insult.

Cade grins. "Far more special than you could imagine."

"Who is she?" I ask, finally finding my voice. "Anyone we know?" I fight to keep my face still, my expression neutral, though I'm unable to do anything about the way my heart palpitates in my chest.

"I reckon you do know her. After all, Enchantment's a small town." He gives me a thorough once-over, allowing a few beats to pass before he says, "A small town with a long memory as it turns out—or maybe that's just me?"

His eyebrow shoots up, and I have no idea how to reply. Is he referring to the black onyx they're using to fortify the new building? Is it truly going to hold the ghostly memories and black deeds of Richters past?

"Care to elaborate?" Xotichl says, the words carrying a surprising edge.

"Not really." The smile he shoots her is grim. "Let's just say this is destined to be no ordinary party."

"The last party you threw, the club exploded and Phyre and Suriel Youngblood died—how do you plan to top that?"

"Turns out Phyre's little pyrotechnic display was merely the pre-show. Each step leads to the next, as they say."

His phone chimes again, claiming his attention.

"Anyway, nice catching up." He turns on his heel, flashes the back of his hand.

"For you maybe." Xotichl folds her arms defiantly over her chest, stiffening when he pauses, glances over his shoulder, and levels his focus on her.

"Careful there, little one. You're venturing into territory that's way out of your league."

His face darkens, prompting me to take a step forward, insert myself firmly between them. Fully intending to defend her should it come to that, but the sight of me standing before him only causes him to laugh.

"Save it, Lita. Xotichl doesn't need a bodyguard. Girl's got her sight back. She can handle herself. Or at least that's what she thinks. Turns out, there's a whole lot you two don't know, but I've done my good deed for the day. You'll get no more from me."

Xotichl fidgets with her glasses, struggles to stand her ground, though it's clear that she's shaken.

We both are.

The two of us unable to do anything more than remain rooted in place, long after Cade's sauntered away.

sixteen

Xotichl

"Are you sure we should do this?" My fingers clasp hard to the edge of my seat as Lita speeds into a turn so quickly I swear the car tilts on two wheels.

"How can we *not* do this? We owe it to Daire, right?" Her eyes find mine, lingering too long for my comfort. At these speeds, I prefer she focus on the road and not me.

"I'm sure he's on to us," I say, the words spilling forth in a shrieky high pitch that startles me as much as it does her.

This isn't like me. I'm usually the adventurous one. First in line to push all the boundaries.

Then again, ever since my sight returned, I'm not my usual self. It's like I've been thrust into an upside-down, out-of-balance world. Left adrift in a turbulent sea with absolutely no hope of ever reaching the shore.

"I'm absolutely positive he's on to us." Lita clasps the wheel so tightly her knuckles blanch. "In case you haven't noticed, he's using his blinkers and slowing his pace when he gets too far ahead. He's definitely leading us somewhere. Not to mention how he waited the full ten minutes it took us to get our act together and go after him."

"Speaking of . . . what the heck happened in there?"

"What do you mean? We were startled, that's all." She nods as though she wants to believe it, but the edge in her voice says otherwise.

"Yeah, we were startled, no doubt. Last place I expected to see Cade Richter was in the dress department, and yet there's no denying we handled it badly."

Lita's shoulders sink in defeat. "I'm ashamed to admit it, but that was kind of a disaster. I have no idea what came over me. It's like I had to keep reminding myself of all the reasons I hated him, and yet I still found myself drawn to him." She rubs a hand over her arm, shuddering at the memory.

"And I could barely speak." I roll my eyes at the memory. "It's like my whole body was frozen and only my mind was still working. Inside my head, I was raging with all the things I wanted to say. I had a whole slew of mocking statements and snarky comebacks ready to go—and yet all I could do was stand there and gape. It's like I'd been robbed of my will. Like I was trapped in a body that refused to obey."

Lita shoots me a worried look, then returns her focus to the road, accelerating so hard my shoulders press into the seat.

"Did he just . . . wave?" I shift my gaze between Lita beside me and Cade's black four-wheel drive racing ahead.

"He did indeed." Her lips sneak into a grin as she shimmies a little straighter in her seat, as though this just became fun.

"So, aren't we just falling into his trap then?"

"It's not a trap." The nod that follows is insistent, though once again, her voice fails to convince. "Okay, maybe it is a trap," she relents. "I mean, there's no doubt he's purposely luring us somewhere. But it's not a trap like you think."

"That is not one bit comforting." I gaze out the side window and frown. Contemplating which would be worse—swinging the door wide open and throwing myself free of her car—or actually going through with her plan. It's a toss-up.

"There's one crucial thing you seem to have forgotten: Cade Richter is a master manipulator. He loves his little games. He practically lives for them."

"Um, yeah. That's pretty much what I was getting at. Hence the fear of us being lured into a trap. His *little games* tend to get violent. Ask Daire."

Lita shakes her head and leans forward, peering through the dust-covered windshield. "Trust me, Xotichl, I know this guy like the back of my hair. He's not going to harm us. He just wants us to see whatever it is that he wants us to see so we can report back to Daire."

"Hand." I peer into the side rearview mirror, watching swirls of dirt and tumbleweeds dance in our wake.

"What?" Lita squints, looking at me for so long I jab a finger toward the windshield, urging her to watch the road and not me.

"The expression is, I know him like the back of my *hand.* Please, watch where you're going!"

"And what did I say?"

"You said *hair.*"

"Seriously, Xotichl?" She frowns, focuses back on the road, which buys me a moment of relief before she returns to me. "That's the take away from everything I just said? What's gotten into you? You're acting all skittish and weird. I've never seen you so fearful. You're always the one assuring me. Remember when you made me spy on Suriel Youngblood?"

I cringe at the memory. Spying on the snake-wrangling, doomsayer preacher was one of my worst ideas ever. Maybe the changes I'm experiencing are a good thing. Now that I can see the world around me, maybe I'm just now, for the very first time, understanding how dangerous it can be. Maybe this new, fearful Xotichl is an improvement over the former, impulsive Xotichl I used to be.

"Trust me, Suriel Youngblood is not someone I'll easily forget. And just so you know, I regretted that decision pretty much the second we arrived."

"Well, you won't regret this." Lita hardens her jaw, lifts her fingers for a moment, only to lower them back to the wheel with a grip that's twice as tight. "And if we do end up regretting it, well, at least we'll have something to talk about, right?"

"Yes. At least we'll have that. I'm always on the lookout for a good icebreaker." I hold hard to the edge of my seat as her car shakes and judders over the deeply rutted dirt road, wondering if I should just close my eyes until it's over.

"We're not going to die, Xotichl. Or at least not today. Not from Cade."

"How can you be so sure?" I sneak a lid open to better see her. "After all, he's the one who killed Paloma."

"He had a different agenda with Paloma. It was a Coyote versus Seeker thing. It was mostly about hurting Daire. Making her feel powerless and alone in the world. And while there's no doubt he succeeded, it's different with me. He won't try to harm me. And I'm afraid you're just going to have to take my word for it."

"You don't seriously think he's still madly in love with you, do you? Because that's the one thing I was sure he wasn't bluffing about."

Lita laughs, lifts a hand to her hair and fluffs up the ends. "Please, I'm not stupid. I don't think Cade Richter was ever madly in love with me. Or even marginally in love with me, for that matter. I don't think he even knows what love is. I know I didn't—not until I met Axel, anyway. What I do know is that Cade's pride and ego are deeply offended by how quickly I moved on. And because of it, I'm pretty sure he'd like to keep me around long enough to make me regret my choice to leave him, which of course I never will. How could I? With Axel, I have everything. I finally know what real love is, and I wouldn't trade it for anything." She glances at me, eyes narrowing when she reads the skeptical look on my face. "Didn't you catch the way Cade made sure to mention his date? *I'm shopping for a dress for my date. This place isn't classy enough for my date.*" She rolls her eyes. "Whatever Cade's up to, you can bet it's well planned. He leaves nothing to chance. Always has an agenda, which we'll learn soon enough. The real question is, why are you so scared? What's going on with you? Why don't you just tune in to the energy of the situation like you usually do? Surely that'll convince you that this will all turn out right."

I frown, unsure how to tell her how untethered I feel. That my newly restored vision seems to be the only tangible thing I can count on. So I just end up blurting out the truth. "I can't really read energy in the way that I used to."

She looks at me. Doing her best to hide her alarm. "You're probably still getting used to your sight though, right? You know, like you're learning to see through your eyes instead of your blind sight. I'm sure it'll come back."

"But what if it doesn't?" I clench my hands in my lap. There. I said it. Revealed my very worst fear that all the progress I made with the help of Paloma's tutelage has taken a permanent sabbatical.

"It will." She nods as though it's already been decided, but I'm not so sure.

I used to know when someone was lying purely by the color of their words.

I used to know when dark energies were lurking by the subtle shift in the atmosphere.

But now it seems I'm as clueless as everyone.

Questioning my instincts.

Second-guessing my gut.

"I don't know . . . I guess I just—" I start to say I have a bad feeling about all of this, but the truth is, I don't feel much of anything. There's a big empty void in the place where my intuition once lived. "The truth is, I really, truly don't know," I finally say, not wanting to lie. "But it just feels . . . wrong. Following Cade—going to the masquerade ball—none of it sits well inside."

I swivel toward Lita, only to find she's already moved on. Already returned her focus to chasing Cade's truck.

I fold my hands in my lap and try to keep calm. Try to find the place of quiet stillness, like Paloma once taught me.

She always said the silence is where my strength lies. That when I find myself anxious, uncertain, or feeling unsettled, I should allow my breath to slow and my thoughts to quiet, so a space can open up for the answers to be revealed. And though it's never failed me in the past, there's no denying it's failing me now.

The silence bears the opposite effect. Leaving me so jumbled and edgy, I turn to the window and press my fingertips hard to the glass in an attempt to steady myself.

Normally I'd be able to read the energy emitted by every run-down adobe we pass, but not anymore.

Still, I grit my teeth and try again, refusing to give up so easily.

Only to shoot toward the dashboard when Lita slams the brakes hard, and says, "This is the last thing I expected to see."

seventeen

Dace

Cade stops his truck in the middle of the street and lowers the driver's side window to better see me. "When I got your text, I was sure it was a joke." He keeps one hand on the wheel, the engine idling.

"Not a joke, I assure you." I lean against the door of the primer-gray, classic Mustang I've been slowly restoring. Arms loose by my sides, legs casually crossed at the ankles, in an attempt to appear open, easygoing, and harmless. In other words, the opposite of what I'm becoming.

"Well, that's your fail." He peers at me through a pair of dark sunglasses. Clueless to the fact that despite the tinted lenses, I can still see his eyes. I can see everything. He's part of me, just as I'm part of him. "So, get to it already. What do you want? I'm busy." He lifts his chin, checks his reflection in the rearview mirror. His usual smug, self-satisfied look deepening when he sees Lita parked a few feet away.

He thinks this scene is his to control.

Thinks he's the one who led them here so he could publicly out me as some sort of traitor.

Little does he know I planned the whole thing.

This is no courtesy call.

He has no idea just how big a traitor I'll turn out to be.

In the end, the beast may consume me, but not before I've defeated every last one of them.

"We need to talk." I push away from my car and crick my neck toward the large adobe estate nestled behind the large wrought-iron gates.

"You? In *my* house?" He works his tongue against the side of his cheek and hocks a wad of spit that lands just shy of my shoe. A feeble attempt to intimidate I choose to ignore. "Hate to break it to you, bro, but this is the closest you'll get. You're not fit to enter. You're not one of us. Never will be."

"You sure about that?" I push my sunglasses high on my forehead and return his look with red glowing eyes.

He laughs. Does his best to appear jaded and unimpressed. But I can see beyond the façade, and he's even more shaken than I originally bargained for.

"That it? That all you got?" He shakes his head, swipes a hand through his hair. "Maybe you should do that again so Xotichl and Lita can see. Unlike me, they tend to scare easily."

He jabs a thumb toward the girls, but I refuse to look. The mere sight of them is enough to conjure a thousand memories of Daire, and I can't afford to be distracted by thoughts of a girl I can no longer have.

He places his other hand on the wheel, shifts into drive, but I can't let him go, not until I get what I came for.

I step forward, moving to stop him as he cranks the wheel hard and noses the truck toward the gate. Sparing me a dismissive glance, he says, "It's like I already said, you can't come in. You can't ever come in. If you were smart, which clearly you aren't, but if you were, you would've known that. You wouldn't have wasted your time coming here."

The gates swing open as Cade eases onto the drive, but I won't be daunted. I will chase him to the front door if that's what it takes.

"I want my job back." I move alongside him.

He brakes, peering at me with a sardonic grin that widens his cheeks. "Not a chance."

"Fine." I shrug, as though it's no big deal either way. It isn't. I have every intention of getting my way. "Just thought I'd appeal to you first, since I heard you were promoted to manager. But I guess I'll go straight to Leandro instead."

"Feel free." Cade laughs, starts to raise the window between us.

"Leandro won't hesitate to reinstate me. Hell, he begged me to come back last time I spoke with him on New Year's Eve. Might make you look even worse in his eyes when I tell him you rejected me. Surely he realizes it's mostly your fault the Rabbit Hole blew. Phyre was just a normal girl, with no real powers to speak of, and still you couldn't stop her from endangering your entire family. Just like you can't seem to stop Daire from thwarting your every move."

His features sharpen, his eyes darken, but he makes no further attempt to drive on.

"Something to think about." I bump the driver's side door and I start to turn away. Acting as though it's an afterthought when I turn back to say, "Oh, and by the way, in case you've forgotten, you owe me your life."

"Is that what you think?" He leans out the driver's side window and frowns.

"That's what I know, and you know it too."

"You saved me to save yourself." He narrows his gaze, tries to look menacing, but comes nowhere close to succeeding.

"Did I look like I needed saving?"

He looks me over. Works his jaw. The seconds tick past.

"Face it Cade, you're not what you used to be. Hell, you can't even shift into your pathetic snake-tongued beast. You're no threat to me."

"What're you after?" His voice is gruff, his features sharpen, but it's the most he's capable of, and I can't help but snicker in the face of it.

"Ultimately—I'm after what's rightfully mine. The house, the town, all of it—my legacy as Leandro's son. But for now, I'll start with my job. Tell Leandro you had to convince me, if you want. Tell him it's your way to keep an eye on me. I don't care how you sell it, just sell it. Though you might have trouble convincing him of anything. I think we all know he's beginning to doubt you. You two are on shaky ground, so here's your chance to prove that you can handle the role of both manager and next in line for Leandro's throne."

"And Daire?"

I narrow my gaze. Not liking the sound of her name on his lips. Especially the way that he said it, with an unmistakable tinge of longing in his tone.

"What about her?" I hold myself still, aware of the beast beginning to rumble and stir, and it takes all of my will to contain it. Won't be long until he makes himself known. But now is not the time. Not even close.

"Does the Seeker know you're here?" He cocks his head, shoots me a look of contempt.

"You think I have to ask permission to visit my ancestral home?" He glares in response, and I take it as my cue to exit. "Tell Leandro I'll report for work first thing tomorrow."

"Never gonna happen," he calls, but I choose to ignore him. I just head for my car and give a quick wave to Lita and Xotichl, hoping they'll do their parts and report back to Daire.

Tell her I was here—that it's too late to stop me from meeting my destiny.

That I've already joined the other side, and it's in her best interests to stay far away.

Hoping they'll succeed where I failed by convincing her to save herself, save them, and forget about me.

Then, without another look, I climb inside my car, gun the engine, and drive away.

eighteen

Daire

With my last client gone, I head into the den, surprised to find Chay sitting on the couch, reading a newspaper and waiting for me.

"How long have you been here?" I stand before the whirring fan blades and twist the ends of my ponytail into a bun I prop high on my head, enjoying the cool breeze on my neck.

"Long enough to feed Kachina, muck out her stall, and nearly finish this paper as a steady stream of clients paraded in and out." He motions toward a glass of iced ginger tea he has waiting for me. "Ice is probably melted by now."

I push away from the fan and move toward it, savoring the stream of cool liquid easing down my throat.

"How you holding up?" He folds his newspaper in half and tosses it onto the table to better focus on me, as I claim the opposite chair and take another sip of my tea.

Though the question is posed innocently enough, the part he failed to voice looms large between us.

How am I holding up now that I'm all on my own without Paloma to guide me?

It's what they're all wondering.

While my friends have provided much-needed comfort and support, sometimes I feel like Chay is the only one who truly understands how empty life feels now that she's gone.

Paloma was his companion, his lover, his closest confidant, and best friend. There's no doubt he misses her as much as I do.

I slip off a blue rubber flip-flop and prop a bare foot on the table. "Honestly?" My eyes meet his, finally able to admit to the truth I've kept buried inside for too long. "Between the gardening, the clients, and looking after me, I don't know how she managed to keep up with it all, and make it look so darn effortless. I always feel two steps behind . . ." I sigh, gaze down at my hands. "She's a hard act to follow."

"But that's just it. You're not expected to follow."

"Aren't I?" I lift my gaze to his. "I'm the Seeker. I have a destiny—and a long list of duties to go along with it."

Chay's expression softens as he fingers the silver wolf's head he wears at his wrist. "No two Seekers are created the same. And for what it's worth, Paloma was once in your shoes. Struggling to find her way after her own mother passed on."

I sit up a bit higher. Eager to know more about the story Paloma never shared. "I know so little about it. She rarely talked about those days."

"Paloma didn't like to dwell in the past." His focus shifts from the wolf to the intricate silver eagle's head ring on his finger.

I nod, knowing I probably shouldn't dwell either. But now that he's mentioned it, I can't resist asking, "What was she like back in the day? How did you meet?"

His lips curl ever so slightly, as he tilts his head back and allows his mind to drift to the past. For a brief moment, I can imagine how he might've looked then. Tall, dark, and ruggedly handsome pretty much describes it.

"I feel like I've always known Paloma." His voice is soft, as though savoring the memory. "She was a lot like you, actually. Beautiful. Strong. Capable. And woefully unsure of herself." He cracks a smile, returns his gaze to mine. "But later, after she lost Alejandro and discovered she was pregnant with Django, the deeply rooted strength inherent in all Seekers began to shine through."

"Is that when you fell in love with her?"

His gaze grows distant. "I fell in love with her long before that."

"Did she know? Did you tell her?"

He grins in a way that creases his cheeks and causes a riot of wrinkles to fan around his eyes. "Oh, I'm sure she knew. It's not like I was capable of playing it cool. Though I was just one of many. Most of us had a thing for Paloma back then. But I finished school early and went off to college, and while I was away, she fell in love with Alejandro. So I resigned myself to being happy that she'd found someone worthy."

I sit with that for a while, wondering if I could do the same for Dace. Be happy for him if he found someone else, someone worthy. While I'd like to think that I could, I'm pretty sure I'm just deluding myself. Seeing him happy with another girl would be a terrible burden I'm not sure I could bear.

"For those who are patient, life has a way of working out." I meet his gaze, realizing too late he'd been observing my reverie. "Paloma and I shared many good years. I prefer to concentrate on the time spent together, rather than the time spent apart."

"You said Paloma was unsure like me, but it's hard to imagine her ever feeling that way. When did she make the switch? What was the one thing that instigated it?"

The question brings another smile to his face, though I can't fathom why. "While I can't pinpoint that in the way you'd like, I can say that confidence is usually the reward for taking the risk of being yourself."

I drum my fingers against the armrests and take a moment to digest that.

Is it possible I've been so focused on being just like Paloma that I lost sight of myself?

"No two people are alike—just as no two Seekers are alike.

Paloma concentrated on her strengths and didn't punish herself for her weaknesses."

"So you're saying I should follow that example?"

"There are worse examples."

"But what if I don't know what my strengths are? What if I feel so overwhelmed by trying to keep up with everything that—" I stop myself before I can dissolve into a full-blown whine. Switching tacks, I say, "I guess what I need is a cheat sheet."

Chay throws his head back and laughs—a deep-bellied sound I'm glad to know he's still capable of.

"You don't need a cheat sheet." He rises from the couch, motions for me to follow his lead. "Though I'm betting you're in need of some dinner."

Chay takes me to a restaurant just outside of town, where he seems to know everyone.

"This is like dining with a celebrity," I say, after the waitress has fawned over him and taken our orders. "And I should know, having dined with a few."

"As the only veterinarian within a fifty-mile radius, you tend to meet a few people." He spreads his paper napkin across his lap and I do the same. And a few moments later, when the waitress returns with two salads, I can't help but grin.

"Since when is that your *usual*?" I stab a fork into a bed of dark, leafy greens. "You on a diet?"

"Never." He lifts his fork to his mouth. "Just making more conscious choices, I guess. Looks like Paloma's lectures managed to stick."

We dig into our meals. The two of us happy to eat in a contented, comfortable silence, until Chay lowers his fork, dabs his mouth with his napkin, and says, "When was the last time you saw Dace?"

I push away from my plate and lean against the vinyl banquette.

"Yesterday when he stopped by to say good-bye. I guess you know why."

He spins the eagle ring around and around on his finger. His mouth downturned, gaze somber. "I'm sorry."

I lift my shoulders in response, try to put on a brave face.

Eating with Chay in the out-of-the-way diner reminds me of the first day we met under similar circumstances. I was scared and uncertain, facing a future I couldn't even fathom. And he was the wise counsel whose presence alone was enough to instill in me much-needed comfort. After all that we've been through, it's nice to know that feeling still holds.

He studies me closely, trying to determine the difference between the truth of my feelings and the fiction of my actions. "You're taking this well."

"As well as I can." My reply purposely vague. After seeing my friends' reactions over my reluctance to steer clear of Dace, I'm a little nervous about approaching Chay.

He lowers his gaze, pulls his wallet from his pocket, and I realize I'm not ready to leave it this way.

"Though any advice would be greatly appreciated."

He tosses a wad of bills on the table and, without hesitation, says, "Don't lose your focus."

I squint, unsure what he means.

"Don't lose sight of what matters most."

"Which is?"

"The people who rely on you to keep them safe from the Richters."

I drop my gaze, having read between the lines. "In other words, don't let my love for Dace—my fantasy that I alone can change him—tame him—slay the beast within and return him to the Dace I know and love—don't let that get in the way of being the Seeker I was born to be. Is that what you're saying?" I sigh, having expected this but still feeling disappointed to hear him echo the same sentiment as my friends.

My gaze meets his, finding the confirmation right there in his eyes. Also like my friends, his faith in me is faltering.

While I hesitate to question his wisdom—partly because he's Chay and I've always relied on his counsel—and partly because he read the bones just as clearly as Dace did—our opinions conflict.

"Chay, you once said that Paloma understood that great privilege comes with great responsibility. That she never dwelled on her tragedies, same way she didn't gloat over her triumphs. She stayed steady, humble, and present, with one eye fixed on the horizon ahead . . ."

His eyes narrow, presumably remembering that night at Leftfoot's, not so long ago.

"Well, that's exactly the model I'm trying to follow. So, I guess what I'm trying to say is, I have every intention of doing the right thing by all of you—and that includes Dace." My hands twist in my lap, unsure how he'll react, but it needs to be said. "Everyone's urging me to give up on him, abandon him without a single look back. I can't do that. I won't do that."

I search Chay's face, but he's guarded, hard to read. So I wait for several nerve-wracking seconds until he forms a reply. "While that sounds good in theory, question is, are you sure that's the right thing to do?"

"It's all I can do. There are no other options as far as I'm concerned."

"Well then, you've made your choice."

We exchange a long look that's broken by the clatter of the busboy removing our plates and the sound of my cell phone chiming.

After taking a moment to read the message, I return to Chay and say, "What did you do with that tourmaline?"

He hunches forward, slides his elbows toward me, and meets my question with a wary gaze.

"I need it."

His eyes grow hooded, his voice gruff. "Impossible. It's not ready. It may never be ready."

I shrug. "I still need it."

"Daire, do you have any idea what you're asking?" He rubs his lips together, shakes his head. "By giving you the tourmaline now, I'd be putting you at great risk. The curse Cade embedded runs deep. The hooks were the most intense Leftfoot and I have ever seen. It hasn't been nearly long enough to be fully cleansed. We're not even sure it can be regenerated."

I pause for a moment, making sure he's finished, before I continue. "While I get what you're saying, thing is, I've done a bit of my own research. Did you know that blue tourmalines are traditionally thought of as a shamanic stone? They've been used in ritual for centuries. Specifically for protection, but also to point the shaman or Seeker, as we're now known, toward safety in times of trouble."

"I'm aware of that. I'm also aware of the irony of Cade using that very stone against Paloma."

"He thinks that's the punch line, but it's not even close." I wave it away, eager to leave the past behind in favor of a future that's mine for the taking. "Blue tourmalines are also used to activate the third eye, as they provide clarity, direction, and enhance intuition."

Chay shoots me an impatient look. "Daire, what are you getting at?"

"I need it. I don't care if it's not ready. I need that stone now. As soon as you can get it to me. We're running out of time."

"I can't do it. I won't risk you falling victim to Cade."

I lean toward him, look him right in the eye. While I regret having to take this approach, his reluctance to help leaves no other choice. "I'm sorry to say this, but if you won't give it to me, I'll get it myself. I know you mean well. I know you're only looking out for me. But this is one risk I have to take. With or without your blessing."

"Can I ask what this is about? And why the urgency?"

I relax into my seat, knowing I won. "I saw Marliz use her tourmaline ring to gain access to the Rabbit Hole. I also discovered that they're enhancing the building with black onyx—making it stronger, more resilient, and ensuring that the energy of their ancestry stays contained in those walls. They're not building the same old Rabbit Hole—they've got a massive mystical makeover planned. The place is enchanted—barricaded and bound by magick. From what I saw, possession of one of their blue tourmalines is the only way in, and I need to get in there before the party begins so I can locate the vortex. With a remodel that extensive, it won't be easy to find."

"I'll get you another tourmaline, then. One that hasn't been cursed."

"I don't think just any stone will work. It has to come from them."

"But if the stone is connected to them, they'll know you're in there."

I lift my shoulders, tuck a lock of hair behind my ear. "That's a chance I'm willing to take."

He holds my look for a moment, then heaves a sigh of surrender and pushes away from the table.

"Also, I just received a text from Lita. She ran into Cade. Dace was with him."

Chay returns to his seat, regards me with a sober gaze. "So it's started." His face is tired, voice resigned.

"Doubtful. Dace would never join forces with the Richters. If he was there, it was for a good reason."

"Daire, if Dace is being led by the beast, then the choices he makes are no longer his."

"Guess that remains to be seen."

Another impasse. Chay sighs and says, "The stone is buried deep at the base of one of our mountains. It'll take most of the night to reach it."

Our eyes meet.

"But I'll do it. I'll bring Leftfoot and Cree for company."

"Thanks." I slide free of the booth, turning in time to catch him looking at me in a way I can't fathom.

"Paloma would be proud."

I squint.

"While I may not agree with your choices, there's no doubt you've just taken your first real step toward trusting your instincts. There's an old saying—when you conquer your fears, you conquer your life. Let's hope it holds true in your case."

I smile, feeling inordinately proud.

"There's another old saying that anger is like drinking poison and expecting the other person to die." He slides an arm around my shoulders and leads me to the door. "And with that in mind, I'll give you that stone on one condition." He swings the door wide and ushers me into the night. "You clear your heart of hate for the Richters, especially Cade."

I stop beside his truck, sure he must be joking. But one look at his face tells me he's anything but. "I'm not sure that's even possible."

"Then you better find a way to make it possible because you're playing right into their hands. The hate you harbor toward them is ripping a hole in your heart, which will serve as a portal. Allowing them access to control you in ways far more effective than any stone could. Hate has an insidious way of taking over—but only if we let it. So don't you dare let it."

nineteen

Daire

Although I didn't think it was possible, Axel looks more distraught than Lita and Xotichl when he learns of Dace's meeting with Cade.

He paces the length of the room, makes a series of U-turns. "I've been guiding him since the day he was born. There was never any indication it would come to this. No warning, nothing. Still, even though he told us, I guess I still clung to the secret hope that it wasn't that bad, that he'd be spared somehow. And yet the evidence speaks for itself."

"How does that work exactly?" Xotichl curls her feet under her legs. "How does one get assigned to a guide?"

"Yeah, and do you know mine?" Lita's eyes light up. "I mean, now that you're open to talking about it—I mean, you are open, right? Since you're the one who brought it up."

Axel drops his gaze to the floor. "I can't discuss it. It's . . . sacred."

"But you're no longer part of the team, remember? You're not even a benchwarmer. For all intents and purposes, you were dropped."

He sighs. Unable to resist her, he says, "Even as guides, we're not created perfect."

"But you were more than a guide, right? You were a Mystic."

"Still, like them, I had my own quirks to overcome. And so we were often assigned charges with similar issues."

"And what were your issues? What are Dace's issues?" I ask, hoping for a fresh perspective, a new angle I might've missed.

"We're both rebels at heart."

I sit with that, trying to decide if it's good or bad.

"We're eager to please but only up to a point. We have a fierce sense of right and wrong, and we'll do whatever it takes to protect it."

Our eyes meet, and I know what he's thinking: *Dace is being led by the beast—his moral boundaries are blurred.*

But I see it differently. Dace's light has always been one of his most defining features—I refuse to believe it could be snuffed out so easily. But when I share the thought with my friends, they respond with the same distrusting look I've grown used to seeing.

"Don't forget, Dace is a split soul," I press. "He encompasses the good half—the light half—while Cade encompasses the dark."

"Not anymore . . ." Lita mumbles under her breath, causing everyone to shift uncomfortably.

"The potential to choose darkness was always there," Axel says. "He did have free will. But he always chose to rise above it. Until . . ."

"Until I came to town."

"It was fated." He shrugs. "Of course, I didn't know that back then."

"So, if you didn't have a road map," Xotichl asks, "how'd you know when to be in the Lowerworld on Christmas Eve to save him—only you ended up saving Daire instead?"

"Usually we don't get the signal until just a few moments before. There's not a lot of time to prepare. But with Dace, I'd been worried for days. I didn't like the way things were progressing, and so I did the forbidden—I peeked at his Soul Book."

We stare at him wide-eyed.

"So it exists!" Xotichl squeals, causing us to shift our attention her way. "It's said that everyone has one. It's a record of all that was, is, and will be. Paloma told me about it early on in her teachings."

"Oh, it's real," Axel says. "And it was strictly forbidden for someone like me."

"But his Soul Book must've been wrong," Lita says. "Because Daire died instead of Dace."

"Words contain energy, and energy is subject to transformation and change. Our thoughts guide our actions, which in turn determine the lives that we lead. Every action has a series of probable reactions or outcomes . . ."

"And Dace deciding to steal a bit of Cade's soul, changed his future?"

"Looks like."

"Was that when you decided to look?" Lita asks.

"I failed that night. I understood his motivation, but I tried my best to urge him against it. Though he was good at shutting me out, and he made that leap without looking back. Shortly after, I stole a glimpse of his book, and you know the rest."

"What about your book? Do you have one? And if so, what does it say about me—about us?" Lita sits up straighter, eager to get a sneak peek into their future.

"It's like I said, energy is subject to change and transformation. Nothing is written in stone . . ." His voice drifts along with his gaze.

Lita frowns, her shoulders deflate, and figuring we could all use the distraction, I say, "Well, the good news is . . ." I pause until I'm sure I have their attention. "Jennika just wrapped a movie, and the costume designer agreed to let us borrow some of the gowns they used, to wear at the Rabbit Hole party."

Sure enough, Lita's face lights up, though Xotichl's grows skeptical. "And the bad news? You may as well spill it. This is Enchantment. Bad news is our specialty."

"The bad news is we have a lot of work to do before we're ready to face the Richters. Anyone up for a little training?"

"I'm on it." Lita heads for the trunk, but before she can reach it, the doorbell chimes. The sound so unexpected, we all stop and freeze.

Axel is the first to respond; determined to make himself useful for living rent-free, he's appointed himself as a sort of butler/house-boy. Though it's only a moment later when he calls, "Daire, I think you better come see this."

I rush out the door and onto the stoop, only to find yet another white glossy box tied with the same type of bloodred ribbon as the last one.

"What dead creature has he left us this time?" Lita snaps, as I kneel down beside it, and Axel follows the set of Coyote tracks, confirming two separate paths of entry and exit.

"You're not going to open it, are you?" Auden asks.

"Of course she's going to open it," Xotichl says. "She has to!" Then seeing me hesitate, she adds, "You are going to open it, right?"

I nod. But instead of unwrapping it the usual way, I call upon the magick I've been relying on for pretty much everything these days in an effort to whip my skills into the best shape I can.

"No matter how many times I watch that, it still freaks me out." Lita shivers as I unwind the ribbon and lift the lid from the box using only intent.

This time, whatever's inside is hidden by several layers of delicate tissue I unfold with my hands, only to find the most beautiful, hand-crafted, black leather raven mask waiting beneath.

"Oh my gosh—it's beautiful!" Lita slaps a hand over her mouth, realizing what she just said. "I mean, I know it's from Cade, but you have to admit, he does have good taste."

"Maybe it's not from Cade," Xotichl says, looking from the mask to me. "What if it's from Dace? You have to at least consider it, seeing as how he's aligning himself with the Richters."

"One visit does not an alignment make," I snap, feeling bad

about the edge in my voice the moment the words are out, but I'm really tired of everyone speaking against him. If by chance he was turning evil, he could hardly be held responsible. He made a choice with the noblest intentions, without fully understanding the consequences. If he could take it back, he would. If he could control the beast, he'd do that too. Still, I refuse to believe he would ever act out against me by sending such a cryptic gift with no note.

"Whoever it's from, the question is: What are you going to do with it?" Auden asks.

I lift the mask from the box and hold it before me.

"Are you going to keep it?" Lita casts a nervous glance my way.

"For now." I return it to the box and pack the tissues around it.

"Are you going to wear it? What if it's cursed? Or worse?" Xotichl says.

"I guess we'll leave that to the pendulum to decide. Come." I usher them inside. "We have training to do, and that's as good a place to start as any."

twenty

Dace

When I get to the Rabbit Hole, the grunt guarding the entrance starts to give me some grief, until I push my sunglasses high on my head, allow him a look at my blazing red eyes, and he waves me right in.

Guess Cade chose to ignore my request.

Yet another regret to add to his growing list.

I slip past a barricade that's well into the process of being torn down, and make my way inside. Barely moving past the entry before I'm stunned into silence. The space is so new and improved it bears absolutely no resemblance to its former, run-down self. Every last trace of the shabby, old dive bar has been successfully eradicated. Leaving a sleek, modern establishment, with high-end, minimalist design to stand in its place.

A sort of luxury Coyote lair.

The walls are an earthy mix of charcoals and browns. The floors are crafted from quartzite. While tall metal sculptures shaped to resemble trees jut from the corners, giving the place a cool, natural vibe.

I move among a row of plush, low-slung banquettes and sculptural aluminum tables that appear to have been crushed by human hands. Noting how the one familiar symbol that remains is the red Coyote insignia marking the barware.

"So, what do you think?"

The voice is Leandro's, and I wait a couple of beats before I acknowledge it.

"A definite improvement." I turn, allowing my gaze to roam the expanse of his face from behind my dark lenses. Searching for some semblance of myself in his sweep of dark hair and shrewd gaze. Though he's never been a father to me, there's no doubt he sired me. Turns out, we have more in common than we could've guessed. "So, you survived the blast," I say. Nothing like stating the obvious. Still, while I came here with an agenda, it's best not to rush it.

"Did you doubt me?" He cricks his neck, studies me with a practiced eye. His suspicion made plain in the look on his face.

I shrug. Hook my thumbs into my belt loops, aiming for a cool and casual stance. "There were many who were wishing you'd perished."

"Oh, I wouldn't say *many*." He laughs, but the sound is hollow, short-lived. "Though I'm sure there were a few. Which leads me to wonder—were you among them?"

I fix my gaze on his, surprised to find the answer comes quickly. That it's not at all complicated and is surprisingly genuine. "What kind of son would I be to wish such a thing?"

His gaze narrows, searching for signs of falsehood, mockery, but he'll find none of that here. I'm glad he survived. More than he could ever realize. Though from the look of it, Leandro's hard to convince. "I'm afraid that's a tougher sell than you think."

"Why would I lie?"

"Same reason most people lie to me. To gain special favor."

"I'm not seeking favors."

"Aren't you?" His brow creases and lifts, his lips fall thin and flat. "That's not what I hear. Cade warned me you'd come. Says you want your old job back."

"Then Cade's a liar."

Leandro tenses, his fingers curl ever so slightly, yet there's no denying his curiosity's spiked.

"I have no interest in being yet another underpaid lackey."

He shifts his weight onto his heels, shoots me an appraising look. "So, what do you have in mind?"

"I want that pay raise you promised last New Year's Eve."

"That so?" His eyes crease in amusement. "And tell me, Dace, what do you plan on doing to earn it? What sort of services are you offering to provide?"

"Whatever's needed. You're the boss, you tell me." I take a moment to glance all around, trying to guestimate just how much this renovation might've cost. No doubt, it set them back a good bit. Still, the Richters are wealthy beyond measure. Whatever the number, they can afford it.

"Turns out, there wasn't a whole lot that came out of pocket." Leandro tries to appear as though he read my thoughts, when in reality, we both know it was my body language that gave me away. "Luckily, we were well insured. Not that it concerns you."

"Doesn't it?"

A group of workers file past, making last-minute adjustments to the furniture placement, the angle of the lighting, as Leandro leans closer and says, "You planning to inherit or claim a portion of the profits?"

"Yes to both." I meet his gaze. "I figure once you go, at least half should be mine. Don't forget, I am part Richter."

"*But not the half that counts.* As you so eloquently stated last New Year's Eve." He tilts his head back, stares down the bridge of his nose. "While I find this all very intriguing, I'm afraid you're testing my patience. I'm a busy man. I have a club that's set to re-open, and a long list of things to accomplish well before then. Aside from the responsibility of running this town and looking after its citizens, who depend on me for their very well-being. So why don't you get to the point. You want a job, is that right?"

"For starters." I nod.

"And why should I hire you when, from what I hear, the gas station just gave you the boot? If you couldn't even handle that brand of grunt work, what makes you think I want you working in my establishment?"

I duck my head, stare at my feet, figuring it's better to remain silent than to rush to my own defense. If Leandro feels the need to exert his authority and show me who's the alpha Coyote, so be it. I'm fine with holding my cards until it's time to play them.

"Excuse my suspicion," he continues. "But it wasn't long ago when you wanted nothing to do with me. In fact, if I'm not mistaken, and rest assured I never am, you saw fit to threaten me. Going so far as to say, *'I'm the mistake you will live to regret.'*"

He pauses, giving me ample time to explain. And since there's no denying anything he just said, I lift my shoulders and admit, "That was then. This is now."

"Yeah? And what exactly has changed?"

"A lot's changed. I've changed."

"What specifically?" He shifts his weight from foot to foot, sneaks a peek at his flashy gold watch. Signaling that I am mere seconds from losing his attention for good.

"Specifically—this." I push my dark shades high onto my forehead, revealing a set of red, glowing eyes. "Turns out, I couldn't control my destiny in the way that I thought. There's no stopping it. No way to fight it. So, I figure if this is what I'm meant to be, then it's time I embrace it."

Leandro moves closer, his expression as unguarded as I've ever seen. He lifts a hand to my cheek, whispers a string of words that at first I don't understand. It's only a few moments later after replaying them in my head that I realize he's saying, *son—my son,* as he gazes upon me with the sort of reverence normally reserved for saints.

Though, I guess to Leandro, my blackened heart and tarnished soul hold a similar appeal.

"I knew it." He's transfixed by my gaze. "I knew it when I saw you last New Year's Eve. Despite your bravado, I could sense the beast growing within. I knew it wouldn't be long before it made itself known—and now this."

He places a hand on either side of my face, thumbs pressing into my temples. That simple, singular touch enough to infuse me with a cache of esoteric secrets and arcane knowledge, until the entire history of the dark arts is coursing through my blood. Much of which comes as no surprise, considering the countless times I eavesdropped on the elders' private conversations as a kid. Still, seeing it unfold firsthand, and discovering the whispers were true, is something else entirely.

In order to be fully initiated into the dark arts—whether it be skinwalking or, in my case, making the full transition into the malevolent beast I'm destined to be—killing a relative is the price of admission.

Turns out, it's the most useful thing Leandro has shared.

It may well prove to be the last conscious choice I'm able to make before the beast fully dominates.

It's an act no Richter has ever achieved. As Leftfoot once said, Leandro is unwilling to spare even the dimmest Richter. Which explains why Cade's transitions are always temporary. Not a single one of them has ever been willing to go all the way—until now.

I have every intention of being the first.

And I know just where to start.

"Father." I clasp his hand in mine. The two of us joined in unspoken solidarity, when Cade calls to him from across the room.

At first Leandro ignores him, but it only causes Cade to shout louder. "What do you want?" Leandro barks, making no effort to disguise his annoyance.

"What do you mean, *what do I want?* What the hell are you doing with *him?*" Cade crosses the room quickly, his voice steeped in outrage, as he says, "You're not seriously considering giving him his job back, are you?"

"Of course not." Leandro spares his son a cursory glance, just long enough to see him visibly relax, before he shifts his focus to me. "I'm giving him your job."

"What the—?" Cade stammers. So enraged by the situation, he can barely get to the words. "Are you freaking crazy? Dace hates us! He's out to destroy us! He's working with the Seeker. They've planned this all along, and you're playing right into their hands!"

Leandro meets my gaze straight on. "Is that true?"

"It was." I take a moment to acknowledge Cade, reveling in the look of defeat plastered across his face. "But not anymore." My glowing red eyes confirm what words can't.

Leandro turns to Cade, voice filled with loathing as he says, "Clear out your office and make room for your brother. Once that's done, check in with the kitchen staff and offer your assistance."

"No. No way." Cade is red-faced and furious. "I've worked way too hard to let you mess it all up!"

"No?" Leandro mocks. "No? And just what are you going to do about it? Go ahead, show me why I shouldn't choose your brother over you. It's been so long since I, or anyone else for that matter, last saw the real you."

As he feels driven by his hatred for me and a true determination to prove himself to Leandro, Cade's face darkens, his body trembles and shakes. Straining with all that he's got to make the shift, but the transformation that once happened so easily he could barely contain it, will no longer come.

"Just as I thought." Regarding his son with a look of blatant contempt, Leandro shakes his head and shoves him aside. "I had high hopes for you, but clearly I overestimated your abilities."

"This is bullshit!" Cade shouts. "It's the worst kind of trick, and you're falling for it! Dace is—"

"Dace is the reason you stand here today. Don't you ever forget that." Leandro glowers. His anger so palpable I can actually feel it streaming off him. "First, you do me considerable financial damage when you flooded the tourmaline market. Then you lied about killing the Seeker, and your brother too, for that matter. Then you put this entire family at risk last New Year's Eve when you couldn't manage to stop the girl and her crazy father from blowing up the place, after instructing me not to get involved because you had it all under control—"

"But I killed Paloma! Did you seriously forget that? Or maybe you're determined to ignore it because you're embarrassed by how easily I succeeded where you failed!"

Though he does have a point, it only serves to feed Leandro's rage. His voice lowered to a whisper that's far more threatening than any scream could ever be. "You've made the tragic mistake of thinking you're one step ahead of me, when the fact is, you have brought shame upon this family by failing it in every conceivable way." He thumps his son hard in the chest, humiliating Cade to no end. "You are no longer useful to me. No longer a revered member of El Coyote. So pull yourself together, deal with your failings, and show your brother a little respect. So far as I can see, Dace is the only one with any hope of someday replacing me." Dismissing Cade with an impatient turn of his head, Leandro slides an arm around my shoulders, and says, "Come. We'll go into my office and nail down the details. By the time we're finished, your new office should be ready."

twenty-one

Daire

When the doorbell rings, I instinctively shout for Axel to get it. Remembering too late he's not home.

I wipe my hands on the front of my cutoffs and head down the ramp. Only to find Jennika struggling to squeeze through the door.

"Mom? What are you doing here?" I rush to help. As equally excited to see her as I am flustered by her ability to continually surprise me with her unannounced, ambush-style visits.

"Told you I'd bring the dresses," she says. The words muffled by the three puffy garment bags piled so high in her arms they cover most of her face.

"You told me you'd *send* the dresses." I help her unload them onto the couch before moving in for a hug.

"Send—bring—what's the difference?" She grins. "The point is, they're here. And just in time, I might add. Which wasn't easy—traffic was insane."

"You drove?"

"All the way from the Albuquerque airport. Now, let me get a look at you. It's been too long since my eyes enjoyed a Daire-sized feast." She draws away, holding me at arm's length to better inspect me.

"And to think it feels like just yesterday when we Skyped," I quip, trying not to cringe under the glare of her probing assessment.

"You look tired." She states the words with the same finality as a judge reading a verdict.

"Nothing a little concealer can't fix." I move to untangle myself from her grip, but she tips her finger to my chin and holds me in place.

"Not what I meant. You're as beautiful as ever, and your skin looks amazing. I'm glad to see you're heeding my warnings and wearing your sunscreen. But behind your eyes, I sense the fatigue of someone with several decades on you. What's going on, Daire? I thought you said all was quiet on the Richter front?"

This time I succeed in pulling away, and I use the moment to steal a quick peek at her ring finger. Relieved to confirm she's still engaged.

Jennika has a habit of bolting from anything that hints of commitment. And for the last nine months since I moved to Enchantment, Paloma's adobe has served as her go-to place whenever things get too heated with her fiancé.

"How's Harlan?" I ask, just to confirm they're still on.

"Good." She grins, shoots a hand through hair that's dyed a pretty, soft blond with bits of buttery yellow streaking through. Though there's no telling how long this look will last. Jennika changes her hair color as often as most people change sheets. "He would've come, but he's on location doing an editorial shoot in Goa."

"Rough life." I crack a smile, but it fails to convince.

"Not nearly as rough as yours." She folds her thin arms across her chest and continues her inventory. Noting bare feet with toes polished a bright turquoise blue, worn denim cutoffs, a white tank top, and hair swept back into a messy ponytail. Not a whole lot to see, and certainly nothing alarming, still she sees fit to say, "Daire, I'm concerned."

"Don't be. I'm fine." I turn on my heel and make for the kitchen. Thanks to Axel, the house is more or less tidy and the fridge is actually full. Last thing I need is for Jennika to see just how chaotic my life has become. Though judging by the look she shoots me when I offer her a cool drink, she's not fooled.

"How long are you staying?" I ask, noting she didn't arrive with any bags. Then again, for all I know her entire stash of worldly belongings is crammed into the trunk of her rental car.

"Haven't decided." She places a hand on her hip and surveys the room. "Guess that depends on you." She shifts her focus to me, and I can't help but flinch under such intense scrutiny.

I can slay demons, stand up to the evilest of Richters, and yet one knowing look from my mom and I'm coming apart.

Last January, when we said good-bye, it was with the firm understanding that I'd keep in touch, keep her informed, and she'd leave me to do what I must. While she may not like my being a Seeker, she seemed to accept it as something she could neither interfere with nor change. But now, although I've kept to my end of the deal, she latches onto the flimsiest excuse she can find to show up at the absolute, worst possible time.

She settles herself at the kitchen table, takes a sip of iced tea, and levels her gaze right on me. "How's Dace?"

On the surface, the question is simple, straightforward, packed with no apparent agenda. And yet it's pretty much the worst thing she could've asked. Dace has become such a hot-button topic, even my friends have stopped referring to him.

Though that's not to say I don't think about him.

Because I do.

Nearly every second of every day.

Dace is always with me, simmering just under the surface. Still, it's been so long since I've talked about him, I'm unsure what to say.

I stifle a sigh, drop onto the seat opposite hers, and decide to lead with the truth. "Honestly, I don't know. It's been a while since we last spoke." My shoulders tense, my fingers twist tightly together, as I wait for her to break into a rousing chorus of the *I-told-you-so* song.

Jennika was never a Dace fan. Right from the start she was fully convinced he was put on this earth with the sole task of breaking my heart. While the assessment speaks mostly of her own well documented fear of commitment—it's strange how it echoes the prophecy.

It took a long time for Jennika to come around. And while she never quite embraced our relationship, she did resign herself to the idea of the two of us being together.

But now, with just a few simple words, I've proven her right.

I pick at the underside of the table, waiting for her to react. Jennika has the tenacity of a pit bull. She will gladly sit here all night if that's what it takes to get me to spill.

"Dace and I are on a break." I cringe when I say it, bracing for one of her sarcastic comebacks. But when she continues the silence, I add, "It's . . . complicated."

"Try me." The diamond stud in her nose quivers and glints. Her green eyes meet mine.

I swallow hard, grasp the edge of the table so hard the table's wood grain leaves marks on my skin. I don't want to discuss it. Can't bear to say the words. And yet, next thing I know, I'm spilling the whole sordid tale. The words spewing so quickly I've no time to vet them.

To her credit, Jennika refrains from all comment. She just nods, sips her tea, and sighs in all the appropriate places, until I'm all out of words, all out of breath, and she lifts her chin and says, "Well, you know what you have to do, right?"

I push away from the table, tilt my chair back on two legs in the way that she hates. "I know what I'm going to do. And, if you're like everyone else, it's not even close to what you're thinking." The words are sharp, but not nearly as sharp as the accusing look on my face.

I was sure she'd follow the usual Jennika script. Use my tale of woe to gloat, tell me she knew it all along. I never expected her to hijack my pain as a teachable moment to reinforce how I need to take down my boyfriend.

"You're acting as though you have a choice, when clearly you don't." She runs a slow finger around the rim of her glass.

"According to who?" I start to say more, start to say something I'll surely live to regret—but then I think better of it and talk myself down. Getting upset won't do any good. If anything, it will only serve to prove her point. If she thinks I'm being irrational, then it's my job to prove just the opposite.

"If Dace is fated to go dark—fated to kill you along with everyone else—then I can't see what you can possibly do to change that. It's your duty to protect the citizens of Enchantment, Daire, or at least that's the story you once told me. If you fail to keep the three worlds in balance . . . well, I can't even imagine the result. There is too much at stake—you can't allow yourself to be led by your heart!"

"It's my duty to protect the citizens of Enchantment, yes, and, in case you've forgotten, that includes Dace! Sheesh, Jennika, I thought out of everyone, you'd be the one who might understand. Nice to know you're against me as well."

"I'm not against you, Daire, I'm merely against your decision. I think you're being reckless, dangerous, woefully misguided, and I'm begging you to reconsider." She pushes away from the table and carries her glass to the sink. Leaning against the tiled counter, she turns and says, "Daire, I get that you love him. I get that it's your first love, which makes it all the more powerful. But if I hear you correctly, then Dace isn't really Dace anymore. He's not the boy you fell for. He's being eroded by this . . . beast, as you call it. And it won't be long before there's not a trace of him left. You need to deal with that now, get it straight in your head before it's too late. You need to prepare yourself for the hard choices to come. You need to be ready to face the inevitable."

"Guess that's where you and I differ. I don't believe it's inevitable. I may be new at love, but if there's one thing I've learned, it's that love knows no boundaries. Not when it's real. Not when it's true. The feelings Dace and I share can never be destroyed by a beast or anything else. We're not like everyone else. We don't fit into a convenient slot. We can't be labeled and catalogued quite as easily as you'd like. Dace did this for me—to help me with my fight against the Richters. He acted with the noblest of intentions, and I plan to honor him with the same level of sacrifice. I won't kill him, and that's all there is to it."

Jennika sighs. Her face is as resigned as her voice when she says, "You know, I have a thousand arguments lined up and ready to go. And yet I know how stubborn you are—and I know you got that from me. I'll never be able to convince you, will I?"

I shake my head.

"But that doesn't mean I won't continue to try." She quirks a brow.

"I've no doubt."

"So, can we call a truce—at least for now?"

"I've been doing that a lot lately."

I settle into my seat, sure that the worst is over, when she moves toward the blue tourmaline I left on the handrail that leads to my office and squeals, "Is this what I think?"

She reaches for the stone, but before she can get to it, I use telekinesis to arc it away from her grip and into my hand, as she turns on me with a face full of outraged disbelief. "Answer me, Daire!"

"Yes." I shove it deep into my front pocket.

"And why is it here? What are you doing with it? And, more importantly, is it still dangerous?"

I answer with an uncertain look.

"I see." Her face is strained, voice grim. "And yet you see fit to carry it around in your pocket?"

"It's . . . complicated . . ."

"You've used that phrase twice now." She folds her arms over her chest, kicks a leg out before her. Staring down the length of her skinny white jeans, she says, "The way I see it, the only thing complicated around here is your reasoning. First, you tell me your boyfriend is destined to destroy the world and everyone in it, but you choose to ignore it because you believe your love will prevail. Then you see fit to hang onto the very same stone that's responsible for killing your grandmother." I start to respond, but one flash of her palm is all it takes to silence me. "Excuse me for saying so, but I can't help but wonder if the two are connected. If you're so devastated by what's happening between you and Dace that it's clouding your judgment and causing you to take unhealthy risks."

"It's not like that. You've got it all wrong."

"Well, until you do a better job of explaining, I'll stand by my opinion."

"It truly *is* complicated. Nothing is black and white. Nothing is what it seems. It's the fundamental rule of Enchantment, and it seems you've forgotten it." She lifts her brow but allows me to continue. "So add this to the list of things we'll agree to disagree on."

"I'm sorry, Daire, but I can't be that glib. What happened to my sensible, if not cynical daughter?"

"I've recently discovered what I suspected all along—cynicism is overrated and overvalued. It's the shield people hide behind in the mistaken belief that it makes them appear cool, strong, and impenetrable. But true bravery isn't about following the crowd or pretending not to care—it's about daring to trust in yourself and staying true to your heart in the face of dissent. True courage is going out on a limb for the people you love because it's the right thing to do." Jennika looks at me long and hard but refrains from further comment. "While it may upset you, while you may find it disconcerting, my drive to save Dace isn't nearly as foolish as you think. I know what I'm doing, Jennika. I've trained long and hard to get to this point. Yet despite the magick I wield, despite the numbers of demons I've slayed, despite the evil I've witnessed first-hand, in the end, I'm putting my faith in the power of love. Everything else pales in comparison."

I stand before her, unsure what comes next. While I'm sure I haven't convinced her, it seems I have silenced her. Still, there's one thing left to say—a promise I desperately need to extract.

"I only ask that you refrain from mentioning the tourmaline to my friends." My gaze pleads with hers. "In fact, please don't mention it to anyone."

"It's not like you to keep secrets, Daire." She narrows her gaze, her suspicions spiked once again.

"It's not a secret. Or at least not entirely. The elders all know. Chay's the one who delivered the stone. Chepi's the one who turned it into a ring."

Jennika flattens her lips.

"Look, I'm not going to lie; it's not like they offered. But they did go along with my request."

"I hope you know what you're doing." She casts a wary glance at my pocket, as though she can see the offending jewel through the denim.

"That makes two of us."

She regards me for a long thoughtful moment. While my words failed to comfort, at least they were honest. The moment interrupted by the commotion of Axel, Lita, Xotichl, and Auden coming through the front door.

"Found another one on the stoop. Looks like this is becoming a habit." Axel deposits a long, rectangular, glossy white box on the kitchen table before he notices Jennika.

"You must be Axel." She extends her hand before I have a chance to introduce them. "Last time I was here, you were invisible. We couldn't properly meet." She says it with such ease I can't help but feel a bit awed at how far she's come. Wasn't even a year ago when she shunned anything having to do with the supernatural and tried to drag me back to L.A. After greeting Auden, she moves in to hug both Xotichl and Lita. Remarking on Xotichl's new glasses, her ability to see, and drawing away from Lita to say, "You are simply radiant. Being in love clearly suits you."

Lita blushes. Allowing for a sight rarely seen. Though as sweet as the moment may be, I can't help but cringe, knowing her happiness is temporary at best.

"Speaking of *love* . . ." Lita nods toward the package. "If I didn't know better, I'd think Cade Richter was in love with you."

"This is from Cade?" Jennika moves toward it, shifting her gaze between the box, my friends, and me.

I move past the comment, it's too ludicrous to contemplate, and use my magick to unspool the ribbon and remove the glossy white top.

"No matter how many times I see that, it's still eerie." Jennika rubs her hands over her arms and stifles a shiver despite the sweltering heat.

"Any animal carcasses in there?" Lita tips onto her toes to get a better view, Xotichl takes a step back, as I unfold the bed of delicate white tissue. Unaware I'd been holding my breath until I uncover a beautiful swath of red silk and heave a deep exhale.

"Is that—a dress?" Jennika leans closer, as I lift the nest of fabric from the box, hold it by the Grecian-style straps, and release glorious swirls of sunset-red fabric that undulates to the floor. The gown is gorgeous, made of fine, heavy silk, bearing a low-cut neckline to rival an even more daring back, a tight bit of gathering that nips in at the waist, before spilling into a series of soft gentle waves that dance just like flames.

An exact replica of the dress I wore in the dream. The one where I found myself at the precipice of a cliff as Cade slid a tourmaline ring onto my finger.

"It's incredible." Jennika looks at me. "Far more beautiful than any of the gowns I brought."

"But why is it red, when it's supposed to be a black-and-white ball?" Xotichl asks.

"Who cares!" Lita says. "It's not like she's going to wear it." Her eyes widening when she sees my reaction. "You're not going to wear it, are you?" She casts me a look I can't quite read. Is it jealousy—derision—caution? It's impossible to say.

"Of course I'm going to wear it." My tone bears the same conviction I wear on my face, aware of my friends staring at me with varying degrees of disbelief.

"Daire, you can't be serious." Lita frowns. "While I agree that it's stunning, wearing that dress will only result in putting you in even more danger than you already are. Nothing's free where the Richters are concerned. Every act of their so-called charity comes with a price, and a steep one at that. Question is, why is he doing this?"

I continue to hold the gown against me, running my palm down the soft, silky front. The cut is exquisite. Every tuck and seam falling right into place. Conforming to my contours so precisely it's as though it was tailor-made.

"So long as there are no blue tourmalines hiding in the hem, I don't see why I shouldn't wear it. Besides, he doesn't expect me to wear it, and that's exactly the reason I will." I splay my fingers against the waist, twirl the skirts around my legs.

"I don't get it," Xotichl says, as Jennika echoes a similar sentiment.

"Listen, so far nothing I've done to stop Cade has worked. So, it's time for a new strategy." I take a moment to glance at each of them, letting them know I'm deadly serious and this is not at all negotiable.

"And I suppose you're going to wear the raven mask too?" Lita scowls, makes no attempt to hide her disapproval.

"I think they'll go nicely, together. Don't you?" I refold the dress and return it to the box the same way I found it.

"Daire, why are you doing this?" Jennika looks at me, and I know the question is not nearly as limited as it seems on the surface.

What she really means is: *Why the dress? Why the mask? Why are you ignoring our concerns? And, more importantly, why do you insist on hanging onto the very same tourmaline that killed your grandmother?*

Jennika means well. They all do. They're only trying to protect me. Still, I look at them and say, "Ever since the very first Seeker went up against the first Coyote, the goal has been to resist the enemy at every turn."

"Um, yeah. Isn't that pretty much the job description of a Seeker?" Lita frowns.

"Up until now, yes. But what if it doesn't have to be? What if there's another way to handle them?"

"By playing right into their hands?" Xotichl screws her lips to the side as though trying to make sense of my words. Reluctant to disregard them outright, yet a long way from accepting their truth.

"Partly."

"You're going to have to explain." Lita shakes her head, looks to Axel for backup, but he just slips a comforting arm around her waist, and wisely stays out of it.

"Ever hear the saying *what you resist persists?*"

Xotichl and Axel nod, Jennika assumes a thoughtful expression, Auden checks his cell, and Lita folds her hands across her chest.

"What it basically means is, the things we resist, the past, the present, the shameful parts of ourselves, have a tendency to become even more prominent. We waste so much of our time and focus on fighting things, ideas, or people we don't like, when, in the end, it only serves to make those things even more magnified in our lives."

"Like when you first showed up at Milagro High, and instead of ignoring you and getting on with my life like I should have, I focused all of my attention on you until it seemed like you were everywhere, and it made me dislike you even more?" Lita says. And while it's not an example I would have chosen, there's no doubt it fits.

"Yeah. Something like that. And, well, what if the same thing could be said for the Richters? I mean, Seekers have spent count-less generations fighting Coyote's advances. But what if we stopped? What if we played along instead? Or at least gave the impression of playing along."

"Well then, I'm pretty sure that would result in the world-plunging-into-eternal-darkness Apocalypse scenario the Codex warns about." Xotichl frowns.

"Not necessarily."

I motion toward the swath of carefully folded silk fabric. "Clearly this is just another one of Cade's taunts. So imagine how he'll react when I call his bluff and show up to the party in full-on, Coyote-style regalia."

They fall silent, taking a moment to imagine how that might look.

"It'll throw him completely off track, which will buy me just enough time to take him down before he even realizes what hit him."

"This is crazy!" Lita says. "Seriously, crazy. And I'm sorry for saying it, but I'm merely voicing what everyone else is thinking. Not to mention that by taking Cade down you also kill Dace. And while you know I'm all for slaying the beast before he can slay us, last I heard, you were dead set against it."

"And I'm still dead set against it. I have no intention of killing Dace, but Cade has to be stopped or we're all doomed anyway. Listen, all I can do is trust in my training, my magick, and the tools Paloma left for me. And when it comes down to it, I pray that not only will my ancestors aid me, but that my love for Dace proves stronger than evil—stronger than death."

Axel shoots me a saddened look, Jennika shakes her head softly and gazes down at her feet, while Auden and Xotichl avoid my gaze, and Lita frowns.

"But for now, the last thing I want to do is argue with you. I know you mean well and I know you're only trying to look out for me, which is a good thing because it turns out I can't do it alone. I've been working on a plan that involves all of you. So we better get started and use what little time we have left."

twenty-two

Dace

I shut the door on my shithole apartment, knowing it won't be long before I shut it for good.

While Leandro offered me a room in the compound, I knew better than to accept.

Much like Leftfoot, everything with Leandro is a test. He may be inordinately proud of the darkness rising within me, but he doesn't entirely trust me. All the years spent apart, combined with my uncensored threats, will take time to bridge.

Besides, having already staked a claim on my inheritance, it's best not to appear too acquisitive right out of the gate. Little does he know, I have no plans to settle for half. Not when I can claim the whole pie.

I climb behind the wheel of my Mustang, now painted a slick cherry-red with an engine under the hood that purrs like a panther. A token from Leandro, who said no self-respecting Richter should be seen driving such a wreck of a car.

Amazing what a bit of magick and a fat wad of bills can do for a ride.

I take the long way to the Rabbit Hole, surveying the land with the satisfaction of knowing it won't look this run-down for much longer. There's hope for the future of Enchantment. Even if I'm no longer a part of it, I plan to leave my mark.

My thoughts are interrupted by my cell phone chiming, though the second I see it's my mom I set it on mute.

Ever since that day at the cave, the elders have made themselves scarce. Yet despite their warnings, Chepi refuses to fold. Insisting some part of the old me hangs on.

While she happens to be right, what she doesn't realize is that it's now so reduced I can't risk talking to her, much less seeing her, even if it's just to say one last good-bye.

The beast stirring within bears an insatiable hunger for the kill, and it doesn't discriminate amongst victims. It's a threat I take seriously, and if she knew what was good for her, she'd take it seriously too.

Daire once told me about the night she spied on Cade after merging her soul with a cockroach. Saw him snacking on the same dregs of unidentifiable bloody, raw carcass he fed to Coyote. Back then, I found the story disgusting.

But now, just thinking about it causes my belly to rumble—my taste buds to spark.

While I haven't yet stooped to that level, the urge grows stronger with each passing day.

Funny how now that I'm turning, everything about my brother makes sense. His urge to slay, consume, and destroy are a perfect match for my own. Allowing for a sense of solidarity I never could've imagined before.

Though that's not to say I won't kill him.

He's at the top of my list.

Killing a relative is the only way to ensure the beast comes fully alive, which will allow me to take down the rest of them too.

I may lose myself, but I'll save Daire in the process.

And that's all that really matters.

I cruise past a seemingly never-ending stream of broken-down adobes. The lights dimming in the windows indicating a sleepy, dump of a town settling in, while I'm just getting started.

Like Coyote, I do my best hunting at night.

I pull up to the back door, arriving at the same time as Leandro.

"How's that for synchronicity?" He grins.

I manage half a grin in return and slip free of my car.

"A vast improvement." He admires the custom paint, the shiny, new rims.

"Thanks." I force the words past my lips, remembering how well he responds to things like praise, appreciation, and overall ego-stroking.

He swings the door open, ushers me inside the club, where I'm so overcome with the scent of Raven I freeze on the spot.

My nose twitching. Vision sharpening. Hunger stirring. Knowing without a doubt that she's here.

Daire.

Lurking in places she knows better than to visit.

"You okay?" Leandro shoots me a strange look and I can't believe he can't sense her. Has no idea his lair has been breached by Coyote's last remaining enemy—not counting me.

I nod, leaving him at the bar where he mixes himself a stiff drink as I hurry down the hall to my office, drawn by the lure of her scent.

When she hears me, she presses hard to the wall in a futile bid to go unseen. Having no idea that ever since the change, my eyes see everything.

I lean against the doorway, indulging a long sweet moment to linger on the drape of her dark hair trailing over her shoulder, the flush at her cheeks, the hollow of her neck, the curve of her thighs gleaming under the glow of security lights.

The sight of her soft, creamy flesh causing my spine to stiffen, my muscles to cord and flex, as my pulse begins to race, and a hunger stirs deep within.

I throw my head back and drag a deep breath, filling my head with her sweet, hypnotic scent.

Aware of the beat of her heart slamming hard in her chest.

The soft whistle of breath passing her lips.

The salty trickle of sweat that's slipped between her breasts.

Her essence so enticing, so alluring, the small remnant of the old me yearns to run to her, confide how much I love her, how much I've missed her. Tell her she's right—we can do this together.

Unfortunately, the beast wholeheartedly concurs. Thinking how much fun it will be to soften her up before he destroys her.

Slowly, very slowly, she slips a hand down her leg, reaches for the knife she's stashed in her boot.

Come. Come to me, the beast coos.

His voice overpowering my own urge to warn her to run while she can.

She grasps the hilt. Removes the sheath until the blade glints silver. Then waits for me to make the first move.

Leaves it to me to determine how this unfolds.

A smart move that buys her another night.

Better not tempt a beast that's not mine to control.

Determined to get away before I lose it completely, I slip into my office, shut the door between us, and bolt it securely.

twenty-three

Xotichl

"Tell me again why we're meeting him all the way out here—in what can literally be described as the middle of nowhere?" I peer through the windshield, unable to free myself of this deep sense of unease, much less pinpoint its cause, other than to say nothing looks as it should.

When we first set out, the sky was perfectly clear and littered with stars—a typical Enchantment hot summer night (albeit a lot hotter than usual). But here, the sky is choked with clouds as thick, ominous, and wide as the sea. And other than countless tribes of tumbleweeds, and the narrow dirt road unspooling beneath us, there's virtually nothing else to speak of.

It's the kind of eerie, desolate landscape often seen in nightmares and horror movies.

A haunting place of dark secrets, bad deeds.

"We came all this way because it's convenient for Luther. It's where he wanted to meet." Auden picks up the speed, places a reassuring hand on my knee.

"Well, don't you think he should've made it convenient for *us*? After all, you're the one signing the contract."

"Exactly." Auden peers at me through a clump of thick, shaggy bangs that fall into his eyes. "And if it wasn't for Luther, there'd be no contract to sign."

"Don't sell yourself short." I frown. "Luther's the one who's set to benefit the most. As they say in Vegas—the house always wins."

"Which means the record company is the one set to benefit most. Then Luther. Then me. Don't forget, I'm just the lowly musician." He laughs, jiggles my knee in an attempt to get me to laugh too or at least lighten up, but it doesn't quite work. "Listen," he says, determined to try again and relieve at least some of my tension. "The location may suck, but I'm lucky to be here. It's not like anyone else was lining up to give me a contract."

"That's because you mostly played the Rabbit Hole and a few clubs in Albuquerque. It's not like this is Nashville, New York, or L.A. It's not like you were really out there marketing yourself."

"Because I couldn't stand the time spent away from you. It never seemed worth it."

"And now you can?"

"Hardly." He leans across the seat to plant a kiss on my cheek, drawing away as he says, "Also, I knew we were okay, but not quite good enough. I wanted to get our sound together before we went wide."

"Yeah, but now it's just you. It's not like they wanted the rest of the band."

"And I still feel bad about that."

"I always thought it was a cool name, but maybe in a way it was a little too prophetic."

He looks at me.

"You know, Epitaph getting its epitaph . . ."

His lips flatten, he focuses back on the road, and we both fall silent. Allowing a few miles to pass before Auden says, "Thing is, my sound still isn't quite where I want it, nor where they want it, but luckily they're willing to work with me."

I lift my shoulders, stare out the side window.

Which probably isn't the reaction he was looking for, since it prompts him to say, "Xotichl, are you not happy for me?"

"No." I look at his crestfallen face, instantly realizing my mistake. "I mean, *yes!* I *am* happy for you. You have no idea. But I also think you're acting too grateful."

"Since when is gratitude a negative?"

"In general, hardly ever. But when you get that *I'm just so lucky to be here I'll put up with anything attitude*—then it's a problem."

"That's hardly the case."

"Isn't it?" I turn to him with a challenging look. "You dropped the band without once looking back, and now we're headed for the ends of the earth because it's convenient for Luther. Never mind that it's completely out of our way."

Auden sighs, lifts his fingers from the wheel, then returns with a grip that appears twice as tight. "It's not quite as simple as that. There's more to it. Stuff I didn't want to bother you with. But the important thing is, once this contract is signed, my songs are recorded, and I'm playing on the radio all over the world, it's going to be pretty tough for your mom to say I'm not good enough for you."

I slink farther down in my seat, not sure I'd agree. Auden is my first and only boyfriend, so I can't say for certain, but I'm pretty convinced that where my mother's concerned, no boy will ever be good enough for her little girl.

At first I thought her overprotectiveness was due to my blindness. Like it stemmed from this instinctual, maternal urge to keep me safe and buffered from the big, bad, dangerous world—especially the big, bad, dangerous world of boys.

Despite Auden's genius IQ, despite the fact that he graduated early so he could attend university, she remained unimpressed. And now that my sight has returned, she's waged a whole new defense for why we shouldn't be together. Turning what should be a happy, if not celebratory time, into a constant series of battles, both big and small. And the truth is, the war she's waging is turning out to be far more successful than I'd like to admit.

It's making me feel torn between them.

I love Auden with all my heart, same as he loves me.

And I just don't get why that isn't enough.

"That must be him." Auden tips his head toward the windshield and the landscape of endless miles of nothing beyond. "See those headlights, right up there where the two roads cross—it's gotta be him, right?"

"Either that or an escaped mental patient turned serial killer who's just waiting for some unsuspecting teenagers to drive past."

"That's it—no more scary movies for you." He squeezes my hand with fingers gone slightly clammy. Guess I didn't realize how nervous he is, and everything I've said since I got in the car has probably only served to make it worse.

I need to try harder. He's worked his whole life for this moment. And I have to stop questioning every last detail.

He pulls to the side of the road, sets the brake, and checks his reflection in the rearview mirror. As I peer through the windshield at the lone car parked on the other side of the place where the roads intersect.

Once again, we have to go to him. He can't even get out of his car and meet us halfway.

I clamp my lips shut before I can break my vow and put a voice to the thought. My dislike of this man is irrational and better kept to myself. He's never actually given me a reason to loathe him like this.

"He has another engagement in Albuquerque," Auden says. "So we need to make this quick."

"Quick works for me." I gather my gown in my hands, while Auden leaps from his side and comes around to open my door. A holdover from the days when I couldn't see, but it's sweet all the same.

It's even hotter out here than it was in Enchantment. And with the blanket of clouds overhead, the air feels so heavy it's like a thermal canopy has been draped over us. Auden folds my hand in his and leads me across the dirt road toward the car with the headlights blazing so bright, I'm forced to lift a hand to my forehead to shield my eyes from the glare.

I lean into his shoulder, seeking comfort in his touch. Determined to enjoy every second I can from this moment on. I've already wasted too much time feeling grumpy, and we both deserve better.

Although Daire has a pretty good plan, and all of us have studied it again and again until we've memorized our parts, there's no telling how this will end. The least I can do is enjoy every last moment of peace I can find with my boyfriend.

I stop just shy of the car and say, "I'm happy for you, Auden. I really, truly am. I'm sorry if I made it appear otherwise."

He drops a kiss on my cheek. "I know, flower." He grins. "You're just looking out for me. You've always got my back." Then he leads me the last few steps to the car, where we angle our faces away from the lights, as Luther climbs out of the car.

"Sorry about the glare. It's so dark out here, I figured we could use the light." Then looking at me, he says, "Xotichl, wow. I've never seen you so radiant." He grins, extends a hand, and not seeing a viable alternative that wouldn't be considered inordinately rude, I clasp it in mine. "How are you getting on?" he asks.

I extricate myself from his grip and shoot him an uncertain look, not exactly sure what he means.

"Auden tells me you got your sight back. That must be a truly incredible experience."

It's all I can do to nod in reply. The heat is so heavy, the air so thin, it's rendered me dizzy, light-headed, like I'm two breaths from fainting.

"Going from a world of total darkness to a world of color and light . . . I can't even imagine how that might feel."

My eyes graze past his absurd ponytail and double hoop earrings, and focus hard on his lips, trying to determine the color of his words. But his speech flows frustratingly clear. "You'd be surprised," I say, finally finding my voice. "My world wasn't nearly as dark as you think."

He quirks a brow, stares down the bridge of his nose.

The moment of awkwardness broken when Auden says, "We should probably get started. We've got to get to the Rabbit Hole, and I know you need to get to Albuquerque . . ."

Luther turns to Auden with a look I can't read. His face obscured when he says, "Right. Let's get on with it then."

He leans into his car, reaches across the passenger seat, and returns with a beautiful designer briefcase stuffed with a thick stack of papers he sets on the hood.

"I know, it looks like a lot." Luther glances at me. "But this should only take a minute. Two at the most. The signature lines are all tagged. All Auden has to do is sign, and you'll be on your way."

"You're not going to at least look them over?" I turn to Auden, assuring myself I'm being supportive, as opposed to mistrusting.

"I've already seen 'em. This is just the formality, right?" Auden looks to Luther to verify.

"If you want to read through it again, s'okay by me." Luther grins in a way that makes his cheeks appear waxy and tight, as though they're unused to the move. "Don't worry about me. I can be a few minutes late. After all, Xotichl's right. This is your future. You can't be too cautious."

Auden lifts the stack of papers, does a quick scan of each page. "Looks good," he says, rooting around in his pocket in search of a pen.

"You serious?" Luther squints at the Bic. "You're not really planning to sign with that, are you?"

"Cap's a little chewed, but it works." Auden looks sheepish, worried he's already blown it before it's begun.

"That's fine for scratching down a song on a napkin, but moments like these deserve something special." He pulls a shiny black pen from his pocket and hands it to Auden. His eyes glinting as Auden rolls the pen back and forth across his palm.

"Are those *sapphires*?" He studies the jewel-crusted cap. "Guess that's the difference between a pen and a writing instrument." He looks between Luther and me. "This thing probably cost more than my car!"

"Oh, it definitely costs more than *your* car." Luther laughs, casting a derisive glance toward Auden's wreck of a station wagon. "Those are real gems on the cap, the barrel is onyx, and the nub is crafted from gold. Twenty-four karats, at that."

"And what's the pattern engraved on it? I can't quite make it out . . ."

"Sun and moon."

Auden squints, angles the pen toward the light.

"Got a thing for astronomy." Luther lifts his shoulder, makes a guilty face. "Anyway . . ." He gestures toward the papers he's spread across the hood of his car, as Auden slips off the gem-covered cap and prepares for the moment he's been dreaming of since he was a kid, but he ends up flinching instead.

"Ouch!" He jams his thumb between his lips as a drop of blood lands on the contract, just below the signature line. "Didn't realize it was a fountain pen. I must've nicked myself on the tip. And worse, looks like I spilled some blood on the papers."

Luther waves it away, pulls a freshly pressed handkerchief from his pocket and hands it to Auden. "Most great success requires a little shedding of blood, right? Guess I should've warned you, most people don't use fountain pens anymore, but I like the formality. Anyway, as long as you're not too badly hurt, I can ignore a few bloodstains. Unless you prefer I come back in a few days with a clean copy?"

"You kidding? I've never been more ready for anything in my life. Let's do this!"

His finger still bleeding, Auden wraps the kerchief around it and goes about signing the documents. Methodically working his way through the stacks, as Luther turns to me and in a lowered voice, says, "I can't tell you how I felt when I first heard him play. I knew at that moment I was looking at a future star. The kid's got the whole package. Looks, talent, the right disposition, a solid work ethic, and a unique sound all his own. Oh, and he's just hungry and ambitious enough to take it all the way. He's going to be huge, Xotichl. You sure you're ready for that level of fame and all that comes with it?"

It's a strange thing to say in the middle of what's supposed to be a celebratory moment. And it's so unexpected, it takes a little longer than I'd like for me to summon my voice. "If you're referring to long nights on the road and even longer lines of aggressive groupies, I can handle it. I'm secure in Auden's love, and he's secure in mine."

Luther meets my words with a look I can't read. Then he gathers the papers and shoves them back into his briefcase.

"Great to have you onboard, Auden." I watch as they shake hands. "And Xotichl . . ." He takes my hand in his and brings it to his lips, in a move so smarmy, it's all I can do not to cringe.

Tipping his head, he returns to his car as I wipe my hand against the folds of my gown.

"Hey, Luther—you forgot your pen!" Auden calls after him.

Luther pokes his head out the driver's side window. "Keep it," he says.

Auden glances between him and the pen. "You sure?"

Luther nods. "Least I can do, considering what you're about to do for me. Besides, you're part of the family now." He guns the engine and waves, leaving us immersed in a cloud of dust and heat.

"So?" I grab hold of his arm as he leads me back to the car. "You gonna keep it or sell it on eBay?"

Auden laughs. "Can you imagine this thing costs more than a car?"

"According to Luther, it won't be long before you'll be able to afford a hundred more."

"Just a hundred?" Auden grins, drops a kiss on the tip of my nose. "I'd like a nice house, a better car, but other than that, my needs are pretty simple. It's a beautiful object, no doubt, but a price tag like that just seems so out of balance, don't you think?"

He stops beside the car, swings my door open, and motions me in. Unaware that the clouds overhead are beginning to clear. Moving so quickly it's like they're racing toward Albuquerque. Their sudden exodus leaving Auden glowing, and luminous, and dripping in starlight. Making for a sight so irresistible, I grasp hold of his lapels and pull him to me. My lips swelling toward his, desperately seeking the assurance that we'll allow each other to live the journey we deserve. That we'll never let the fear of losing each other interfere with the people we are destined to be.

It's a lot to ask from a kiss. But I guess Luther questioning my readiness to deal with Auden's success left me more disturbed than I cared to let on.

I refuse to be a needy, jealous girlfriend.

I refuse to let Luther's insinuations take root in my head.

"We did it, flower." Auden draws away, brushes a palm calloused from years of guitar playing across my cheek. "I couldn't have done it without you."

He kisses me again, and while I can no longer see the lovely swirls of pinks and golds that once circled our heads, that doesn't mean they're not there.

"Wow." He grins. The kiss has left him as breathless as me.

"Wow, nothing," I tease. "That was merely a tiny hint of the celebration to come."

"You mean there's more?"

"Oh, much more. So much more. More than you could ever imagine." I push away, slide into the car.

"And exactly how long do I have to wait for this *more*?"

"Long enough for Daire to take down all the Richters, which, according to her, shouldn't take all that long."

He kneels beside me, kissing me again with all that he's got. Drawing away when he says, "Oops, guess I'm still bleeding. Here . . ." He licks his finger and uses it to clear the smudge from my cheek.

Then wrapping the kerchief back around his finger, he heads for his side of the car, and begins the drive back to Enchantment.

twenty-four

Daire

Getting ready to head out to the Rabbit Hole is like getting ready for prom.

Not that I've ever been to prom.

Though I have spent enough time on various prom-themed movie sets to know it involves fancy dresses, giddy friends, and a certain amount of nervousness.

What it doesn't involve is a blowgun stashed in a boot, an athame strapped to a thigh, a buckskin pouch secured to a complicated up-do, and a plan to stamp out evil from the face of the earth.

"What do you think?" Lita stands before the full-length mirror, looking smoldering in her black, slinky gown and the Venetian-filigree skull mask embedded with shiny, black crystals.

Axel's eyes widen, his mouth drops, but no words come, which makes Lita laugh.

"You look lovely." Jennika directs a final shot of hairspray to her curls, before she stands back to admire her handiwork. "You too, Axel."

The mask he chose is nearly identical to Lita's, except his is white to go with his slim-cut white suit that, according to Jennika, was recently worn by one of the world's leading heartthrobs on a big-budget remake. Not that Axel cares about fashion or Hollywood for that matter. Lita is pretty much the center of his universe. Everything else is just background.

Lita edges out of the way so Jennika can give me a final swipe of lip gloss before adjusting the raven mask. "As your mother, I should probably be concerned about the cut of this dress." She gestures toward the plunging neckline, which is only slightly more modest than the dip in the back. "But I have to concede you look stunning." She bites her lip, blinks several times to ward off the tears. "I just hope you know what you're doing."

Me too.

Keeping my doubts to myself, I swirl the skirts around my legs, and say, "Think he'll like it?" I watch as the color seems to shift from orange to burgundy to a rich, deep scarlet.

"I hope that was supposed to be a joke." Lita frowns. "But either way, you are freaking me out." She glares at me through the mirror, and I remind myself she speaks more out of concern than anger. "I'm worried about you." She softens her tone along with her stance. "We all are . . ." She shakes her head, leaves the rest unsaid. "And I see you're still wearing your key. Unless you plan to leave it behind?" Her voice rises with hope that's soon dashed when I shake my head and center the black, silk cord at my chest. Though when I pull the blue tourmaline ring from a pocket hidden deep in the folds of my dress and ease it onto my finger, she clutches a hand to her throat and sags against Axel as though she's seconds from fainting. "Oh my freaking Opossum—is that what I think?" She fans herself with her hand, her reaction a little overdramatic, though I guess it's not completely unwarranted. "Why am I the only one reacting?" She glances between Axel and Jennika. "Did you guys know about this?"

Axel shakes his head while Jennika reluctantly nods in assent.

"So, it was a secret?" Though most of her face is obscured by the mask, her voice betrays her annoyance.

"Listen . . ." I turn away from the mirror to better address them. Guess it's time to explain before this gets any worse. "I need you to trust me. I know what I'm doing. Seeing me in this dress, wearing this ring, is the last thing Cade expects. It'll throw him completely off his game, which will allow me just enough leverage to get a head start."

Lita studies the toe of her shoes, as Jennika picks at the hem of her sweater. And while that's not exactly the picture of solidarity I was after, at the moment, it's all that I've got and it's time to get moving. "So what do you say we head out and put our plan into action?"

Axel's the first to react, steering Lita toward the door as Jennika follows. "I'll be here if you need me," she says. "I'm not leaving this place until you've safely returned. And if by chance you don't . . ." She swallows hard, squeezes my hand so tightly my knuckles crack in protest. "Then I'll go after those Richters myself. And trust me, not a single one of them wants to deal with me when I'm angry." Her gaze is fierce, the tilt of her chin determined, leaving no doubt she means every word.

Wanting it to be the look I take with me, I say a quick good night and head for Lita's car.

The first thing I notice when we get to the Rabbit Hole is the abundance of floodlights. As though anyone could possibly miss it in a one-club town.

The second thing I notice is how those floodlights reflect off the glossy black onyx exterior, making it shine as bright and imposing as a monolith.

Last I was here, it was still partially concealed by the barricades. But now that it's unveiled, it's abundantly clear that the days of humble adobe are gone. This new Rabbit Hole is modern, sleek, and twice the size of the last one. The lack of windows and cool, stone walls giving it the look and feel of a massive mausoleum, which, I guess in a way it is. The material specifically chosen to impart staying power and strength while serving to house the spirits of Richters long past.

Though, as I already know from my previous visit, the real transformation happens inside.

Lita whistles under her breath. "Sheesh—I feel like I've been teleported to someplace way better than Enchantment. It's so luxe and loungey, and . . . I hate to admit it, but it really is pretty amazing."

I take a good look around, noting how different it looks from the night I broke in, when I was forced to find my way using the dim, yellow glow of the security lights.

Until Dace and Leandro arrived, and I clung to the shadows in a bid to remain undetected.

And though I did manage to sneak out without being caught, I'm convinced that Dace saw me.

There was a moment in the hall, when we were just a couple of steps from each other. And though it took all of my will not to barrel straight into his arms, I know beyond a doubt he sensed my presence just as surely as I sensed his.

The fact that he chose not to alert Leandro provides a small shred of hope that I cling to.

It's the hope that's carried me through the loneliness of time spent without him.

It's the hope I will lean on tonight.

Dace is still on my side. Despite what everyone thinks, he's determined to help me.

Our love is enough to conquer the beast.

"Not as crowded as I thought it would be." I shake free of the thought and check out the bar with the mosaic snake sculpture hanging overhead, the glass tiles shimmering in a way that makes it appear to be slithering.

Lita grasps Axel's wrist, checking the time on the watch she gave him for their three-month anniversary. "Trust me, they'll show. No self-respecting denizen of Enchantment would miss a chance to dress up and guzzle free well drinks. Another ten minutes and we'll be fighting for space."

As it turns out, it's only five minutes later when the room begins to fill, and Lita points toward the door. "Isn't that Jacy and Crickett?" She nods in their direction. "I haven't seen them since last New Year's Eve. Funny how even with the masks, it's easy to spot them."

"You should go talk to them." I follow her gaze, watching as her former friends nervously fuss at their hair and cling to their dates. The tourmaline pendants they received in the New Year's Eve swag bags hanging from their necks, much like all the other women in the room, while, according to Lita, the men got leather bracelets with tourmaline chunks woven in.

Lita crinkles her nose, wanting me to know she doesn't like the assignment. "We have nothing in common. I wouldn't even know what to say. Besides, shouldn't we wait for Auden and Xotichl? They should've been here by now."

"Xotichl sent me a text. They're running late. But they'll be here."

"They better be." Lita frowns. "We've got a lot depending on them."

"I'll handle that, you handle them." I nod toward her former friends. "There's a good chance they might know something useful. Last time I saw them, they were definitely under Cade's spell. For all I know, they still are." When she continues to hesitate, I add, "In case you haven't noticed, they're totally staring at Axel. You may as well give them a better look."

Lita's eyes gleam from the other side of her mask. The chance to gloat in front of her former friends is too good to miss. After taking a moment to adjust Axel's lapels and push a stray curl into place, she marches him across the room, leaving me to wander free on my own.

I move among the clusters of low-slung banquettes, past the

large, iron sculptures that look just like trees, until I stop, frozen in place, with legs turned to lead.

My mouth goes dry.

A shiver slips over my skin.

While my knees tremble ever so slightly.

Just like the dream, I feel him before I see him.

But when I turn to acknowledge him, his dark, fathomless eyes are all I need to see to know part of him is missing.

He's already transitioning into the beast he's destined to be.

I press a hand flat against the bodice of my dress and fight to steady myself. Determined to speak my piece while I can.

"Dace—" I start, but he's quick to interrupt me.

"You look beautiful." His gaze seeks mine, but with his eyes no longer reflecting, I can't bear the sight of it. "You're truly a vision. Stunning—breathtaking—ravishing . . ."

When I close my eyes, I can easily pretend that nothing has changed. But the moment I open them, the illusion is gone, and I find myself wishing he'd stop.

I clear my throat, lift my chin, and center my gaze just to the right of him. Disappointed that he doesn't seem to realize what I've done. Doesn't recognize my gown as the one I described from the dream. Doesn't find it the least bit odd that I'm wearing red to a black-and-white ball. Leaving me to wonder what else he's forgotten—about me—about us.

"Thanks," I say, my voice tight and clipped. "I'm surprised you don't recognize it—it came from your brother." Dace's face darkens, his eyes so feral and red, it prompts me to move on. "You're not wearing a mask."

He rubs a hand over his chin, a holdover from the Dace I once knew. "Trust me, Daire, I am. It's all I can do to maintain this face—you don't want to see my other one. I pray you won't have to."

I straighten my spine, square my resolve, but it doesn't do a thing to make me feel better. The sight of Dace struggling makes my heart ache. I need to find a way to appeal to him, remind him of the light still residing inside . . .

His gaze slips down the length of me, pausing on the deep V of my gown before focusing on the small golden key resting at the center of my chest. His expression so guarded, I can't help but wonder what he might've done with his. Is he still wearing it? And, more importantly, does he remember what it once meant?

"Dace," I say, my voice urgent, afraid of losing him completely. "The other night, when you caught me breaking in, why'd you let me go? What kept you from telling Leandro?"

His eyes close. His hands curl to fists. His struggle so palpable, I decide to drop it and instead tip onto my toes, press my lips to his ear, and whisper so that only he can hear. "Please try to remember who you really are. Please try to remember that you weren't always like this. You and I are fated for each other but not in the way the beast wants. You have to fight him, Dace. You have to come back to me—to us. Together we can beat Coyote and forge the future we want. Please, Dace, don't let go of your light." I draw away, eagerly reading his gaze, only to find my words fell on deaf ears.

Aside from his red glowing eyes, he looks pretty much the same. But inside, he's guided by instinct, a shard of memory, and a beast so sordid and sinister it would just as soon kill me.

He cocks his head, shoots me a curious look. But I drop my hand to my side and take a step back. I can love him with all of my heart, and I do. But for the first time ever, I realize I can't do it alone—it takes two to make this work.

My eyes glitter more brightly than I'd like, and with my throat so scratchy and dry, I have to push the words past. "Please don't ever forget that it's your belief in your darkness that snuffs out your light. You may have made the wrong choice—but you did so for all the right reasons. You did it for me—for us—and it's not over yet. You still have the choice to save yourself. But if you continue like this, no amount of light, no matter how insistent, could ever penetrate the walls you've raised to block it. They're your walls, Dace. Which means you're the only one capable of knocking them down."

He meets my words with a cold, vacant stare, and I turn away, having done all that I can.

It may not look at all like I'd hoped, but it's time to put my plan into action.

twenty-five

Dace

"Saw you talking to the Seeker. What's going on there?"

I watch Daire cross the room, like a blaze of red in a sea of dull nothings. "Turns out, I was wrong about her." I find Leandro's gaze from behind his ridiculous coyote mask, holding the look for as long as it takes to determine my truth.

He slaps an arm around my shoulder, chuckling as though I've made him inordinately proud. "If you knew how many women I've said that about!" He laughs a conspiratorial laugh. "Still, they do have their uses." He winks for emphasis, as though I might've missed the implication.

"Exactly how many times?" I ask, my voice as humorless as my gaze.

"What?" His forehead creases. The mirth fades from his face.

"Exactly how many times have you said that?"

He studies me closely, unsure how to react. Unsure of me. So I force my expression into one of solidarity. As though we're just two guys comparing our trophies. Which gets him to relax just enough to give me the answer I seek.

"Hundreds," he says. "Thousands." His eyes shine with the memory of an endless stream of conquests, and I can't help but wonder if my mother is featured among them. "In other words, you have a lot of catching up to do, son. But not to worry, I know just where to start . . ."

He squeezes my shoulder, starts to lead me across the room, but I've no interest in hooking up with anyone from Leandro's stable.

"What's your problem?" He glares, clenches his jaw.

"Guess I'm not as much like you as you thought."

His features sharpen, his lips flatten with unspoken fury.

"I like to work for it. Feel a sense of accomplishment. It's no fun when it comes too easily."

He pauses. Waits a few beats to see if there's more. Then, determining it's just me being weird, he throws his head back and roars.

"You are full of surprises," he says.

"You have no idea." I force a grin.

"What happened to your mask?" He casts a critical eye at my face. "You really shouldn't be walking around like that." He motions toward my red glowing eyes. "You're going to scare people. I told Cade to leave you one in your office." His gaze darkens as he looks around the club for his most disappointing son. Ready to call him out on the grievous offense the second he spots him.

"He left it." I shrug. "I choose not to wear it."

"In case you've forgotten, you're a member of Coyote now." Leandro leans toward me, his voice low and menacing. "It was sealed in the ceremony."

The ceremony. How could I forget? What may be commonplace dark magick for them was all new to me. Bearing no resemblance to anything Leftfoot ever taught me. And while the beast in me was delighted, it took every ounce of will left over from the old me to keep them from actually killing a real horse to symbolize the death of my former spirit animal. Which also raised some suspicions.

"I'm much more than Coyote," I say. "I'm about to surpass every last one of you."

"That may be true, but there's still one thing left to do. And until that time comes, don't you forget I'm the one in charge around here." The words are as sharp as they're intended to be.

Still one thing left to do . . .

I close my eyes, lift my chin high, and inhale long and deep. Scenting my brother among the throngs of bodies. He reeks of anger, vengeance, and the endless loop of revenge fantasies he needs to sustain him. But the truth is, he's pathetic, weak, and sorely lacking the appropriate amount of fear for someone in such a precarious state.

Then again, he has no idea of what's to become of him.

No idea Leandro has designated him as the one to kill so I can make the transition into my destiny.

"Here." Leandro removes his mask and thrusts it at me. "I insist that you wear it."

Knowing better than to protest, which will only serve to arouse his suspicions more than I already have, I snap the mask onto my head and return my focus to my brother, tracking his every move through the eyes of Coyote.

twenty-six

Daire

With Dace under Leandro's wing, Lita and Axel talking with Jacy and Crickett, and Xotichl and Auden expected to arrive any moment, I weave through the crowd in search of the vortex. Needing to at least be in the general vicinity long before the Richters can reach it, I retrace the path I memorized the night I broke in. Not entirely sure I'm on the right track since Dace and Leandro's unexpected arrival kept me from actually locating it.

Still, I'm sure it exists. Portals are contrived of the purest form of energy. They can be blocked but never destroyed.

All around me, throngs of people continue to gather. Seemingly immune to the lingering vibration of pain and destruction—the evil wrought, the lives lost (including Phyre)—that occurred here through the years.

For me, the sensation weighs heavily. You can level a structure and rebuild from scratch, but the energy of past events never quite dissipates. The essence remains. And the Richters' use of black onyx ensures those memories are sealed for eternity.

I pause near the spot where Dace found me, and when the

tourmaline ring starts to warm, I take it as a sign that I'm either in the presence of the vortex or that Cade Richter has lured me into his trap.

Figuring it's a win either way, I move forward. Instantly aware of a shift in the atmosphere, a heightened vibration, I gather my skirts and pick up the pace. Making it only part of the way when I'm stopped by a shaky hand with clammy fingers grabbing hold of my wrist.

Cade.

Cade is here. The vortex is near. Leaving me with no clear idea of just who's controlling this stone.

He jerks me back against him, nudges his nose into the hollow of my neck, and drags a long, steady breath. "Nothing like the scent of Raven at night," he says, his voice betraying an uneven pitch. "Though I must say, you do look enchanting." He twists hard on my arm, turns me to face him. "Still, I can't help but wonder where you're headed in such a hurry?"

I wrench free of his grip, put a more comfortable distance between us. Rubbing the place on my wrist where his fingers left marks, I bite back a scowl and force myself to play along. "Where do you think I'm going?"

"I would hope you were looking for me." He grins in a way that pulls his lips tightly, creases his eyes until they're just barely visible, and causes his head to jerk to the right. Making him appear manic, more than a little demented, and I'm not sure what to make of it.

The sinister, snide, mocking Cade is the one that I'm used to. The one I can deal with. This unbalanced version is a bit of a mystery.

"It's good to see you, Daire. I didn't think you'd come." He casts his gaze downward, drags his mask over his face as though caught in the grips of a sudden bout of shyness.

"Hard to pass up such an interesting invite," I reply, studying his intricately detailed mask, bearing a silver moon eclipsing a golden sun.

When Shadow eclipses Sun—the Seer shall fall

The choice is no accident. The message anything but subtle. It's Cade's way of telling me he knows about the prophecy—that he considers himself the Shadow, destined to rule.

"So you liked the invitation? I wasn't sure if you would." He lifts his chin, regards me with a hopeful gaze. His energy so chaotic, I can't get a read.

"What's not to like?" I grin flirtatiously, choose my words carefully. Convinced the slightest misstep will set him off, and it's a risk I can't take. For now, it's best to play his game his way.

"I worried the raven might send the wrong message, but I'm glad you could see past all of that and glean its true meaning." His eyes are shrewd and appraising. "It was meant to be symbolic, as you've clearly figured out. Something which, I have to admit, makes me inordinately proud."

I nod encouragingly, needing to hear more. I have no idea where he's going with this.

"It's the end of our old roles, Daire. It's time we shed Coyote and Raven and move into a new day. It's time for Richter and Santos to join. With the kind of power we wield, the possibilities are endless. You and I could rule the world. And the thing is—I know that we're ready. Your presence here tonight, wearing the dress and the mask that I sent, well, clearly you feel it too."

My smile grows tighter, but he's so caught up in his delusional world he doesn't seem to notice my struggle to keep this farce going.

It's hardly the first time he's tried to convince me to join his quest for world domination. Still, he's never been quite so . . . earnestly poetic before.

My gaze runs the length of his crisp white tux, his bloodred bow tie and cummerbund. Funny how Dace chose to wear black and his brother white. Yin and Yang, just as Cade stated in the dream where he slipped the blue tourmaline ring onto my finger.

"I understood immediately." I lean toward him, hoping to foster a sense of intimacy and trust. "But what I can't help but wonder is whether you broke Coyote's neck as well? You know, as a symbolic gesture to signal the end of your role." I adopt an innocent expression as though I'm merely curious and not at all baiting him.

"I'm embarrassed to say that it didn't even occur to me. But now that you've mentioned it, it makes perfect sense." His gaze glimmers. It actually *glimmers*. And if I peer close enough, I can catch the tiniest bit of my reflection staring back.

I blink once, twice, making sure it really is true—that Cade's eyes actually mirror in the way Dace's once did.

The startling sight, combined with his willingness to kill his beloved Coyote in an effort to please me, forces me to reevaluate everything I thought I knew about him.

While it's never been clear how a spirit animal's death might affect its owner, considering Cade and Dace's mystical connection, I can't take the chance. "I don't think that's necessary," I purr, touching his arm briefly, before using the momentum of a group of people brushing past to take a tiny step back, inching closer to what I hope is the vortex.

"It's your call, Daire." His voice catches on my name in a way that's unnerving, as though it elicits untold emotion. "You're probably surprised to hear me say that, but how else can I convey the seriousness of my offer? Besides, you've pleased me immensely by wearing the dress and the mask. I never imagined you'd actually go through with it—and I have to say, it looks even better than I dreamed." He pushes his mask high onto his forehead, filling his eyes with the sight of me. Not seeming to notice the space slowly increasing between us.

"I could never reject a gift of such generosity and beauty. I felt like Cinderella the moment I slipped it on and saw how perfectly it fit." I gaze down the bodice, to the deep V, and smile shyly, all the while risking another step back.

Cade's gaze follows mine. His fingers twitching, his weight shifting from foot to foot. His movements as awkward and jerky as a marionette with loose strings.

"Yet I did find it odd that you chose a red gown for a black-and-white ball." My right foot slides back. The left one soon meets it. "I couldn't quite make sense of that. Care to explain?"

"Easy." He grins, causing his eyes to flash clear and bright. "You're not like the rest of them, Daire. Girl like you should always stand out in a crowd." He centers his gaze on my chest, and I have to fight every instinct not to move my arm to cover it. Though it's not long before he catches me looking and drops his gaze to his feet, doing the shy act again. Which is strange enough in and of itself, but when I catch sight of his fingers trembling and clenching by his sides, it's a sure sign of the strange inner conflict that rages inside. "The mask—the dress—I had them made especially for you." He scrapes the sole of his shoe against the stone-tiled floor. "But you really need to toss that ridiculous key. It's ruining the look." He lifts his gaze to meet mine, and I watch the glimmer fade until he's back to being the Cade that I'm used to. The dark, overconfident Cade. The one whose eyes absorb everything around him. "And what's with the shoes?" He thrusts a disapproving finger toward Jennika's designer motorcycle boots peeking out from the hem.

"You don't approve?" I sneak the hem up just a bit, allowing for a better look. The scowl on his face telling me I've only succeeded in making it worse. "Well, on the plus side, they're a lot easier to run in than stilettos."

His fists curl tighter. "And what exactly are you running from?"

"Well, normally, that would be you. But here you are, right here before me, and I wouldn't even consider it." I press a hand to the outside of my thigh, ready to summon my athame should I need it. Peering past his shoulder as Auden goes through a series of sound checks and the crowd starts to head for the dance floor. Won't be much longer until he heaves his last breath.

"Somehow, your words fail to convince. No matter what I do, you still see me as the enemy," he says, so lost in the thought, he fails to notice when someone bumps into him and sends him reeling into my space.

So much for the progress I made.

"I assure you, that's hardly the case." I wiggle my fingers by my side, hoping for a tingle of energy, some kind of hint that I'm on the right track, that somewhere nearby a portal awaits.

"If only I could believe that." He cocks his head, shoots me a suspicious look.

"Well, for starters, I'm here, wearing the dress and talking to you." I chance another step back, wishing Auden would just get to it already and get the plan underway.

"True." Cade moves along with me. Either in an effort to stay close or he's totally on to me—it's impossible to tell.

"And I'm doing everything I mentioned despite the fact that you're responsible for my grandmother's death. That's got to mean something." I stand firmly before him, the vortex now just a few feet away, according to the energetic swarm playing at the back of my hands. And while I have every intention of breaching it, I need to get there long before Cade. It's his job to chase me.

He dismisses my words with a shrug. "I know what she meant to you, but Paloma was determined to keep us apart, and you have to admit, we wouldn't be here now, just you and me, if I hadn't killed her." His delivery so matter of fact, I know without a doubt that whatever is going on with him is far worse than I thought. The old Cade would've taunted me to no end. Detailing exactly how much he enjoyed killing her. This new Cade is completely unpredictable, which makes him even more dangerous.

"I loved her," I say, knowing I shouldn't push it, shouldn't veer from the script. But it's impossible to fake my feelings where Paloma's passing is concerned. Besides, it's just a matter of time before Cade Richter is history. "Not a day goes by I don't miss her," I add. Despite Chay's warnings, with each spoken word I can feel my anger mounting until it's all I can do to keep it in check. "Yet it's true that Paloma never would've understood these . . . feelings . . . we share for each other." The words taste bitter on my tongue.

Cade makes a conciliatory face and reaches for my hand, and as repulsive as I find him, I need to play along for just a few seconds more.

"People die, Daire." He huffs under his breath, his face reddens with outrage, as though angered by the lack of justice in the world—as though he doesn't actually wear Paloma's blood on his hands. "It's the circle of life. You, more than anyone, should know that. Sheesh." He drops my hand, his fists curl in outrage. The burst of anger lasting only a moment, before he softens and says, "It hurts, I know. But I'm so glad to see you getting past it and focusing on the future you deserve."

I cast my eyes downward, use the pause to sneak another step back.

"You've lost so many so quickly, it almost seems unfair. Still, there's a reason for everything and each step leads to the next. Now that you're on your own, with Paloma gone, Dace having moved on, and Jennika—"

"What about Jennika?" I cut him off before he can finish. The sound of my mom's name on his lips is enough to make me forfeit my whole plan and kill him right here.

"Relax." He slips the mask over his face and laughs, making for a strange, muffled sound. "I was just about to say that even Jennika will one day move on. Jeez, Daire, when'd you get so sensitive?"

But the way his head tilts, the way his voice catches, leaves me to wonder if that's all there is to it. He's unstable. Untrustworthy. Which makes him capable of just about anything.

"Anyway, enough of all this. It's time we set aside our differences. Come." He reaches for my hand again. "You're lucky I found you when I did. Do you know there's a kill order issued with your name on it?"

"Yeah. You're the one who issued it. Remember?" I drop the façade, having reached my limits for him and his madness.

"Don't be ridiculous. You have no idea what's really going on here. But if you stick with me, you just might get out alive."

I look past Cade's outstretched hand and glance toward the stage.

The game is over.

The plan is in motion.

And little does he know, I've got him right where I want him.

With the sound checks complete, Auden introduces the band, as Xotichl uses the amethyst pendulum she wears at her neck to locate the Richters. While Lita plucks two of the three feathers in her hair and uses them to enhance herself, Auden, Xotichl, and Axel with magickal and transformative powers, saving the eagle feather—the one for sending wishes and prayers—for later. And Axel pulls the rattle from Lita's bag and readies it before him, waiting for Auden to launch into his song.

When he reaches the drum solo, Auden butts the head of his guitar into Paloma's drum he's propped up beside him, as Axel shakes the rattle. The two of them sending a mystical vibration throughout the room, as I brace myself, praying it works.

This is it.

There is no plan B.

I close my eyes for a moment, say a little prayer of my own, and when I open them again, I turn on my heel to see that it worked.

The vortex is just a few steps behind me, and thanks to the drum and the rattle, it's visibly illuminated in a way only my friends and I can see.

I spin on my heel, begin to sprint toward it, when Cade grabs hold of the back of my dress and I respond with a fist aimed straight for his jaw. My knuckles slamming hard into his flesh, sending him reeling, spinning, slamming onto the floor with his mask knocked clear across the hall.

Though it's only a matter of time before he's on me again—or at least that's the plan.

I need him to chase me.

But not before I put a solid distance between us.

Freeing my buckskin pouch from my hair, I loop it around my neck, gather my skirts in my hands, and charge through the vortex.

twenty-seven

Xotichl

Auden steps away from the drum and leaps from the stage. Grasping my hand tightly in his, we run alongside Lita and Axel in a race toward the vortex, while the Richters race to catch up.

Problem is they're not exactly alone. From the looks of things, they're taking half the club with them.

The idea was to lure the Richters on a chase through the portal while the elders worked their magick to block off the exits. Ensuring the safety of the citizens of Enchantment, while trapping Cade, Leandro, and the rest of them to deal with Daire's wrath, while we serve as backup in case she should need it.

But with all of these people joining in on the chase, it's not going as planned.

Lita shoots a worried look over her shoulder, searching for Auden and me, but a crush of people rush past, and the next thing I know, I've lost Auden's grip and I'm stumbling straight for the floor. My hands out before me, just about to connect, when someone hitches onto the back of my dress and yanks me to safety. Sparing me from what surely would've been a case of death by trampling.

"Thank you." I push my hair from my eyes and fight to catch my breath. "I think you may have just saved my life."

"Perhaps it's me who should be thanking you."

I look into the face of a man with black, opaque eyes and a hideous grin. Despite the evidence before me, I tell myself it's not what I think. I'm clearly imagining things.

"I thought you were going to Albuquerque?" I take a quick inventory of his squinty mean gaze, absurd middle-aged pony-tail, and wannabe hipster double-hoop earrings. Could only be Luther.

"Turns out I was needed here." His grin grows as wide and empty as the look in his eyes.

"Who needed you—Auden?" My gut churns with dread as my mind searches for an easy explanation.

"Auden?" He makes a face of distaste. "No, flower. As it turns out, Auden's offered all that he can. Gotta admire his level of am-bition though. If you must know, it was Leandro who called."

My gut roils, practically screaming *I told you so!* "How do you know Leandro? I don't understand." Though the second it's out, I realize I do. In fact, I'm beginning to understand more than I ever wanted to.

"Oh, but you're beginning to understand now, aren't you, flower? Clever girl that you are. The record company I work for is owned by the Richters. Leandro's my cousin. Thought for sure you would've figured that out. But I guess you can't really *see* nearly as well as you used to. You can't really see much of anything, can you? Or at least nothing of any real importance or depth. So sad to watch someone with so much power, and so much unlimited po-tential, become as dumb-downed as everyone else in this town."

"You did this! You're behind this!"

"While I'd love to claim all the credit, turns out, it was all you. Think, flower, what was always the one thing that kept us from altering your perception until now?"

My stomach clenches, a stream of bile rises high in my throat. *My blindness.*

As Paloma once told me, *The Richters need your sight to alter your*

perception. If you can learn to look upon your blindness as a blessing, I
can teach you how to see that which remains hidden to most . . .

"Oh, and it goes even deeper." He grasps my hand in his, and
before I can stop him, he sends a stream of images into my head.
Images so awful, so horrific, my knees buckle and give.

No.

My hands find the floor.

The rest of me follows.

No, it can't be!

I look up, my gaze pleading with his. "You have to undo it! You
have to—"

He looms over me. Shoots me a malevolent grin. "A signed contract is binding. A contract sealed with blood is binding for eternity. And speaking of blood—" He reaches toward me, swipes a
thick finger across my cheek. Tracing over the exact same place
where Auden accidentally bled on me. "Looks like someone's
been marked." His sardonic laughter bleats in my head. "Turns out,
this was one of my best and surprisingly easiest gets. A twofer—
who would've guessed?" He ducks his head. "Now, if you don't
mind, I hear there are worlds to breach, not to mention a Seeker
to kill. Can't think of a better way to celebrate the end of your
world!"

He races toward the vortex, vanishing as quickly as he appeared.
As I struggle to my feet, struggle to digest this hideous turn of
events. Vaguely aware of a hand shooting out from behind me, as
a hurried voice says, "There you are, flower. I've been looking all
over for you!"

And before I can respond, Auden is pulling me through the
glimmering veil.

twenty-eight

Lita

I glance over my shoulder, searching for Xotichl and Auden. Catching only a fleeting glimpse of them, before a surge of people intervene and they seem to vanish from sight.

Where are all these people going? This wasn't part of the plan!

I look at Axel, wondering if he's thinking the same thing as I am. But he just tightens his grip and pulls me past the shimmering veil, where we pause long enough to get our bearings and confirm this is nothing at all like it was the last time I visited.

Whenever there's a party at the Rabbit Hole, the Richters like to host their own private party within the party. It's considered a big deal to get an invite, mostly because it's all very cloak and dagger and shrouded in mystery. Involving things like blindfolds and cigarettes, which, I later learned, were used to appease the demons guarding the entrance.

But now it's nothing like that.

Not only are there no demons, but what was once a bizarre luxury cave with gilded antique furniture and priceless pieces of art, is now just a burned-out shell leading to a wasteland of mile after mile of dull yellow sand that, according to Daire—who gave specific instructions to get through the tin walkway, the luxury cave, and then the second vortex beyond that leads to the valley of sand—this isn't supposed to come until later.

"The landscape's all wrong." I cling tightly to Axel, afraid of losing him in the throngs of people rushing around us, seemingly with no real direction in mind. Their eyes glazed, their movements jerky, almost robotic, as though they're not quite acting of their own accord.

"That's the least of what's wrong." Axel's features sharpen, his eyes crease with worry. "Check out the tourmaline pendants those girls are wearing."

I follow his gaze to see the gems glowing, blinking, as though a magickal switch was turned on.

"Jacy and Crickett are wearing those pendants—and Daire has the ring—we have to help them!" I'm filled with adrenaline, motivated by my need to rescue them all, until I take a good look at my surroundings, watching as the world descends into chaos, and realize I'm way out of my league. This goes far beyond any abilities a couple of feathers might've bestowed upon me. "This is a disaster!" My shoulders sink, my eyes burn, I'm falling apart, succumbing to the pressure, along with the growing certainty that it's about to get worse. "How could this happen, when it was all going as planned?"

Axel responds with a grave face, as he pulls me alongside him through the valley of sand. "Looks like the Richters were in control all along."

twenty-nine

Dace

When the drum sounds, when the vortex illuminates, Leandro lifts his drink high and clinks his glass against mine. "Just like clockwork." He grins, takes a final sip, and abandons his scotch on the bar. "Would you like to do the honors?"

I shake my head, causing him to doubt me again.

"You go first," I say, in an effort to appease him. "But go easy on her. Don't be too rough. I have a big finale planned for the end. And I want the Seeker lucid enough to enjoy it."

Leandro's grin grows wider. I'm finally speaking his language. "Just so you know, Gabe will want a shot at her. Heck, Marliz too. She's always hated her."

"Then they better get in line. And you better get moving before she gets too much of a head start."

With a face filled with fatherly pride, he takes a moment to pat me on the back, then he's gone in a flash. Leaving me to study my brother from across the room. Still lying prone in the hall where Daire punched him.

Get up, fool.

His head swings. His eyes veer toward mine.

If I didn't know better, I'd think that he heard.

"Leandro's right." I move toward him, closing the distance in a few quick steps. "You're an embarrassment to all of us."

He glares, curses under his breath, and struggles to his feet. His jaw marked by Daire's fist. His mind a torment of heartbreak and rage.

Killing him is going to be ridiculously easy.

I brush past him on my way to the vortex. Knocking his shoulder so hard he stumbles, loses his balance, nearly ends up right back on the floor. "Get a grip," I tell him. "Leandro's going after the Seeker, and you're in enough trouble already. If you're smart, you'll get moving and get to her first."

thirty

Daire

The sand comes too soon. And what's worse is there's even more of it than the last time I was here.

Still, I try to stay positive. Try to assure myself that while it's not quite what I was expecting, it might prove better this way. If nothing else, it guarantees that there's no place for the Richters to hide.

I close my eyes, lift my arms to my sides, and indulge a moment of quiet, contented solitude. Knowing the elders are out there, working their magick and closing the exits, while my friends are on their way to provide backup in case I should need it.

Though I don't plan to need it.

Aside from the sand, it's all going according to plan.

Soon, very soon, I will avenge every last Seeker who was ever felled by a Richter.

El Coyote will be begging for mercy.

As the head of the clan, Leandro is first on my list, with Cade following close behind.

The roar of feet pounding in the distance tells me they're well on their way. The moment I've been waiting for about to come to fruition.

My heart thrums with anticipation.

I center my focus and ready my blade.

Having waited so long for this moment, I can hardly believe that it's here.

I wave my athame high over my head, signaling to my friends that all is well. It may not look like we planned, but there is nothing to fear.

"Keep running!" I shout. "Make for the hill and wait for me there."

On the lookout for Lita, Axel, Xotichl, and Auden, only to discover my friends aren't there—it's the crowd from the party instead.

A tsunami of masked people in formal attire cresting straight for me. Their tourmaline pendants and bracelets flashing and blinking as they plod through the sand as though driven by an outside force.

With only a few feet left spanning between us, the ground gives way, the sand collapses, and we're sucked deep into the earth. Careening toward the Lowerworld, where we crash in a heap of disjointed bodies.

I free myself from a tangle of limbs and scramble for my knife that came loose in the fall.

Fingertips barely grazing the hilt when Leandro captures it with the heel of his boot, looms before me, and says, "Thanks, Seeker. That went exactly as planned."

thirty-one

Daire

Leandro glowers before me.

Kicks my athame well out of reach.

That one simple move signaling my plan is a fail—and yet there's no denying I've got him right where I want him. Now all I need is my knife.

I flatten my palm, splay my fingers to the side, and try to summon my athame. The familiar tingling sensation crawling over my flesh a sure sign it's working, until Leandro hooks a mean right that lands squarely on my jaw.

My head snaps back, my feet fly up from under me, as my body spirals toward the dirt, and my mind reels with the absurdity of what I'm now facing: My boyfriend is a demon and his father just clocked me.

I roll onto my side, blinking past the constellation of stars swirling past, to see Leandro leading an army of demons, Richters, and anesthetized partygoers, on a rampage through the very land I vowed to protect.

The Lowerworld is in chaos.

The Upperworld will soon follow.

Turns out, when Auden beat Paloma's drum, it didn't illuminate only the Rabbit Hole portal like we'd planned.

It illuminated *all* of the portals.

Swinging those glowing doorways wide open—allowing the Richters an all-access pass to dimensions long denied them.

Once again, Coyote was one step ahead.

Orchestrating, if not second-guessing, my every move.

With the crowd quickly dispersing and Leandro long gone, I get to my feet, retrieve my athame, and duck behind a small grove of trees, where I hope to go unnoticed until I can figure a way to regroup.

Reaching for the buckskin pouch at my neck, convinced that if there was ever a time to call upon the aid of my ancestors and talismans, it's now, I remember something Paloma once told me: *Someday you will need to call on us like never before—use your light.*

Well, I'm using my light, my talismans, my will, my intent— I'm using every trick my grandmother taught me and calling to them with all that I've got. But after a few moments of silence, there's still no sign of them. Not even Raven comes to my aid.

I'm alone.

Truly alone.

Just like the lone raven that soared above Paloma's grave the day I buried her.

Seems my ancestors, along with my spirit animal, are dead set on ignoring me.

I push away from the trees, determined to locate my friends and do what I can to gain some semblance of control, when Chay whispers my name from a few feet away.

"Our magick failed." He lumbers toward me. His face griefstricken, hand clutching his side. "We were down here working. It was all going as planned. But then . . ." His voice fades, both of us knowing there's no need to finish when the evidence surround us.

"It's a disaster," I say. "I thought I had it all under control, but once again, Coyote was pulling the strings."

I start to yank the tourmaline ring from my finger, convinced Chay was right. I never should've made him dig it up. It's only served to enable Coyote by allowing them direct access to me.

"Don't." He shakes his head, places a hand on my arm, as I shoot him a questioning look. "If it's truly working against you, then it won't be long before the Richters find you. They'll want to celebrate breaching the three worlds by killing the Seeker. Which means you still have a chance to get to them before they get to you."

"Leandro already had a go at me." I rub the sore spot on my face where his fist met my jaw. "But then he took off. Guess raiding the Upperworld held more appeal."

"He won't be the one to kill you. He'll save that particular victory for one of his sons." The words are spoken in a straightforward manner, though his eyes betray the magnitude of his grief.

"How altruistic of him." I roll my eyes, crack a sardonic grin, noting the way Chay grimaces in response. "How do you know so much, anyway?" I study him carefully, convinced there's more going on than he's willing to share.

"As a veterinarian and a life-long citizen of Enchantment, let's just say I'm well versed in the ways of Coyote. I always figured this day would come."

"It was fated." I shut my eyes tightly, briefly; the words cut to the bone. Remembering the day I first learned Dace was my fated one. How happy I felt. How secure my future seemed. Never once daring to think we were fated to this . . .

My gut pings with grief, I find it hard to breathe, and I instinctively reach for the key that hangs from my chest—the symbol of Dace's and my love. My fingers curling around it, seeking the assurance it's never failed to provide.

I can't give up.

Won't give up.

The Richters have taken enough already—they won't claim Dace too.

I lift my hand before me, watching as the tourmaline glimmers and glints as though it's taken on a life of its own, then I glance all around. Taking in a once peaceful world now left in ruins, and it's only bound to get worse.

"This marks the start of the prophecy." Chay's voice is gruffer than normal, as though each word is a struggle. "It may have nothing to do with the ring."

"Either that or once again Cade got impatient and decided to jumpstart the event."

"While we may never have the answer, perhaps you can find a way to make the stone work *for* you. What is it you told me about its properties?"

"It's a shamanic tool, it activates the third eye, and in times of trouble, it can guide one toward safety . . ." My eyes grow wide with understanding. "So, you're saying I should use it to lead me to the Richters instead of it leading them to me?"

His eyes shine as much as they're able under the circumstances. "Either way, you're bound to meet. But at least this way puts you in control of the situation."

It doesn't take long to concede that he's right. But before I enact my new plan, I first need to know that the elders are safe. "Where are the others?" I ask. "Leftfoot, Cree, and Chepi?"

"They're all here, somewhere. Figured it was best to separate so if worse came to worst, the Richters couldn't take us all at once."

I close my eyes. Hardly able to believe the danger I've put them all in.

"Hey now. There's no time for regrets." Chay tips a finger to my chin. "We've been part of this fight from the start. Long before you were born. What happens from this moment forward is not your fault. You hear?"

I nod because he expects me to, but I can't quite shake my remorse.

"If you're going to worry about anyone, save it for Jennika."

My eyes snap open.

"I couldn't stop her. She insisted on coming."

"Tell me you didn't really just say that," I plead, wondering how it's possible for this to get any worse. Though the look on his face confirms it's the truth. "Is she at least armed?" Figuring what's done is done, it's better to veer toward the practical. "And what I mean by that is—is she armed with something other than a fierce maternal instinct to save her cub no matter the cost?"

Chay attempts a grin but doesn't get very far before his lips flatten and his face pales from the strain. "She told us she's quite proficient at archery, so Leftfoot set her up."

"Proficient?" I frown, allowing a quick trip to the past when she took a few lessons during filming breaks on a movie set, but I don't remember her adding it to her short list of hobbies. "At best, she's an amateur," I say, growing inexplicably angry at Jennika for overstating her skills and putting herself in grave danger.

"Well, it's going to have to prove good enough." Chay brushes a hand across his forehead, coming away with a film of sweat coating his fingers. "Anyway, you ready?"

I look at him.

"Fun's just getting started."

"You call this fun?"

"Like anything, it's all in the perspective."

He slips his Eagle ring from his finger, holds it high above his head, and emits a quick series of whistles that perfectly imitate the Eagle's high-pitched peal.

"What're you doing?" I ask, worried he'll attract Richters and demons before I'm ready to face them.

Chay flattens a hand to his belly. Seeing my look of concern, he jabs a finger toward the sky, gesturing toward the beautiful Eagle soaring in ever-widening circles above. "He's hunting for Richters," he says, watching his magnificent spirit animal at work, which only makes me wonder what happened to mine.

"Will he bring them back to us?"

Chay tries to laugh, but it's as unsuccessful as the grin. "Not likely. But if you follow, he'll lead you to them. Think of him as a backup to the tourmaline."

I shift my focus to Chay, adding up all the signs of physical distress he's displayed since he arrived and becoming even more convinced that something's gone terribly wrong. "If *I* hurry? What about you? It's your spirit animal. Aren't you coming with me?"

He shakes his head sadly and flips open his jacket. Revealing the place where blood continuously pumps from a wound hidden inside his shirt. "Looks like you're not the only one who met up with Leandro." His complexion pales, his gaze grows blunted, distant, and when I rush to help, he pushes me away.

"I'm a healer! I can help you!" I cry, mentally reviewing the short list of quick fixes and remedies.

"That's a side gig." He grasps my hands and folds them in his. "You're the Seeker first and foremost, which means you cannot afford to get distracted by me. Go, Daire. You've got a job to do. I'll be fine."

"But what if you're not?" My lip quivers, my eyes sting, and if I didn't know better, I'd swear that my heart has splintered into a thousand jagged shards. "I can't do this alone! I can't lose you too!"

"But someday you will." His gaze is resigned, leaving no doubt he's fighting to hang on long enough to convince me to leave. "If not today, then someday, and it's perfectly okay. Paloma is waiting for me, and when my time is up, I'll go gladly. I'm ready to find her. So don't you worry. My breath may cease, but my soul will transcend. So go, Daire. Trust in your abilities. Trust in Paloma's teachings. Trust in the wisdom of your ancestors. But most importantly, trust in your heart. It will never lead you astray."

My eyes meet his, and I instinctively know he means Dace.

"Love is a powerful force. If anyone can save him, it's you. So go. Go do what you were born to do."

I cup a hand to either side of his face, tip onto my toes, and press my lips to his forehead. Hoping he can somehow intuit all of the words I'm too shaken to say. Then, with a heavy heart, I turn on my heel and race to catch up with Eagle.

thirty-two

Xotichl

The second I discover we've landed in the Lowerworld, my first instinct is to flee.

The place I once begged to visit—the place I once held so dear—the place that bestowed me with what I once considered the most incredible gift by restoring my sight—has descended into a scene so hellish, it's like a mirror image of the wasteland of emotions warring inside.

I pound my fists into the dirt.

I thrash, kick, and scream with all I have in me.

Driven by an all-consuming hatred for this place—blaming it for fueling my dreams and encouraging me to believe the old me wasn't quite good enough—that I needed improving.

But mostly, I hate myself for relinquishing my blind sight with barely a thought, in a desire to be *normal*, like everyone else.

It's the reason I couldn't get a read on Luther.

Why I couldn't warn Auden against signing that contract.

Couldn't warn Daire that something awful was afoot.

And because of it, the three worlds, like our lives, are in ruins.

Those weren't sapphires embedded on that pen, they were blue tourmalines from Cade's mine.

And the blood Auden spilled on that contract—the blood he accidentally spilled on my cheek—ties us to the Richters for all of eternity.

Because he agreed to beat the drum that illuminated the portals allowing Coyote unhindered access to the worlds long denied them, Auden will have unlimited riches, unsurpassed fame and success.

He'll live the life of his dreams.

But the fame will be fleeting.

The success comes with a shelf life of one single lifetime.

While our souls are doomed for all of eternity.

"Flower, hey—you okay?" Auden crawls up alongside me, brings a hand to my tearstained cheek. "Are you injured?"

I shake my head.

"Scared?"

"Not in the way you might think."

"So what then?" He brushes a hand through my hair, tucks the strands back behind my ear. His touch so tender, his gaze so caring, I can't bear to tell him the truth.

Though I guess he reads the look on my face because he takes my hand and says, "How long have you known?" His voice is somber, face grave.

"Probably not as long as you."

"Xotichl—" He squeezes my hand. "I'm so sorry. I messed up. I wanted this so badly, but only because I wanted you to believe in me. I wanted your mom to believe in me—I wanted to be good enough for her—to get her approval . . ."

My throat grows hot and tight. "Oh, Auden. Don't you get it? No one will ever be good enough for my mom. That's just how she is when it comes to me. But you've always been more than good enough for me—isn't that what really matters?"

"It should've been. But I was so desperate for her blessing that I . . ." He shakes his head, squints his eyes closed as though he can't bear to see or be seen. "And now, because of it, I've endangered you."

"Maybe, maybe not."

Auden opens his eyes, looks at me.

"Just because our plan's a fail doesn't mean we can't improvise. There's got to be a way to turn this whole thing around and I'm determined to find it. I've had enough of the Richters. They won't get our souls that easily, not without a fight." I get to my feet and entwine my fingers with his. Putting on a brave face and the voice to match, I say, "First, we need to find our friends and make sure they're okay. Then we'll deal with Luther and the Richters once and for all."

thirty-three

Lita

The second the sand drops from under our feet, Axel pulls me tightly to his chest and wraps his arms snugly around me in an effort to cushion the fall.

He's always there for me.

Always looking out for me.

In just six short months he's become such an integral part of my life, I can't imagine ever being without him.

We crash to the ground, with Axel on the bottom, me on top. And after determining we both survived seemingly unharmed, I bury my face in his chest and seek strength in his touch. Figuring I'm going to need it, since, from what I can tell, the world's gone to hell.

"You okay?" Axel loosens his grip, gets us both to our feet, as I adjust the straps of my dress and conduct a quick inventory of myself.

"Yeah," I say. "Or, at least, I think so. That mask is long gone, but good riddance. I'm just glad I let Daire convince me to wear these boots." I raise the hem of my dress, gaze down at the hideous pair of hiking boots I was reluctant to wear. "The stilettos I had in mind never would've survived that fall." I grin, jostle his shoulder, try to get a response. But he's already drawing away. "What? What is it?" I follow the direction of his strangely glittering gaze, watching as he stares wide-eyed at a sky glowing red.

"It's the Upperworld." He turns to me, his face filled with pain. "It's been breached."

I study him closely, alarmed by the way his irises lighten until they're almost iridescent in color. "Maybe it's just more of Cade's stupid magick tricks. I mean, it wouldn't be the first time. Last Christmas Eve he made the sky bleed fire. Practically firebombed the whole town."

"It's not Cade." His tone is as regretful as his face. "I can hear the cries of my people in agony."

He starts to withdraw. His movements so effortless, it's as though he's being willed by a much greater force.

"Axel!" I grasp his hand, force him to face me. "What are you doing?" I cry, though the answer is clear. His eyes reveal everything. "No." My voice shakes, though it's nothing compared to my knees. "No! You *cannot* go back there! You live here now!"

"Lita . . ." He turns long enough to cup his hands to my cheeks, his touch so soft I could easily be distracted if his gaze wasn't so final.

"Are you freaking kidding me?" My voice is shrill in a way that would normally embarrass me, but not anymore, not when everything I cherish is about to fall apart. "You come into my life, make me fall head over heels for you, just so you can dump me the second the worlds go to hell?" I clutch his arm tightly, try to force a reply, but when he fails to speak, I try another approach and appeal to his practical side. "Axel, I don't know what you're thinking, but you *cannot* leave me out here on my own. It's dangerous, there are demons, and I'm completely unarmed!"

"You're not unarmed." He plucks the last remaining feather from my hair and brushes the vane softly against my cheek. "It's a miracle you didn't lose it in the fall. It must be an omen."

"A miracle? Since when does a feather qualify as a miracle?" Hating the very sight of it, I bat it with the back of my hand, push it away. "Like that's ever going to defend me against a Richter!" I glare, so angry, so incredibly insulted, I could scream. Though somehow, I manage to refrain.

"It's not just any feather. It's an Eagle—"

"I know what kind of feather it is!" I rub my lips together. Bite back a barrage of words I'll only live to regret. Knowing it's better to appear rational, if not entirely calm, I force myself to say, "Axel, I swear if you leave me here, I will—"

He presses a finger to my lips, which only tempts me to bite it. Not that it'll do any good. He'll just bleed a bit of gold, before the wound seals right up as though it never existed.

"*Believe*, Lita. That's all I ask of you. Belief and intent are at the heart of all magick. It can't possibly work without them."

I start to push his hand away, but the second my fingers meet his, I find myself clasping it instead. "And who exactly am I supposed to send a prayer to? You? You gonna answer my wish once you get there?"

"If I'm able."

"And if you're not?"

He squeezes my fingers, holds my hand close to his chest. "Honestly, I'm just looking to get my own prayer answered. But, Lita, you need to know that prayers are like wishes. If you waste them on the frivolous, they won't be there when you need them for something serious. So please think long and hard before you put this to use." He places the feather into my hand and curls my fingers around the quill.

"You're serious. You're really doing this, aren't you?" My voice cracks, hardly able to believe this is happening. That Cade's prophecy of our doomed romance is actually coming true.

Axel cups his palms to my cheek, his glimmering lavender eyes conveying all the things that words fail to. But it's too painful. I can't bear to look. So I shutter my eyes, tip onto my toes, and bring my lips to meet his. Allowing myself to revel in a touch so light, so mesmerizing, so loving, so fleeting . . .

And the next thing I know, he's disappeared into a burst of blazing red light.

thirty-four

Daire

I follow Chay's Eagle to a fat nest of demons amusing themselves by terrorizing a warren full of rabbits.

Which is why they don't notice me.

"Bunnies? Really?" I wave my athame before me. "You know, the rules are actually pretty simple, and yet you always seem to break them. So, allow me to remind you. First, there will be no terrorizing, killing, or eating of the spirit animals—"

They stop with the menacing and turn their attention to me, waiting to hear what comes next. That's the thing about demons—while they're definitely hideous, evil, incredibly dangerous, and prone to causing massive destruction, they're also easily distracted.

Not to mention stupid.

"And second—"

My gaze moves among them, searching for the leader. Deciding it's not the one that snarls, growls, and goes after me first, I still don't hesitate to slice my athame straight through his thick, scaly neck—if for no other reason than to send a message to the rest.

His body jerks and twitches in a brief adrenaline-laced jig, before collapsing to the dirt alongside its head.

"As I was saying before I was so rudely interrupted—" I shake the remaining crud from my blade and position it before me, ready to take the next wave. "The Upper- and Lowerworlds are strictly off-limits. Which means you can either leave now or deal with me. Your choice."

They come at me in a wave of tails and horns and oversized monstrous heads, and my athame carves 'em up as easily as a Thanksgiving turkey. Counting each severed bit as a small sign of victory, all the while knowing I probably shouldn't be enjoying it to the degree that I am.

It's not like there's a shortage of evil. There are plenty more where they came from.

Not to mention that somewhere, out there, Coyote is waiting.

I stop with the fancy moves and quips and concentrate instead on finishing the job. Methodically eliminating them one by one, until the entire nest is eradicated and I follow Eagle to the next one. Then the one after that. And all those that follow. Eventually slaying so many demons, the spirit animals begin to come out of hiding and work alongside me.

A posse of Rabbits, Turtles, Bison, Ram, and Bobcats are soon joined by countless others intent on reclaiming their turf.

Though, once again, Raven is notably absent.

Horse too.

But with so much left to do, I can't get distracted. I keep a close watch on Eagle as he soars a wide arc before me, just a few feet ahead, signaling another lot of demons lurking nearby. Swooping past my shoulder just as I'm about to close in, he veers so close his feathers graze my cheek like a kiss, before he winks out of sight.

A chill pricks the back of my neck, blankets my skin.

My knees go weak.

As my fingers tremble so severely, I nearly drop the athame.

My body instantly acknowledging the truth my mind fights to deny.

Chay.

Another one lost at the Richters' hands.

I sag toward the ground, staggering under the weight of the loss. So gripped by grief, it's a moment before I notice the peal of voices shouting close by.

Driven by rage, heartache, and vengeance, I spring to my feet and race toward the noise. Wondering at the spirit animals' unwillingness to follow, when I burst onto a scene that explains their reluctance.

Even with her back turned toward me, the sight of her gorgeous mane of glistening amber waves spilling down her back, her black leather corset, unearthly translucent skin, and skirt comprised of countless slithering, writhing, live snakes, leaves no doubt I've crossed paths with the Bone Keeper.

The one who rules the lowest level of the Lowerworld.

The one who presides over the Day of the Dead, collecting the bones of the deceased as admittance to the afterlife.

No wonder the spirit animals prefer to steer clear—she's as terrifying now as the first day I met her.

"So, the Seeker returns." Her voice is throaty and deep, as she glances over her shoulder, revealing the beautiful version of her face. The large, black onyx eyes—the lush generous mouth used for swallowing stars. A stunning façade that can instantly shift to a sun-bleached skull with horrible empty sockets standing in for the eyes. "While you've done a fine job of demon slaying, don't get any ideas. Demons serve me no purpose, which is why I left them to you. These are mine, you'll get no part of them." She gestures toward a large group of Richters who had the misfortune of falling into her trap.

It's the one commonality we share—the Bone Keeper hates Coyote almost as much as I do. For centuries, their dead have denied her their bones, and the Bone Keeper never forgets what's owed her.

The ones still alive huddle wide-eyed and terrified, watching as her endless army of snakes sink their fangs into the flesh of the fallen. Painstakingly stripping them of muscle and meat, exposing the bones that she covets.

I gaze upon the lot of them, searching for three in particular. Hoping they're not among the heap being flayed by the snakes. I have my own torture planned.

"While I'm not here to interfere with . . ." I gaze among the wreckage, looking for the correct way to phrase the horror show she's directing. ". . . your *bone collecting,* I feel I should warn you— that one is mine." I point to the one on my list, leaving no room for doubt who I've set my sights on, as I pick my way through countless beds of snakes.

Ready to stake my claim, when the Bone Keeper's pale bony hand locks hard on my wrist. "I don't negotiate." Her eyes blaze on mine.

I place my hand over hers and wrench free of her grip, rubbing the place where her nails nearly broke through my skin. "Funny, that's not how I remember it." I glare, recalling the deal we wagered on the Day of the Dead when I got the souls and she kept the bones. "Not to mention, today is not *Dia de los Muertos.* You have no claim to them."

She grins. Her lips stretching wide to reveal a row of glittering teeth, a tongue sprinkled with stardust. The display oddly enticing, until her face transforms into a skull and the illusion is lost. "In case you haven't noticed, the worlds are merged, Seeker. The old rules no longer apply."

"A temporary reprieve that's soon to be remedied." I push the words past, speaking with far more confidence than I currently own. "And as it just so happens, that one is the first step toward making it happen." I brush past her until I'm standing before him. Enjoying the look of sheer terror on Gabe's face as I press the tip of my demon crud-covered athame to the underside of his chin. Admittedly disappointed it's not Leandro or Cade, though it's still a good start. "You can have his bones for all I care. But I want to be the one to destroy him."

"My, my." The sound of the Bone Keeper giggling is so unnatural, I can't help but cringe. "Seems the Echo's not the only one who's gone dark around here."

"What do you know about it?" I glance over my shoulder, shifting my focus between her and Gabe.

"Same thing I've always known about it. It's going to be fun to see how this ends. Though probably more so for me than you—I'm pretty sure your luck is about to run out."

"Luck? You think I'm relying on luck?" Now it's my turn to laugh, the sound bitter, sarcastic, and not at all satisfying. I return my focus to Gabe and shove the tip of my blade into his flesh, releasing a bright trail of red. "Luck has no place where duty's concerned. I've trained hard for this moment. I'm merely doing what I was born to do and no more."

"If you say so," she muses. "Still, it's a rare spectacle to watch a Seeker kill a human. That's Coyote's game, not yours."

"Looks like the rules have changed."

"Have they? Or is that how you justify your rage over all that you've lost?"

I glare from over my shoulder. If she wasn't so formidable, she'd be next on my list. "What do you care?"

"I don't. It's all the same to me. In the end, I'll get your bones too. And from the look of things, it won't be much longer. Speaking of . . . have you seen him? Have you seen the Echo turned beast?" Her jaw lifts. Her cheeks widen. The sound of bone scraping bone as disturbing as nails on a chalkboard—until she heaves a long sigh and her face transforms to the flesh-and-blood version. Her skin as translucent as wax paper, her eyes adopting a lascivious gleam at the memory.

And though I'd like to look away, pretend to ignore it, if she has any idea where Dace is, I need her to tell me. Tightening my hold on Gabe, who, oddly enough makes no attempt to escape, I turn to her and say, "Listen, anything you can tell me about Dace's whereabouts would be greatly appreciated."

"I'll bet." She returns to watching over her snakes, signaling she has no intention of helping me, so I switch my focus to Gabe.

"You're done," I tell him. "Your reign of terror ends here. Now."

"So hurry up and do it already," he says, arcing his head back and offering his neck.

Evil Gabe Richter is begging to be delivered?

My knife stills in my hand.

Is this some kind of trick?

I follow his gaze to where the Bone Keeper directs her snakes to drag down another one of his cousins and begin the process of flaying flesh from bone while he's still breathing.

The sight so disturbing, the agonized screams so wrenching, it's all I can do to keep it together. I've seen some sick stuff in my time, but this is about as bad as it gets. No wonder Gabe prefers to die at my hand.

"You're not going to kill me," Gabe says, though the truth is, I can barely make out the words over the din of tormented screams—frenzied squealing and shrieking—the hum of snakes hissing and slithering—the slow, agonized rattle of death—accompanied by—*the Bone Keeper screeching?*

I whirl in her direction, watching in confusion as she casts a wide, silvery net over her bounty, calls to her snakes, and flees with her cache of bones rattling behind. Returning to Gabe just as he flips the knife from under his chin, ducks out of my grip, and moves to stand beside Dace.

requiem

A seeker must learn to see in the dark, relying on what she knows in her heart.
                                        —Paloma Santos

thirty-five

Dace

The sight of Gabe racing toward me as though I'm some kind of savior is funny at best—misguided at worst.

He would've been better off taking his chances with the Bone Keeper.

Or even the Seeker.

Though I plan to enlighten him soon.

"Get her!" he shouts. "She's right there—ripe for the killing!" He jabs a thumb toward Daire, as though I might've missed her.

As though my newly heightened senses aren't capable of scenting her, tracking her, intuiting her every inhale and exhale.

Still, I don't deny myself the chance to fill my eyes with the sight of her. Soaking in a beauty so radiant, so luminous, she appears lit from within.

"What the hell are you doing looking at her like some lovesick fool? She's gonna get away if you don't do something soon! Leandro warned me to leave her to you, but if you're not gonna kill her, then—"

"Then, what?" In an instant my hand circles his neck. "Tell me exactly what you plan to do to the Seeker."

"What the hell are you doing?" he gasps, features distorted with outrage. "Let me go, you idiot. I'm on your side!"

"That may be." I lift him into the air. Lift him so high his feet fumble for stability, his toes strain toward the ground, as his body jerks like a fish on a line. "Thing is, I'm not on yours." He dangles from my hand—fighting, kicking, screaming bloody murder. Or rather, he would be screaming bloody murder if I hadn't cut off his air supply.

I gave them all a head start.

Encouraged Leandro, Gabe, and Cade to get to Daire first, so she could have the pleasure of slaying them all.

Imagining how it might feel to watch Raven finally conquering Coyote after all this time.

It's a sight I would like to have seen.

But it seems plans, like destiny, are subject to change.

And with the portals swinging wide open and Coyote left completely unchecked, I'll have to claim this particular kill for my own. But at least Daire can watch.

I drag Gabe's face closer to mine, peer into his bloodshot eyes, and loosen my grip just enough for him to remain conscious. Be a shame for him to miss out on last rites.

"You shouldn't be surprised to find yourself here. Surely it's no secret just how much I've always despised you. You're an embarrassment, a misogynist, a thug, annoying as hell, and just so you know, your jokes aren't funny. Turns out, that's a bad combination, Gabe. That kind of behavior is no longer tolerated in these parts."

"Are you freaking crazy?" Gabe's eyes bulge in an effort to choke out the words. Guess it's hard to properly enunciate when your neck is locked in a vise-tight grip.

"Nope, not crazy." I tighten my hold. "You're the one who's crazy for thinking, even for a second, that we're on the same side. I don't belong to Coyote. I don't belong to anyone. As you're about to discover, I'm something far worse than your small mind can conjure."

The second he digests my words, the bravado that once seemed permanently tattooed on his face is replaced by terror. Seems I've finally gotten through.

"Any last words?" The question is asked merely out of formality. Inside, the beast thrums with anticipation and he won't be denied much longer.

Gabe's jaw falls slack, his tongue flops around a good bit, but all that comes out is a sick, muffled gurgle I don't have the patience to even try to decipher.

The beast hungers.

Demands to be fed.

And I am but a humble servant, his to command.

Sorry, Daire. While I wanted you to have the pleasure of slaying Gabe, the sooner this happens, the better for everyone.

"You know, I have no idea what you're trying to say. And, the truth is, I'm not at all interested. Guess this is good-bye then." I clench my fingers, watching his eyes fill with dread as his body gives one last amusing attempt to claw at my hands, kick at my knees. A mildly entertaining death dance that ends with a single flick of my wrist.

His neck snaps.

His head falls limply to his side.

And it feels so damn good I do it again.

Dedicating this kill to Daire, I twist Gabe's head all the way around until it's facing the opposite way.

Inside, my heart swells with accomplishment—a voice shouts in victory.

We can do this.

I can help her.

An essential part of me still exists!

I warned her away—just in case I was wrong—but now that I'm still in control—I'll never have to suffer another day without her.

I can see it as clearly as I can see her standing before me. Daire, me, and the beast—working together to rid the world of Richters!

It's the last thing I think before the beast fully awakens and I'm completely overtaken.

The last thing I speak is her name cried out in agony.

I've lost.

He's won.

Whatever remained of me is now gone.

Stretching and expanding in size until he's consumed every last shred of the person I once knew as *me*, he kicks Gabe's broken body aside and centers his sights on the dark-haired girl in the red silk dress standing just a few feet away.

thirty-six

Daire

His glowing red gaze narrows on mine, offering all the proof that
I need to know the beast seized control.

The boy I fell madly in love with—the boy made entirely of
goodness and light—has been snuffed out by the bloodthirsty
creature that glowers before me.

My hands tremble.

My knees threaten to fold.

Overcome by the enormity of all that we've lost, along with
the harrowing truth that he did this for me.

Convinced that the darkness was his to control—only to discover too late that fate serves its own agenda.

Aside from the eyes and the tufts of black feathers beginning
to form at the crown, he's as handsome as ever. Though I can't be
deceived by his looks. The moment he killed Gabe, he became
fully initiated.

Won't be much longer before the shift is complete.

Still, I lower my knife, refusing to use it until I'm absolutely
sure no part of him exists. As long as the beast continues to
breathe—a part of Dace may manage to cling.

At the sight of me standing defenseless before him, he throws his head back and roars a deep, guttural laughter. But it's not Dace who mocks me. It's the beast. Aware of how much it may hurt, I remind myself to never forget this.

"Sure you want to do that, Seeker?" The words are brusque, but the tone is lazy, as though he'll take his time to slay me his way. "Not that I blame you. Knife like that could never save you. I don't care whose essence it contains."

Despite the implied threat, the words give me hope that I'm on the right track. If he truly remembers the day I told him about Valentina's spirit being sealed on my athame, then clearly a shred of him has managed to survive.

I flip my hair out of my eyes and lean toward him. Determined to appeal to whatever part of Dace still exists, when the last remaining pin securing my updo is released, and I watch as his eyes lovingly follow the course of curls settling in untidy waves over my shoulders.

Though the moment he catches me looking, his admiration is replaced by such deeply penetrating menace, it's all I can do to stay calm.

"You saw what I did to my cousin," he growls. "Saw how easy it was."

"I watched the whole thing." I press my knife to my side. "I could hardly keep from cheering. I hated Gabe too."

He cocks his head, curls and uncurls his fingers, as though weighing my words.

"You did the world a favor, Dace. Heck, you did Marliz a favor. Gabe really was embarrassing, annoying, a total misogynist, a major thug, and his jokes were truly stupid. Good riddance, I say."

"And you know what I say?"

He moves toward me and it's all I can do not to flee. Repeating to myself over and over that Dace is in there. Somewhere. He has to be.

"I say you should've run when you had the chance."

"I won't run from you, Dace." I square my shoulders, remain

fixed right in place. If I can keep addressing him by his name, it might manage to penetrate. "Not while you're still in there—and we both know you are. It doesn't have to be like this, Dace. You can beat this. You can—"

Before I can finish, his jacket begins to shred at the seams, as impossibly long talons shoot from his fingers and a crown of black feathers fully encircles his head. "Seems the evidence would speak otherwise." He shrugs, causing the sleeves to fall to the ground just beside him.

I tighten my grip on the athame, try to follow Chay's advice and listen to my heart. But with the beast quickly closing the gap between us, any wisdom my heart may contain is drowned by the blare of impending defeat.

I take an awkward step back, but the move comes too late. His reflexes now lightning fast, his strength greatly multiplied, he easily catches me by the wrist and squeezes it so hard I'm afraid it might snap.

"All those incessant workouts, all of the magick, and daily six-mile runs, and you're not even going to try to put up a fight?" He hauls me up against him until my back is flush to his torso, tightening his grip until my fingers fall limp, the athame drops to his feet, and he kicks it well out of sight long before I can even attempt to summon it back.

"I'm here to fight the enemy, not you. You seem to forget that we share the same goal. We're both after the Richters, and there's no reason we can't defeat them together."

He laughs, nudges his face against mine. The move releasing a hail of feathers that spill onto my cheek. "I work alone," he growls, the sound primal and deep. "I've no need for partners." He runs a finger down the center of my chest, lingering for a moment over the key, as though it sparks a distant memory that makes him reluctant to proceed.

I suck in a sharp breath, praying I'm right, when he centers a talon as long and sharp as a switchblade right over my heart.

"Unlike you, I don't rely on knives and blowguns and silly talismans that only work on a whim," he says. "My body is the only weapon I need. I could kill you in the span of a heartbeat."

"That must make you feel very powerful," I mumble, trying to ignore the increasing numbness spreading the entire length of my arm, and focus instead on the way his finger caresses my flesh, as though protesting his words.

He drags his nail along my flesh while his lips find my ear—his razor-sharp incisors rasping my flesh. "Looks like you're about to find out."

I squirm, try to get some blood to flow to my fingers. Instantly regretting it the moment I realize the beast misreads it as fear.

"First you'll gasp," he says, spurred by my distress. "Despite my numerous warnings, your denial is so deep you won't see it coming. Then the blood will begin to gush from the wound, ruining your pretty red dress. And not long after, you'll be forever erased from this world."

While there's no doubt he could easily accomplish the task, his touch is soft and sweet, his voice as soothing as a lullaby—completely at odds with his words.

Besides, if he truly meant to kill me, he would've done so already.

"Your twin already tried that. Didn't quite work out like he planned."

"Maybe so, but this time you're on your own. No Raven, no elders, no little glowing man to help you. You're at my mercy now, and trust me, I have none."

I'm not so sure about that . . .

At the sound of leaves rattling and feet shuffling, the beast spins toward the noise, taking me with him. The two of us watching as Leftfoot ducks free of the bushes, his hands raised in surrender.

"Let her go." Leftfoot risks a cautious step forward. Stopping just a few feet away, head bowed in offering, he says, "Take me instead."

"Instead?" The beast laughs, his hot breath hitting my cheek. "Why would I choose when I can just as easily take both of you?"

The talon remains on my chest, but that's as far as he'll go. And although I shoot Leftfoot a look, warning him away, he continues to approach.

"I'm the one who taught you to soul jump. I'm the one who introduced the idea of claiming the darkness. I'm responsible for who you've become."

The beast roars with laughter. "In that case, I'll be sure to thank you before I kill you. Now don't interrupt me again . . ."

He returns his attention to me, at the same time Leftfoot dives for his feet. The move so sudden, so unexpected, I have no time to stop him.

The beast shrieks in outrage, tosses me aside, and goes straight for Leftfoot. But before he can reach him, he falters, stumbles to the ground, and heaves a cry of agonized pain as he fumbles to his feet. Inadvertently slicing a talon across Leftfoot's throat before lumbering away with the shaft of an arrow jutting from his left shoulder.

The entire scene unfolding so quickly, I've barely made sense of it when Jennika rushes from her hiding place in the bushes with a bow clutched in her hand.

"Why did you shoot him?" I scream, eyes wild as I drop beside Leftfoot and press my hands to his wound in an attempt to slow the bleeding.

"Are you kidding me, Daire? It's not like I had any choice—he was going to kill you!" She glares at me, her hatred of the beast/Dace clearly marked on her face.

"No—he wasn't. If that was the case, he would've done so already!"

"Yeah, and how do you explain that?" She motions to Leftfoot.

"It was an accident. He lost his balance when you shot him."

"So it's my fault?"

"It's—" I shake my head, seeing no point in arguing. I pull the scarf from her neck. "Here, keep it pressed here." I place the silk over the wound, and her hands over the silk, as I get to my feet, start to move away.

"Where are you going?" she cries, her face panicked and pale, eyes wide and terrified as she looks between the old medicine man and me. The two of us helplessly watching the life force fade from his eyes.

"I'm going after Dace."

Her eyes meet mine. "You know you have to kill him," she says. "For God's sake, Daire—you have no choice."

I grasp the buckskin pouch at my neck and bid one last plea to my ancestors, begging them to come to Leftfoot's aid. Then after looping it around Jennika's neck, I look at her and say, "I know you're not a Santos, but you were once deeply loved by one. The power of Django's Bear resides in this pouch. He'll come to your aid, but in order for that to happen, you've got to believe."

She folds her fingers around it, her gaze settling for a moment on Gabe's lifeless body with the grotesquely twisted head, before she turns to me. "Daire—I'm not joking. If you don't do it, I will. You have a duty to protect us—or have you forgotten?"

Though the words are spoken like a question, one look is all it takes to tell me she's already decided I've failed them. That I chose love over duty. That I can't be trusted to save them.

I turn away. All too aware that time's running out. That I need to handle this before someone else decides to complete what Jennika started. I follow the trail of blood and destruction Dace left in his path.

thirty-seven

Daire

For something so large, the beast moves lightning fast. And with the Lowerworld plummeting into a state of complete devastation, it gets harder and harder to discern his tracks.

Trees are toppled. Shrubbery flattened. While once-beautiful flower beds have been crushed by numerous upended boulders and rocks. And with Eagle long gone, combined with Raven's continued absence, I'm left to rely on the ring, hoping it will lead me to the Richters, where I'm sure to find the beast.

I hold the ring before me, making careful study of its glimmering facets, the subtle shifts of hue that seem to change with my escalating anxiety. Trying to get a feel for just who's controlling this thing, though the truth is, there's no way to know for sure until I put it to use.

Going on the assumption that it's working for me since it once permitted my access to the Rabbit Hole while remaining undetected by Leandro and Cade, I engage in the opposite version of the hot-and-cold game. Every time the stone grows hot, presumably leading me to safety, I change course until it cools and I'm (presumably) moving toward the enemy. Figuring that, either way, we'll end up face to face. I just hope it's on my terms, my way.

Though after roaming for what feels like miles with still no sign of them or anyone else for that matter, I'm about to give up and try something else when the stone grows notably cooler and I stumble upon a haphazard trail of mutilated demon carcasses bearing damage so severe, only a beast could've caused it.

With my athame missing and my buckskin pouch now with Jennika, I'm down to the blowgun still stashed in my boot.

Same blowgun Dace left in my care, making me promise to use it on him.

A thought that's as inconceivable now as it was then.

Despite what he's done, I refuse to abandon him.

If he really wanted to kill me, he would've done so already.

He could've easily crushed my windpipe, spiked a talon straight through my heart. And as soon as that was done, he could've ripped both Leftfoot and Jennika apart.

So what stopped him?

Certainly not Jennika's dart.

No, Dace is still in there. Exerting whatever control he has left.

Question remains—how much longer can he keep the beast contained?

All along, Dace understood the nature of the beast far better than I did.

Held no illusions about the sort of power it would wield.

Then again, he's lived with it for much longer than I first realized. Making its debut on New Year's Eve, when Dace connected with the snakes and convinced them to attack Suriel. Which, in effect, turned out to be his first kill. The one that served to whet the appetite of what's grown into an insatiable bloodlust.

With each dark deed, the darkness inside Dace increases. Like fertilizer, feeding and strengthening a beast that's meant to destroy us.

And now, with Gabe dead, Dace's initiation into the dark arts is secured. Next time we meet, he'll be fully transformed.

With a terrain of charred earth underfoot, a blazing red can-

opy of clouds drooping overhead, and the agonized screams of
spirit animals and guides called to battle, I follow the trail of car-
nage. Reminded of the story Paloma once told me about the day
my father was buried—how the funeral unfolded under a crimson-
scorched sky.

Funny to think I may end under similar circumstances.

With the stone nearing the point of freezing, I better my grip
on the blowgun and push my legs harder, until I'm sprinting up a
grueling trail littered with random switchbacks and bends that
grows increasingly narrow and steep with each passing turn. Ultimately leveling off to a place where the atmosphere thins, the
clouds that once drooped overhead now sag below, and the dirt
gives way to a slab of rugged red rock.

I make for the edge of the cliff and peer into the void. The toes
of my boots teetering precariously over the ledge, when I realize
a moment too late that everything about this scene—the dress,
the ring, the surrounding landscape, even Cade standing behind
me—perfectly mimics the dream.

Did he lure me here?

Did he plant the dream in my head?

Or did the ring merely lead me to my destiny and demand it be met?

"Don't jump!" Cade calls, half serious, half in jest. "Odds are, I
won't save you this time."

"So, you had the dream too." I turn to face him. "I've always
wondered about that." My gaze roams the length of him, taking
in his perfectly groomed façade—the pristine tux, the freshly shined
shoes, the triumphant grin on his face. Three worlds have fallen
into a state of absolute devastation, and, as usual, he looks as impeccable as ever.

But at least I know what happened to Raven.

"Dream? What dream?" His eyes flash. His tongue works the
inside of his cheek. As I switch my focus to poor Raven—locked
inside a gilded cage, a gleaming tourmaline stone hanging from a
black silk cord at his neck, while Coyote lurks beside him, licking

his chops as though he can't wait to devour him. "Though, now that we're on the subject, I guess I should thank you for making *my* biggest dream come true. After all, I'm finally here in the Upperworld, and I couldn't have done it without you. Told you we make a good team, and yet you never seemed to believe me."

The Upperworld?

That's where this is?

Though my time there was brief, the surrounding landscape is nothing like I left it. It's completely unrecognizable. This is even worse than I thought.

"Yes, the Upperworld, Seeker." He grins, seemingly thrilled by my failure to conceal my shock. "Wasn't like this when I first made the climb. And though it took some doing, I must admit, I'm quite satisfied with the results. I like this look a lot better. It was a little too heavy on the sparkle and greenery before. This new landscape is much better suited to Coyote's needs."

Rugged barren mesas, treacherous cliffs, only trace amounts of shrubbery, and absolutely no viable place for the spirit animals and guides to take cover—I can see why Coyote approves. They've never liked a fair fight.

"As I'm sure you're aware, the Richters have tried to breach this place for centuries, millennia actually, but never once had a hope in hell of succeeding until I came along. I can't wait for Leandro to acknowledge all I've accomplished." His face glows with the prospect. "I've surpassed every Richter who came before me. And the funny thing was, it was so easy! You and your band of idiots really took to your roles, played it straight by the script. You've all done such an amazing job, it's a shame there's no one left among you to appreciate it." He slaps a hand to his mouth and makes an exaggerated mock guilty face, as my gut churns in trepidation at what he'll say next.

"I'm sure you've heard about Chay and Leftfoot, right?" He pauses, waiting for me to respond, but when I continue to glare, he goes on. "Don't look so sad, they were practically elderly. It's not like they had loads of time left. I did them a favor by sparing them the humiliation of dementia and adult diapers that inevitably comes with old age."

"Why are you trying to sell it?" I study him carefully, noting how he's taking credit for acts committed by Leandro and Dace, never mind his need to explain. The old Cade delighted in mocking and taunting—he practically lived for the chance. Never once did he try to justify his acts or soften the blow.

"I'm not trying to sell it!" His fists curl at his sides as his eyes narrow on mine. "You just happened to look saddened by the news, and—"

"And that bothers you?" I take a step toward him, chancing a quick look at Raven, making sure he's more or less okay, before I return to Cade. "My sadness makes you feel the need to defend your actions?"

His features sharpen, his face darkens, but that's as far as he gets. As far as he's capable of getting. And we both know it.

"I thought I made myself clear. You're not the one running the show here, Seeker. That would be *me*. And just so you know, your friends aren't faring so well either. Believe me—" He grabs the dome of Raven's cage and dangles it so precariously, Raven lets out a long, gurgling croak as his purple eyes roll back in his head and his claws clutch the perch in a fight to stay upright. His distress so palpable I'm about to intervene, when Cade lowers the cage to the ground and says, "Your little bird here is getting off easy. As for your friends, well, Lita was a lot better off when she was with me. But now, thanks to you, Seeker, Lita's all on her own. Though it's not like I didn't warn her. Just like I predicted, Axel didn't waste a second to ditch her once the three worlds opened wide. Didn't think twice about trading her in for the glowing girls back home. And to think all he left her with was an eagle feather, as though that could possibly help. My guess is she became demon bait not long after. But don't look so glum, you'll be happy to know that Xotichl and Auden are alive and well, and as it turns out, Coyote's in control for all of eternity. Seems they fell for the oldest trick in the book. It was almost too easy. Amazing what people will sacrifice for a taste of popularity. Of course, Lita knows a thing or two about that. Or, should I say, *did*. Lita *did* know. Lita's not present tense anymore."

I keep my face neutral. He's trying to get a rise out of me, and I won't take the bait. I'm just hoping his failure to mention Jennika is because she managed to slip under his radar and not because he's saving the juiciest bit for later.

"Let's face it, you failed, Seeker, in every conceivable way. You failed your friends, your ancestors, your Raven." He nudges the cage with his foot, moving it closer to Coyote, who thumps his tail in approval. "You've failed everyone. But most of all, you've failed yourself. And now, I'm afraid you've lasted way past your expiration date. You're beginning to smell a bit . . . *fowl*, as they say." He laughs heartily at his joke as I make a point of rolling my eyes. "Anyway, enough of that. It's time for me to finish what I started. Which means it's time for you to reunite with your ancestors."

The gap that separates me from the next gorge easily spans six feet, if not more. Still, I'm pretty sure I can nail the leap if it should come to that.

But only if it comes to that.

"So how do you plan to do it?" I ask, stalling for time as I get a better grip on my blowgun, remembering how he loves a good monologue.

"What? And wreck the surprise?" He kneels beside Raven's cage, giving firm instructions to Coyote to wait for the signal, before returning to me. "What happened to your mask?" He places his hands on his hips and frowns as though he just now noticed it was missing. "I always imagined you wearing it when I snuff the light from your eyes and Coyote devours your spirit animal."

"Guess you'll both have to improvise. Besides, I don't see you wearing your moon and sun."

"I have no need for symbols when it's about to be done."

"Is it?" I take a step toward him. "Is that what you think?"

"That's what I *know*. Shadow is about to eclipse Sun, which means you, Seeker, will fall. I've rescinded the offer for you to rule alongside me. Turns out, you're not up for the task. And for the record, I saw right through your façade. Your clumsy attempts at flirting and feigning interest in me were painful at best."

"Really? How about when I clocked you and sent you spinning on your ass—how'd you feel then?"

"Nice try, Seeker. Trying to distract me from the task. You're outmatched. The game was never yours to control. Don't believe me? Take a good look around. The prophecy is in motion and there's no way to stop it. Oh, and just so you know, I won't miss you when you go."

"No, I don't suspect you will. But not for the reason you think."

He quirks a brow, cocks his head to the side.

"I'm not going anywhere, Cade."

"You're funny."

"I'm a lot of things. As you're about to see."

I raise Dace's blowgun. The one he insisted I use on him and aim straight for his brother. Confident the beast will spare Dace's life like it did New Year's Eve.

"You're not going to use that relic against me?" Cade smirks, not taking me the least bit seriously. Unfortunately for him, it's a mistake he won't live long enough to regret.

I close an eye, center my aim, and shoot.

Watching the dart soar straight for its target. The moment I've been imagining about to come to fruition.

Until Cade ducks, the dart breezes over his head, and the next thing I know, the top of Cade's head is barreling into my gut.

My feet fly up from beneath me, my back smacks hard on the slab, and my head quickly follows. The blow so unexpected, it knocks the breath out of me.

I squint into the space, struggling to see past the constellation of tiny white stars blurring my vision. Just barely able to make out the sight of Cade looming over me, fist raised high, ready to strike.

"Say good-bye, Seeker." He grins, about to nail the same spot his father had a go at, when his eyes meet mine and, once again, I catch a glimmer of my own reflection staring back.

That's twice now. And the thing is, Cade's eyes never used to reflect.

While they used to glow red when he was in full-blown demon mode, they never mirrored. They could only absorb, like the abyss that they are.

It's what enabled him to control people by changing their perception—he absorbed their energy until they were his to control.

He's just about to make contact when I jump to my feet and catch him by the wrist. "You sure you want to do that?" I twist his arm until he grimaces. "'Cause it kind of seems like you don't."

"Keep dreaming," he grunts. Though his tone, like his face, is full of bravado, there's something off about him. Something more than just the strangeness of his gaze.

For one thing, if he was serious, he would've pushed me away and punched me already. My grip's not that tight.

But instead, his fingers flex uncertainly. As though he's purposely leaning into me, only pretending to try to free himself from my hold, while secretly enjoying the contact of his skin on my flesh.

Just like his brother, he's reluctant to make good on his threat.

Until Leandro's voice rumbles from across the divide.

thirty-eight

Daire

"Enough, Cade! What're you waiting for, a good-bye kiss?" Leandro's voice booms from across the canyon. "Kill her already. If
you have any hope of redeeming yourself, do it now! You've failed
at every single thing you've set out to do. Kill the Seeker, Cade, or
I'll come over there and do it for you!"

Cade wrenches free of my grip. Looking between Leandro and
me with a conflicted gaze, his body involuntarily twitches and
shakes, while his creepy Coyote snarls and yelps beside Raven,
who clings to the backside of his cage.

"I didn't fail!" Cade screams. His face, like his voice, is choked
with rage. "I'm the reason you're here! I'm the one who opened
the portals! *Me*—not Dace!" He slaps a hand over my throat, tries
to squeeze his fingers around it but doesn't get very far before he
lets go and approaches the ledge.

"The role you played was minor at best," Leandro yells. "Now
go ahead and do it. Kill the girl, and be done with it!"

Leandro continues to berate him, as Cade paces precariously
close to the edge. Twitching and mumbling to himself as I scramble to my feet, retrieve my gun, and take aim.

Just about to shoot when Cade whirls on me and says, "Dammit, Seeker, put that thing down! Do *not* make me choose!"

Choose?

I hold my breath in my cheeks, delaying the shot. So caught off guard by the words, I'm not sure how to react.

Did he really mean choose between Leandro and me?

"Clock's ticking, Cade—do it already!" his father shouts, as Cade seems to visibly crumple before me. His shoulders sagging, his head bent, gaze downcast. He digs his knuckles into his eyes. Pinches hard at his cheeks. All the while mumbling a string of unintelligible words under his breath. Making him appear deranged and distorted, like a person gone completely unhinged.

"What the hell have you done to me?" His eyes are shadowed and bloodshot as he glares at me accusingly.

And suddenly, with that one simple question, it all falls into place.

The reflection in his eyes.

His reluctance to kill me.

It all makes sense.

And it proves Dace was right! There's only one force more powerful than evil—love.

Cade is a perfect example of that.

He's changed by love. It's the love in his heart that won't allow him to kill me.

"I haven't done anything. You brought this on yourself," I say, reminded of something Phyre said the day we discovered her in possession of Dace's soul. When she saw the piece of darkness in Dace and wondered if Cade contained a piece of his light.

At the time, I was too worried about saving Dace's soul to pay much notice to her philosophical musings, but now I realize her suspicions were right.

"When you fed off the love Dace and I shared by using it to

strengthen yourself, what you failed to understand is that darkness cannot exist in the same space as light. The love you ingested obliterated your darkness, it changed you from the inside."

A look of pure horror crosses his face, but little does he know, that's only part of the story. What I fail to voice is my suspicion that when Dace made the soul jump into Cade to steal a chunk of his darkness, he left behind a piece of his light.

Just like the dream, their connection is no longer relegated to the mystical, it's veered into the physical.

Part light, part dark.

The yin and the yang.

Connected.

Bound.

Each containing a piece of the other.

Leandro continues to rage from across the gorge, which only serves to confuse Cade more.

"Don't listen to him." I raise my voice in an effort to drown out Leandro's. "There's nothing wrong with you. In fact, it's pretty miraculous if you think about it. You're getting a second chance to do the right thing and redeem yourself. Don't fight it, Cade. Don't fight me . . ." I lower the blowgun to my side and approach him slowly. He's so unstable there's no telling how he'll react.

"Back off, Seeker!" He swerves out of my reach and looks across the canyon with a face full of longing. "And stop looking at me!"

I do as he says. Holding perfectly still until he relaxes enough for me to chance another step toward him. "Cade, don't you recognize what's happening here?" I gesture to the surrounding landscape. "This is just like the dream. I know you had it too. It's where you came up with the idea for the dress."

He rakes an agitated hand through his hair. Shuffles his feet uncertainly.

"And look, I'm even wearing the ring." I lift my hand, urging him to see. Watching his features grow blunted, his eyes glazing at the sight of it. "But it's not as bad as you think. You're not in love with me. You've just never experienced such a strong emotion before, and you're so overwhelmed by its power, you're projecting it onto me. You once claimed that true magick exists only in the darkest of men. And maybe you're right. But the thing is, you're no longer that guy. If you allow your light to shine, you'll be capable of the kind of miracles that'll make your magick look like the work of a third-rate birthday party magician."

His shoulders soften. His pacing slows. And I breathe a little easier knowing I've managed to reach him.

Until Leandro hurls another long stream of insults, and Cade rushes toward me, fully intending to harm—only the light now illuminated inside him won't allow him to strike.

Won't allow him to do the only thing required to make his father proud.

It's Leandro he loves.

It's Leandro he lives to impress.

He's spent the last sixteen years in a desperate bid for his father's approval, only to be eclipsed by the twin they both once despised.

Even when Cade was at his darkest, it was the one bit of humanity that managed to survive.

I could kill him in a second. And yet, knowing what I know, it no longer feels right.

No longer a monster—the light has rendered him human. And like the Bone Keeper said, killing humans is not the Seeker's game.

From across the canyon, Leandro approaches the ledge. "That's it, Cade," he shouts. "You've had your chance. I should've left it to your brother like I promised. It would've been over by now. But since you can't seem to handle the one thing I'm asking you to do, I'm coming over there to take care of it for you!" He crouches down low, ready to make the leap, when the beast appears by his side, dragging Chepi behind him.

thirty-nine

Daire

The chasm yawns between us, and I pray I really can nail it. If I'm wrong about Dace, Chepi won't stand a chance.

I gather my skirts, do as Paloma taught me, and think from the end. The image of myself landing safely on the other side firmly entrenched in my head, when Chepi shouts, "Daire—no! Stay where you are!"

Leandro roars with laughter as though the scene just became greatly amusing, as Chepi turns her focus to the beast. The resigned look on her face telling me she's not the least bit surprised to see what's become of her son.

Is that why she tried so hard to shield him from his mystical legacy, along with the horrible truth behind his conception?

Did she suspect all along that this day would come?

Just as I thought, Dace is completely transformed. Far surpassing anything Cade was ever capable of becoming, he's transcended into something so sinister, so horrific—it's impossible to turn away.

His towering height, rippling muscles, blazing red eyes, and crown of black feathers circling his head, making for a sight that's as stunning as it is diabolical. And by the way Leandro stands beside him, beaming with pride, it's clear he agrees.

Refusing to see him as he is, Chepi insists on appealing to the shred of humanity she's convinced still exists. And while I was in full agreement just a moment ago, watching her now, so defenseless and vulnerable, reminds me of what Jennika said.

It's my duty to protect her.

If it turns out I'm wrong, the beast will soon kill her.

"You've outlasted your usefulness, old woman," Leandro taunts. Looking between the beast and Cade. "Do it!" he urges. "Both of you, strike now! You have one last chance to redeem yourself, Cade. Kill the Seeker while Dace kills his mother. Rid the world of these obnoxious do-gooders, and you'll make me proud beyond measure."

Cade sneaks up from behind, but even in his unstable state, I'm a lot less worried about what he might try, and a lot more worried about what will become of Chepi. One swipe of the beast's hand is enough to see her permanently eliminated from the world, and I'm the only one who can possibly stop him.

From somewhere within the earth's core, the ground begins to tremble and quake, as the sky glows a dark, blood-drenched red. And when a coil of wind begins to stir at my feet, there's no denying the prophecy has begun.

Won't be long before the wind becomes a tempest and all three worlds are ravaged by flames.

Unless I can stop it before it gets to that point.

With Chepi in Dace's grasp, I can't take the chance that I'll miss. So I inch toward the ledge, raise the blowgun to my lips, and aim for Leandro instead. Taking my shot at the same time Cade yanks hard on my dress and jerks me back toward him. The move causing the dart to veer wildly off course before disappearing into the chasm.

The beast snarls and roars. Grasping Chepi by the throat, he holds her up high as though considering the most efficient way to destroy her. As I wrench free of Cade's grip, swerve out of his reach, and reload my weapon. Fully aware the attempt was half-hearted at best, staged to make Leandro think he's serious, and I don't have time for his games.

I center my aim, ready to shoot, when Cade rushes from behind. Leaving me no choice but to nail him with a swift roundhouse kick to the jaw that sends him reeling and skidding across a long swath of rock that rips a hole in his sleeve and burns off a good portion of flesh.

"Dammit, Cade," Leandro shouts. "Get up! If you kill her now, the world will be ours! We are two kills away from ruling the worlds!"

The beast growls, the sound deep, guttural, echoing through the ravine. His glowing red eyes fixed right on mine as I center my aim on Leandro again.

Releasing the dart just as the beast lifts a hand, about to remove Chepi's face, when, at the very last second, he changes course, pushes her out of harm's way, and removes Leandro's instead.

His features falling away like a discarded mask, Leandro's pulpy mess of a mouth screams briefly in outrage, before collapsing inertly beside his old face.

Chepi looks on in horror, presumably thinking the same thing as me.

Another Richter felled.

Another relative killed.

No telling how the beast will react.

Though one thing is clear: Dace has now managed to outshine his twin in every conceivable way.

Cade turns on me in a fit fueled by rage, grief, and deeply rooted shame. Having failed at his one and only chance to make his father proud by slaying me.

With his fists clenched to his sides, his whole body shaking, he throws his head back and howls in a way so primal, so chilling, Coyote quickly chimes in.

But no matter how desperately Cade yearns to transform into the two-headed, snake-tongued, monstrous version of himself, he can't make the shift.

Blaming me for his failure, he lurches my way as Coyote continues to howl by his side, and I aim the blowgun straight toward him. All the while begging him to stop, to not go through with it, to give up the fight while he can.

"It's over. He released you. You don't realize it now, but he has. It's just like you always wanted, we can work together. But instead of me joining your side, you can join mine."

His hands curl to fists and he stops dead in his tracks, leaving only a handful of feet yawning between us.

"C'mon, Cade. You don't have to do this. With you and me working together, we can stop the prophecy."

"It's too late, Seeker." While his gaze is filled with loathing, his fists can't seem to respond.

They're useless.

Unable to strike.

So he turns to Coyote still howling beside him, focusing hard on Raven's natural-born enemy until his lids begin to droop, his knees give out from under him, and his body falls unconscious to the ground.

"No!" I scream, scrambling to put some distance between us. Only the move comes too late. My boot catches in the hem of my dress, my blowgun flies free of my hand, and I land in an unarmed heap of shimmering red silk. Unable to do anything but stare helplessly before me as Coyote, now soul-merged with Cade, bares his teeth and lunges straight for me, as Raven furiously rattles his cage, trying in vain to escape.

Raven and I both watching as Coyote descends.

Knowing it won't be long until we fall and the prophecy is fulfilled once and for all.

With no defenses left, I lift my ring high. Hoping it might distract Coyote from his mark, and watching in horror as the gem catches the last fading rays of the sun and transforms my gown into a swirling circle of flames.

I scream. Try to smother it by rolling onto the rock.

Only to realize the flames do no harm, the element is mine to control.

At the first whiff of smoke, Coyote yelps, tries to change course, but it's too late.

I've already rolled to the side.

Already retrieved the blowgun.

Already taken aim at the center of his forehead.

Already taken my shot.

His snout veering so close, the last thing I feel is his hot, fetid breath hitting my cheek, before his eyes roll back in his head and he falls limply at my feet. A single poisonous dart jutting from his head—a steady stream of blood pumping from the wound.

My gown smoldering, I leap to my feet, and race toward Cade, only to find he bears the same injury as Coyote.

I press my hand to his forehead. Try to stop the blood from gushing. Telling myself head wounds always bleed more. That it's not nearly as bad as it seems. Though it fails to console.

Finally, after all of this time, I've managed to kill him.

Funny how it doesn't feel anything like I imagined it would.

I brush a hand across his forehead, try to think of something comforting to say to ease his transition, when I realize he's singing.

Thinking it's the same song he hummed when I spied on him via the cockroach, I lower my ear to his lips and realize I've got it all wrong.

Cade is using the last of his strength to remind me of the prophecy.

> *When air sears and water fades*
> *When tempest winds ravage fire-scorched plains*
> *When Shadow eclipses Sun—the Seer shall fall*
> *Causing three worlds to descend into darkness eternal*

"You can't stop it, Seeker." His voice is a rasp. His lips curl at the sides as though he takes great pleasure in reminding me of my fate. "The prophecy is in motion. You are destined to fall. Leandro was wrong. I didn't fail. I never once failed him . . ."

His eyes close.

His breath ceases.

And when the flames die, and the sky dims all around me, I realize he's right.

The prophecy is here.

But it's not because of him.

It's because I snuffed the Sun and left the Shadow to rule.

forty

Daire

Chepi screams, grabs hold of his arm, but the beast shakes her off, kicks Leandro's body aside, and makes for the ledge.

Each step causing the sun to shrink.

The sky to darken.

So by the time he's clinched the leap and is standing before me, the three worlds are black.

I can feel his hot breath rising before me. His hunger so palpable, I can sense it stirring within. It's the only way to track him now that I can no longer see him.

With only one dart remaining, I raise the blowgun to my lips and tighten my grip. Remembering a time when I was afraid of the dark and couldn't fall asleep without the glow of a nightlight, until Jennika found a way to convince me there was nothing to fear.

You must adapt to the darkness so the light can find you.

Such an uncanny match for the Seeker's creed that Paloma shared with me when I first started training: *A Seeker must learn to see in the dark, relying on what she knows in her heart.*

I suck in a lungful of air, tracking the beast as Chay's last words play in my head: *Love is a powerful force. If anyone can save him, it's you. So go. Go do what you were born to do.*

I was born to protect—to keep the Richters contained—and the three worlds in balance.

I don't have to look far to see how I've failed on every count.

My friends are all missing or dead.

The worlds are in chaos.

And though the Richters are finally defeated, the beast has now taken their place.

There is only one force more powerful than evil—love, Dace claimed.

Listen to your heart, Chay said. *It will never lead you astray.*

What I know in my heart is that the choice is no longer mine to make.

Destiny has made the choice for me.

If I have any hope of surviving, any hope of sparing my friends, Dace's heart is where I must aim.

I squint through my tears, guided by the hum of his breath to locate my mark, grappling with the horror of piercing the very flesh I once cherished.

He lumbers closer.

I steady the gun to my lips. Whispering one final plea: *Dace— please, if you're in there, stop now—don't make me do this!*

He snarls. Growls. Continues his approach. Taking a swipe at me as he did with Leandro, and only narrowly missing.

One more step and he's on me.

One more step and I'm history.

I close my eyes. Rely on my instincts to guide me.

My cheeks wet with tears as I release my last dart. Its softly whistled hiss closing the distance between us, before slamming hard against the small golden key that hangs from his neck and ricocheting right back where it lands in a muffled thud at my feet.

I missed.

The three worlds are now his.

I'm so sorry.

It's the last thing I think before the beast comes barreling toward me.

forty-one

The Beast

An old woman calls out from behind me. Her voice echoing from across the divide. She's mistaken me for someone else. Insists on calling me by a name I don't recognize.

She's a nuisance.

Can't leave well enough alone and be glad she was spared.

Still not sure why I didn't kill her when I had the chance. Something inside just wouldn't allow it.

It's a mistake I won't make again.

I shift my attention to the girl standing before me. A vision of emerald-green eyes, shining dark hair, and a tattered silk gown, she clings to a slim wisp of hope that died long ago, the darkness has rendered her blind.

Unlike me. I got the night on my side.

I close the few steps between us, inhaling the wondrous perfume of her flesh, wondering how anything could smell so enticingly sweet, as she whispers a prayer to a boy she once loved, then levels her weapon at me.

Her aim is true, but her heart is reluctant, filled with regret.

A battle between the emotion and intellect, duty and longing.

It's no wonder she misses and the dart strikes the inexplicable small golden key that hangs from my neck.

Must be some sort of protective amulet left over from the days I was human.

I take it as proof that I'm here for a reason.

I loom over her, searching for the look of betrayal, outrage, and fear I saw on the last one but find only a resigned acceptance instead. Even when I throw my head back and release a loud and thunderous roar, she continues to gaze at me with love in her heart.

I raise an arm high. Arc it straight toward her. But once again, my hand falters. Leaving me staring mutely into her beautiful face, overcome by something I can't quite identify, when my body goes numb and I drop to my knees. Swaying helplessly for a handful of seconds, before my legs give out, my heart sputters, and I land hard on my side.

The girl drops beside me, casts a worried gaze at my face. The expression she wears telling me, *this is it.*

The beast is dying.

But strangely, he's not dying alone.

The talons shrink.

A hail of black feathers spill to the ground.

As the girl brushes a tender hand to my forehead and says, "It's not this breath, but the one that follows that determines whether you live or die. Focus on the next one, Dace, and the one after that. Please, whatever you do, try to keep breathing."

Dace?

It's the same name the old woman called me. Must mean something to them.

The girl takes my hand in hers, places that small golden key in my palm, and folds my fingers around it until the truth comes roaring back and it all falls into place.

It's more than just a talisman—it's a key to the past. A passport that leads to a future I can no longer have. Unlocking a cache of memories that return in a rush—the girl has a name—an identity—a revered place in my life. The knowledge streaming through me as quick as a flash.

"Turns out, you were right," she whispers, her eyes wide and glittering. "There's only one force strong enough to overcome evil—love. Our love."

She brings her lips to my cheek as I heave a breath so ragged I'm sure it's my last. No time left to tell her how sorry I am to leave her with so many unrealized dreams. How lucky I was to know her—to love her—for the short time I did.

forty-two

Daire

It's a half prophecy.

A half victory.

Half dark—half light.

Just like the twins who started it all.

Though the Richters have finally been stopped, with Dace dying before me and the three worlds gone dark, it's hardly worth celebrating.

I crumple beside him, throw my body over his. Clinging to the promise of the whistle and wheeze in his chest, while cursing the injustice of a destiny that demands more than I'm able to bear.

His pulse fades.

An ominous gurgle seeps from his lips.

The death rattle.

Won't be long before it ceases for good.

I lift my face to the sky and release a wail of sorrow so deep, the earth rumbles beneath me, a blast of wind buffets my body, as a shower of hail pelts down from above.

Once again, the joke is on me.

I'm powerful enough to manipulate the elements but woefully helpless when it comes to saving my loved ones.

I settle beside him, trace a finger across the width of his brow, and remove my tears that spill onto his cheek. "You once said that miracles are nothing more than the truest expression of love." I press my lips to his ear. "If you still believe that, then feel my love now, Dace. And breathe. Please breathe . . ."

"It was Leftfoot who taught him that." The voice drifts from behind me, and though I can't see her, I recognize it as Paloma's.

She's here!

I can feel her essence all around me.

Seems my earlier prayers weren't ignored after all.

"It was Jolon who taught it to Leftfoot. Jolon was a wise and gifted healer. It's said he shared a direct link to the divine. He worked many miracles but took credit for none—claiming a healer never works alone. All healings are based on the compassionate help of the spirits, he said. And it's true. It's why we are here for you now."

The moment she says it, I can feel the presence of Django, Valentina, Alejandro, and all the rest of them. Countless generations of Santos ancestors gathered around me, prepared to guide me.

Paloma rests a hand on my shoulder. Her touch so reassuring, I return to Dace with a heart full of hope. My hands moving over his torso, seeking a wound. Though it's not long before I determine that the outside is as perfect as ever. It's the inside that's failing.

"The damage is internal. Something tells me it's his heart that's failing." I strain to see through the dark to the shadowy figures who guide me. Though they remain unseen, I can still feel them, and it's Django who speaks next.

"Daire, my beautiful baby girl. I've been watching after you since the day you were born, and I'm so incredibly proud of you. Not only have you faced the very thing I tried so hard to flee— you've succeeded in all the places I failed."

"The only way to heal Dace, is to love him." The voice belongs to Valentina. "Jolon was right about miracles—they're nothing more than love in action. But you'll have a hard time working one if you can't find it within you to love yourself first."

I swallow hard, reach with one hand for the key that hangs from Dace's neck, while grasping my own key with the other.

"When you curse your destiny, you curse yourself," Django says. "I'm a prime example of that. But you are the Seeker, Daire. And Dace was so proud of you he gave you the tool that allowed you to take him down. He understood all too well what you would be called to do, and he forgave you long ago. Now it's time for you to forgive yourself. Time for you to love yourself. It's the only hope Dace has, but you can't give what you don't have."

Love myself.

A pretty tall order considering the circumstances.

Still, I'm committed to trying. I have everything to lose if I don't.

My father's words reminding me of the day I visited Paloma's grave—when I faced the mountain and rededicated myself to my legacy and the destiny I was born to claim.

No matter what becomes of me—I won't go down easily. The Richters will pay for the heinous acts they've wrought on this town—on my loved ones—on the Lower-, Upper-, and Middleworlds, which are mine to keep balanced.

From the moment I killed Cade, I made good on at least half my word. Though the three worlds still need to be dealt with.

Still, no one ever promised a clean victory. And Paloma always warned that a Seeker's life is one of incredible sacrifice.

But what if it doesn't have to be?

As I've already seen, prophecies are not concrete.

What if the future really is mine to design?

I lean toward Dace, pushing our keys together until the edges are evenly matched. Clearing my heart of regret and replacing it with a surplus of love, I lower my lips to meet his and kiss him with all that I have.

But it's not enough.

His breath hitches. Falters. And I have no idea what to do

next—until Paloma whispers, "It's just like I taught you, *nieta*. You've got to peer through the darkness and see with your heart—if you are to see his."

I shutter my eyes, blocking out everything but the boy lying before me. Cutting through the darkness, I delve inside his body, peering at a heart choked by a tangled web of darkness that must be removed if Dace has any hope of surviving.

Now turn on your light.

With my hands centered over his chest, I summon my light and project it toward him. Watching it chip away at the darkness until it's nearly diminished, allowing his heart to swell and expand.

But before the darkness can be completely eradicated, Dace heaves a harsh breath, followed by another.

"Not to worry," Valentina says. "The bit of darkness that remains won't harm him. Everyone has a shadow side. This just makes him human. Though there's still more to do, your fix is only temporary."

I peer into the dark. "He's breathing—what more can I do?"

"While your light has served to illuminate his darkness—when you killed his twin, he took a piece of Dace's soul with him," Paloma says. "Without it, I'm afraid he won't last."

No.

No!

I rock back on my heels. Hardly able to believe I had it all wrong. I was sure that the only way to kill Cade without harming Dace was to catch him in beast mode or, in his case, Coyote mode. Turns out I was wrong.

One brother down.

Won't be much longer until the other one follows.

"But there is a way . . ." Django hovers by my side. "I've seen your soul, Daire. It's strong—fueled by so much love and light I'm betting you have plenty to spare."

I glance over my shoulder, and for one fleeting second, I see him, really see him, materializing before me. The father I've only known from old photos is smiling and nodding and encouraging me to act before it's too late.

I return to Dace, unsure how to proceed.

"Think of it like a soul jump," Paloma says.

"Only this time, you'll leave a piece of your soul behind," Valentina chimes in. "You'll be bound forever—but isn't that what you both want?"

Bound.

Fated.

In the way we always dreamed.

Finally, the nightmare that started this journey gets a new ending.

I focus on Dace with all that I have, vaguely aware of my body collapsing as I enter his world and my soul merges with his.

Viewing Dace as a young boy, eagerly exploring the world.

Dace as a teen, the very first day he laid eyes on me.

Dace as the beast, calling on every scrap of what remained of his will to spare me from his drive to kill.

His love for me matched only by my love for him—I leave him with a piece of my soul and slowly extricate myself.

Finding myself back in my body only to discover the world is still dark.

My ancestors are gone.

And Dace is lying inert before me.

I've failed.

Truly failed.

Nothing left to do now but wait for the end.

The thought leaving me strangely still and bereft—until Dace drags a long inhale and pulls me into his arms.

forty-three

Xotichl

The second the world falls dark, Auden clasps tightly to my hand and we fall into a state of communal stunned silence.

There's no need to speak, when we both know what it means.

Daire is dead.

The beast has won.

The dark days have dawned.

And our lives are over before they had a chance to really get started.

Though, for Auden and me, our lives were in jeopardy well before that.

"Auden, I—" I want to share my regret at not being able to see how the Richters were manipulating us all this time, when I notice a sliver of space opening up all around him.

At first it's subtle. No more than a glimmer. Though it's not long before it expands into a glorious nimbus of light that circles around him. Stretching and pulling at the edges until he's completely illuminated.

"Auden," I whisper. "You're glowing! Can you see it?"

"Are you serious? I can't even see my own hand." He raises it between us and wiggles his fingers to illustrate his point.

"Wait—" I fall silent for a few seconds, long enough to see if my suspicions are right.

"Xotichl, what is it?" He squeezes my fingers, but the glow is now gone and I can no longer see him.

"If I'm not mistaken, I think I might've just found a way to get us out of here." The sound of my voice bouncing off Auden's form causes him to light up again, confirming I'm right. "It's kind of like echolocation, except instead of sensing the sound wave of the object before me, I can actually *see* what's before me."

"You can *see* me? Now? Seriously?"

"I can't see you in perfect detail, but I can definitely determine it's you. You know, when I first started seeing Paloma, I asked her to show me how to do it, especially when we discovered I was guided by Bat. But Paloma said she could do me even better and taught me how to rely on my blindsight. And yet, ever since my vision returned, my blindsight was lost. Until now."

"What do you think changed?"

"I think it's because I was never afraid of the dark. Before I met Paloma and started reading energy, eternal night was the natural state of my being. Whatever the reason, as long as I keep talking, I'm pretty sure I can lead us out of here." I take a step forward, tug on Auden's hand, expecting him to follow, but he remains firmly in place.

"Where are we going, flower? If it's dark here, it's dark everywhere. Doesn't matter where you lead us. It's all the same in the end."

While he makes a good point, there's no denying I've just been offered a gift, and I refuse to ignore it. "Honestly," I say. "I have no idea where we'll end up. But we'll never get farther than here if we don't at least try. As long as our friends are still out there, I refuse to call it quits. At the very least, we need to determine what happened to them."

forty-four

Lita

The second the world turns dark, I sink to my knees in surrender.

Overcome by a combination of exhaustion and I-no-longer-give-a-crap defeat, I officially call an end to the fight.

I've been running from demons and hiding from Richters for too many hours to count. And now, with Daire clearly dead, I don't see the point in continuing.

There's nowhere to go.

Nothing to see.

It's just a matter of time before evil claims me.

I drop my head in my hands. Give myself permission to cry. But surprisingly, the tears just won't come. Instead of the panic I assumed I would feel, I find myself immersed in a strange wave of calm.

I guess there really is peace in certainty.

Even if the thing you're certain about is your own grisly demise, it's still better than the anxiety that comes with not knowing.

And it's not like I don't see the irony.

When Axel first left, it felt like the end of the world. But clearly I was wrong. The end doesn't feel anything like I imagined it would.

It's not at all panicky.

Doesn't make my heart ache so badly I'm sure it's about to implode.

It just feels final.

Imminent.

Sure to find me when it's good and ready.

With nothing more to do than wait, I settle onto the ground and curl up on my side. Resting my head on my arm, I tuck my chin to my chest and allow my eyes to drift closed, when something floaty and soft tickles the tip of my nose.

I gasp. Leap to my feet. Convinced some kind of foul creature, most likely a cockroach since they're definitely set to inherit the earth, is building a nest in the neckline of my dress, I frantically bat at myself, until it tips from the bodice and glides to my feet, where I discover it isn't even remotely close to an insect.

It's the eagle feather Axel gave me right before he left.

Same feather I stashed in my bra, figuring it was useless.

But now, with nothing to lose, I hold it before me and squint into the dark. Striving to make out its lilting form but unable to discern anything more than the shadowy curve of its vane, I close my eyes and make a wish.

One that isn't the least bit frivolous.

If Axel is right, if belief and intent really are the spine of both miracles and magick, then I can't afford to not take this seriously. Gathering every shred of faith that remains, I project it onto the feather. Refusing to feel silly, refusing any emotion other than my unwavering devotion to see that it's done.

Imagining how the scene might look. How it might make me feel, both inside and out. Until I'm so consumed with the vision, I snap my eyes open, expecting to see it manifesting before me, only to find I'm surrounded by black.

I settle back onto the ground, bring my legs to my chest, and wrap my arms around them. Consoling myself with the thought: *At least I tried. At least I gave it all that I had.* When a hand clasps onto my shoulder, and Xotichl says, "Hey, Lita. You okay?"

forty-five

Dace

"How much do you remember?"

Daire lifts a hand to my brow, and I'm quick to reach up, clasp it in mine. All the while giving silent thanks for the darkness that shrouds me.

While I'm glad the beast has been slain, while I'm grateful to be reunited with the love of my life, unfortunately, I have full recall of every heinous act.

Every evil urge.

My rampage lives on in a spool of horrifying images that'll haunt me for the rest of my days, and I couldn't bear for her to see me this way.

But to Daire, I just say, "I remember plenty. Enough to know I'll never be able to make up for all that I've done—"

She places a finger to my lips, halting the words. "The Richters are gone. You spared Chepi's life. And while you could have easily killed me, you always stopped short."

"And what about Leftfoot?" My voice croaks. I bury my face in my hands. Tormented by the image of my mentor and friend with his slashed and bloodied neck. "He wasn't a demon. Wasn't even a

Richter. He was like a father to me. How am I supposed to make peace with that?"

Daire falls quiet, taking a moment to gather her thoughts before she speaks. "It was an accident—Jennika shot you with an arrow and in your attempt to flee, you accidentally cut him." I turn my head to the side, reluctant to believe her. "Look, you may never make peace with your actions, but you have to accept the things you're unable to change. Otherwise, peace will elude you in all facets of life, not just the ones of your choosing."

I pull her to me. Fold my arms tightly around her. Aware of her soft even breath, the cool smoothness of her skin. Marveling at how close she came to dying at my hand—but for some reason, even in full-blown beast mode, I couldn't go through with it.

Though the all-consuming desire to make Leandro pay for what he did to my mother never abated.

I'm glad he's finally gone.

I take solace in knowing he can never again harm anyone who has the misfortune of veering into his path.

Though it does nothing to erase the harm he's already caused.

Still, if Chepi's learned to live with it, found a way to look past the painful memory of how I came to be, then maybe, someday, I can learn to accept it as well.

"So, where do we go from here?" I return to Daire.

"First, we find a way to return order to the worlds, then we locate our friends." Her voice is determined. "And then, once that's done, we celebrate this event like the victory it is."

"Any ideas on how to begin?"

Daire grins. Although I can't see it, I can feel it in the way her energy lightens and lifts. "That's where Raven comes in."

I remain quiet, the question posed by my silence. Raven's locked in a cage, somewhere in the distance.

"Raven flies into the dark to bring forth the light."

"Another soul merge?" I ask, my voice betraying my worry. Although she hasn't mentioned it, I can feel her presence thrumming inside me. Unlike the beast, hers is a presence I cherish. She's the reason I'm here. The reason behind every breath. And while I'm grateful beyond words, I worry another attempt will leave her depleted.

"Not to worry," Daire says. "After all of this time, I finally understand what Paloma was really trying to teach me. I don't have to merge with Raven to call on the power of Raven. He guides me. He's *in* me. All I have to do is access his truth. There's an old story about Raven stealing the sun from Coyote, who was determined to keep the world shrouded in darkness. It was back in Valentina's time. She was one of the earliest Seekers, she went to great risk to document the events of her life, and she's often the one who comes to me in times of distress. Despite the centuries that separate us, my life often mirrors hers. But now, with the Richters finally gone, I'm determined to get a much happier ending than Valentina could secure for herself. It's like I owe it to both of us."

"And how does Raven fit in?"

"By realizing the underlying truth of the story. The light Raven brings forth isn't just out there, it's in here." Daire grasps my hand, presses it tightly to her chest. "Paloma always told me to use my light—claiming it's the one thing that would lead the way. At the time, I chalked it up to more woo-woo, *abuela*, Seeker-speak. I didn't really give it a whole lot of credence. But there's no denying it was my light that brought you back. And I'm hoping to use that light to illuminate the three worlds again. It's time I use my connection to the elements for something more than an outlet for grief."

She lets go of my hand, gets to her feet, and stands tall beside me. Humming the first few lines of a song under her breath, when she's interrupted by the distant clamor of footfalls.

More Richters.

Or, perhaps even demons.

Who else would charge so freely through the night?

Guess I didn't get them all like I thought.

I stand before Daire. Feet spread wide, hands clenched by my sides, as she continues her song, not missing a beat. With no place to take cover, we're completely exposed. Still I'll do whatever it takes to keep my girl safe.

I take a step forward, ready to face the threat, whatever it may turn out to be. The bit of darkness Daire failed to eradicate thrumming, stirring, enlivened by the possibility of another bout of violence, an act of revenge.

Only this time, unlike the last time, the darkness is mine to control.

I will do what's required and no more.

I won't be ruled by revenge fantasies—won't cause any more harm than is actually warranted.

The ground shakes under my feet.

A fierce wind whips through the land.

As the night sky cracks open, releasing a hard-driving rain.

And still the enemy approaches.

Daire's singing the songs of Wind—Fire—Earth—Air—the very harmonies revealed to her after surviving a series of brutal initiations during her training. But while the songs allow her to manipulate the elements—they fail to restore light to the worlds.

"Come," she says, interrupting her song. "We're stronger together."

I hesitate, reluctant to turn my back on the enemy when there's so much at stake.

"Did you actually believe what you told me?" she asks. "When you said that love is the only force more powerful than evil." Her voice is impatient, and with good reason. Still, when I hesitate, she says, "Love is the reason you're here. Love is what saved you. And that's all the proof that I need. Now I'm hoping it's strong enough to save us all. So forget about protecting us with your fists, and take hold of my hand, before it's too late."

Without hesitation, I do as she says. The two of us standing together in a wall of love and solidarity, with a whisper of hope held tight in our hearts. Waiting for either the sun to rise or the world to end.

Either way, we'll meet it together.

forty-six

Daire

It's always darkest before the dawn.

Or at least that's what I tell myself to explain away the earth rumbling under our feet, the wind lashing our bodies, and the torrent of rain pelting our heads.

If I'm the cause, if I'm the one manipulating the elements, and there's no doubt I am, why is it I only seem capable of destruction?

I grip Dace's hand tighter. Buoyed by his energy, his love, his willingness to believe in me and my ability to reverse all that's been done—all the while humming the four songs under my breath. Earth, Air, Water, Fire—songs that came at great risk. Songs that were only revealed after passing their tests.

Their lyrics connecting me to the elements, in much the same way Dace was once connected to Cade. Each depending on the other for its very existence.

The tips of my fingers begin to vibrate and thrum, and it's not long before I realize it's the result of my contact with Dace. Our combined energy making for a force that's palpable, alive.

And suddenly I understand the very truth of our existence. It wasn't just the twins who were connected—we are all connected.

Each and every one of us has a role, a duty, to sustain one another and keep the world balanced.

This is exactly what Paloma meant when she told me I never walk alone. While she was mostly referring to my ancestors and a power far greater than I—I now realize it goes so much deeper than I first realized.

Like the vision I saw in one of the very first dreams that started it all—the moment Dace kissed me and a spark of images blazed through my mind until I finally understood what it was trying to tell me—that I'm an integral part of everything—and everything is an integral part of me.

The thought filling me with so much joy, I shutter my eyes to keep from crying. Captured by the wonder of how it's possible for my heart to feel so very full when I've lost nearly everything I once held so dear.

But the truth is, I haven't lost anything.

I can feel Paloma beside me, egging me on.

I can hear Valentina whispering words of encouragement into my ear.

I can sense Django's presence all around me, telling me how proud he is of his little girl.

They're all here. Every last one of them. And we will do this together.

"Think from the end," I tell Dace. "Locate the sun in your mind, and position it high into the sky. Feel its warmth. Revel in its light. Believe in your ability to work a miracle, and merge your soul with that of the earth—the elements—the spirit animals. You have to want this with all your heart—more than you've ever wanted anything in your life. And you have to place your full intention on seeing it done. Oh, and, in addition to that, you also might want to use every bit of magick Leftfoot taught you. If we can manage it—there's no reason we can't pull this off."

My voice continues to soar; carried by the wind, it echoes through the canyon.

I sing with all I have in me.

Sing until my voice grows hoarse and scratchy.

Aware of Dace glowing beside me—his magick returning life to the earth as the harsh red rock beneath our feet gives way to a soft, squishy lawn.

I can hear Raven call; breaking free of his cage, he lands on my shoulder. His cry soon joined by Paloma's White Wolf, Django's Bear, Chay's Eagle, Valentina's Raccoon, and many more I can't immediately recognize.

All of us joined in solidarity—the desire to restore peace and balance to the worlds.

And when Dace squeezes my hand, urging me to open my eyes, I'm met with the glorious sight of a bright golden sun rising before us.

Without my even noticing, at some point during my song, the rain stopped, the earth stilled, the wind died, and dark conceded to light.

And what the night once disguised as the enemy, the light of day has revealed to be our bedraggled group of assorted friends and family.

Xotichl leads the way, as Auden and Lita flank either side, and Jennika, Chepi, and Leftfoot bring up the rear.

All of them filthy, weary, and more radiant than I've ever seen them.

forty-seven

Daire

"Django came." Jennika looks at me, her eyes wide, as though she can still hardly believe it.

"You actually saw him? As in, he manifested himself before you?" I ask.

She smiles, wraps an arm around my waist, and kisses me smack in the middle of my forehead. The move upsetting Raven, who moves from a perch on my shoulder to a nearby tree. "Unless I was hallucinating, which is entirely possible . . ."

"Don't," I say. "Don't doubt your experience. If nothing else, a few visits to Enchantment should've taught you that there's more that remains hidden than seen."

She rests her head on my shoulder and sighs. Indulging a moment of silence, before she goes on to say, "Is it possible that one of the worst nights of your life could also turn out to be one of the best?" I look at her, waiting for more, but she just shakes her head, choosing to keep the specifics to herself. "A very long story for another day. Let's just say it was an amazing reunion. Not only did Django help me to heal Leftfoot and save his life, but he also helped me to save my own. I'm finally ready, Daire. I'm finally ready to stop running and take a chance on building something that may or may not turn out to be permanent, but either way, I'm perfectly okay with it." I hug her tightly, knowing she's referring to a future with Harlan, and I couldn't be happier. I've been rooting for them since the first day I met him.

"I have so much to tell you, but it can all wait. Just know that I'm so incredibly proud of you. And while I never quite doubted you, I did fear for you."

"But that's your job, right?" I grin. "I mean, it's not like you're planning on giving that up just because I saved the three worlds from complete devastation."

"Of course not, don't be silly." She wipes a finger under my eye, removing a mascara smudge more out of habit than any real belief that it could possibly work. I'm a mess. Filthy in the way only a long hot shower could possibly remedy. Still, the fact that she even tries, makes us both laugh.

"Would you like to touch-up my lip gloss too? I'm pretty sure the last of it wore off somewhere between my seventh and eighth demon kill."

"I wouldn't even try." She laughs. "You look far more radiant than you could ever imagine. Besides, you should probably check in with your friends." She nods toward the place where Lita stands. "Lita in particular. She's not doing so well."

Without another word, I head in her direction. Pausing briefly near Dace, who's talking with Leftfoot and Chepi.

"Don't," he says, his face bearing the remorse of remembering his acts as the beast. "Please don't be so forgiving. I don't deserve it. I nearly killed you—both of you."

"But you didn't," Chepi says. "I knew you were in there. I never once doubted you."

"I did," Leftfoot says, causing Dace to look away in deep shame. "Until I saw the look in your eyes just after you cut me. The moment I saw your regret, I knew it was an accident."

My eyes meet Dace's, and while Chepi and Leftfoot are a long way from convincing him, at least it's a start.

I continue toward Lita, only a few steps yawning between us when she turns to me and says, "He left me. Just—left me. *Me.* Lita Winslow. Can you freaking believe that?"

"He must've had a good reason," I say. "Axel loves you. He wouldn't just up and leave unless there was a really good motive driving him to do it." The words come quickly, easily, though deep down inside, I'm not nearly as sure as I claim. Reminded of how Paloma warned of something like this. Said no good would come of their budding relationship. Turns out, she was right once again.

"Sure there was a reason." Lita swipes her palm across her face, collecting a handful of tears she transfers to her dress. "He probably has some shiny chick waiting in the Upperworld. Someone who bleeds gold or maybe even platinum, for all I know. Hard to compete with someone like that. Even for me."

"Doubtful." I place a hand on her shoulder, try to steer her away from self-defeating thoughts. Knowing all too well just how easy it is to get so sucked into that way of thinking, and what a chore it is to find a way out. "Lita, seriously. Anyone could see that what you two shared was real. After all, you're Axel's first love, and—"

"I didn't say he *loved* his platinum-bleeding, glowing girl. Maybe he just—" She stops, shakes her head, as though she can't bear to continue down that path. Plucking the feather from the bodice of her dress, she rolls her eyes and says, "He left me with this. I don't even know why I keep it. It's not like it worked."

She starts to toss it, but I catch it well before it can reach the ground.

"Did you make a wish?" I ask.

She nods. Swipes a hand over her eyes.

"Then don't trash it. Allow enough time for the dream to manifest." I press the feather back into her hand.

"I did. Believe me I did. I allowed all the time I can possibly spare, and now I'm officially over it. So. Totally. Over it."

"You sure about that?" I peer over her shoulder trying to make out the form in the distance.

"Did you miss the part where I said *totally*?" She sighs, swipes a finger under each eye, fluffs up her curls, and readjusts the bodice of her dress to better enhance her cleavage. Sometimes Lita wears her beauty like armor—a defense to keep people at a safe distance. But just beneath the glossy veneer is a vulnerable girl who's terrified of being revealed.

"Well, that's too bad." I shoot her a sympathetic look. "Guess it's true what they say about timing being everything. Looks like Axel arrived a few seconds too late."

At the sound of his name, she spins so fast she's like a blur of tangled hair, runny mascara, and a black silk gown with a broken strap and severely shredded hem.

But one look at Axel's face, and it's clear that to him, she's the stuff of dreams.

And it's exactly that look of sincere admiration and love that gets Lita's game back.

"So, you think you can just ride up on your dark horse like some knight in glowing armor, and I'm supposed to forget you ditched me and left me to fend for myself?"

"Lita—please." Axel slides from Horse's back, revealing the gorgeous, dark-haired girl perched right behind him.

The sight of it causing Lita to inhale a sharp breath, her eyes narrowing, hands trembling ever so slightly, she says, "Oh. Oh, I understand. I understand everything now. Well, that's just great, Axel. That's really just so nice . . . so sincere of you . . . so . . ." Her eyes fill with tears, her features crumple in the unbearable pain of his betrayal. "Whatever," she mumbles, turning her back, she starts to move away but doesn't make it very far before Axel grasps her by the arm and hugs her tightly to him.

"It had to be done." His voice is tight, face pained. "And I promise to spend the rest of my life making it up to you. But, Lita, please, you've got to believe me when I say it wasn't my choice. It had to happen this way."

Lita holds her ground, refuses to melt. "You're gonna have to do a much better job of explaining. I nearly died out there. More than once." She presses her palms to his chest, pushes him away, as Axel looks over his shoulder, pleading with the girl to step in and help.

"This is Zahra." He nods in her direction as she slides from Horse's back and moves to join us. "She's Daire's spirit guide," he adds, causing my eyes to grow wide, my throat to go dry, as I take in her swirl of dark curls, her gleaming brown skin, her unearthly irises, the same silvery/pink hue as the gown that she wears.

It makes so much sense, I don't know why I didn't see it before.

The girl who tried to stop me from fleeing the Upperworld is my spirit guide.

"Axel was never meant to be here." She stands beside him. Her stoic face and regal stature such a sharp contrast to a voice that rings soft, mellifluous, and instantly reassuring.

Though it doesn't quite work on Lita.

"So, let him go back already. I mean, I don't even know why you both bothered to come here. Clearly, that's what he wants, so why rub my nose in it?" Lita turns her back on both of them and folds her arms across her chest. Her angry stance serving as a thin disguise for her undeniable state of absolute heartbrokenness.

"I'm afraid it's too late for Axel to return," Zahra tells her, but Lita refuses to budge. "From the moment you made your wish on the eagle feather, the deal was sealed."

"What?" Lita drops the pretense, whirls on both of them. Her head jerking back and forth between Zahra and Axel. "What are you talking about? What does she mean?" She turns to me as though I might have the slightest idea of what's truly going on, but I just shrug in response. I'm as clueless as she is.

"Until the portals were opened, Axel was unable to return to the Upperworld. So, the moment he saw an opening, he seized upon it."

"You don't have to explain it to me. It's not like I didn't witness it firsthand."

"Well, you say, that, but, as it turns out, there's a little more to it. At first we all thought he was there to help. With the portals wide open, granting the Richters access, it took us a while to gather our wits and forge a proper response. Though, it wasn't long before we were able to contain them to this very space, which, to his credit, Axel helped to accomplish. But once things were more or less under control, he confided that his only reason for returning to the Upperworld was to request permission to be permanently released from his duties, his status, so he could permanently live here with you."

Lita presses a hand to her chest, centers her gaze on the toe of her severely scuffed boot.

"To be honest, I thought he was being incredibly foolish, as did most everyone else. I couldn't imagine why he would choose a life in the Middleworld with all of its inherent pain and difficulties when he could enjoy a much easier existence with us."

"And what did you say?" Lita lifts her gaze to meet Axel's, her expression guarded, though the surge of hope in her voice gives her away.

"I told her that a life that included you was well worth any difficult or painful moment that might come my way."

Lita swallows hard, blinks several times to hold back the tears, but it's no use.

"And I told him he was being utterly foolish," Zahra says, and from the look on her face, her opinion hasn't changed. "So, we came to a compromise and decided to hold him until you used that feather to wish for his return. We had to make sure you felt the same way about him as he does about you."

Lita remains where she is, her bottom lip trembling, cheeks misted with tears.

"He's given up his gifts, his magick, to be human. To be with you." Zahra watches impassively as Lita, unable to keep her emotions in check, rushes into Axel's outstretched arms. Not the least bit swayed by their reunion, Zahra shakes her head and says, "This is all fine and good now. But what you all conveniently forget is that she's only sixteen. She has no idea what she'll want in a year, never mind for the rest of her life."

"Seventeen," Lita says, burying her face in Axel's neck. "I had a birthday. I'm sorry you missed it."

"The fact is, you're young. Impressionable. With a teenager's romantic notion of love. There's a very good chance you won't always feel this way once the reality of a long life together sets in."

"Zahra—" Axel reluctantly removes himself from Lita's embrace. "I think we've already seen firsthand that none of us can predict the future. Even when the future has been predicted for us, it's subject to change. So while I thank you for granting me this wish, it's time for you to let me enjoy the beginning of my new life with my girl."

He slips an arm around Lita's shoulders and leads her away, and that's when I notice the most remarkable change I've failed to notice until now.

I mean, sure Axel's eyes have transitioned from a soft, unearthly shade of lavender to a deeper, more human shade of violet. And yes, his complexion is a lot less pale and translucent now that real human blood flows through his veins. But whereas before his movements used to cast only light, now I watch as the two of them walk together, casting individual shadows.

Zahra turns to me then, her disapproval beginning to fade. "I'm not here to claim you, if that's what you think."

"You couldn't if you tried." I fold my arms across my chest, but more out of fatigue than anything else. She may be a cynic, she may be one of the least romantic persons I've ever met, but the truth is, I can't help but like her. Mostly because she reminds me of the way I used to be before I came to Enchantment. Before I realized the value in things like friends, family, and love.

"Turns out, I'm glad you fled." She regards me with an amused gleam in her eye. "In retrospect, I can't imagine what might've become of us if you hadn't escaped."

"But would any of this have happened without my participation?" It's a question I've avoided asking myself.

"Maybe, maybe not. Though I'm inclined to think it would've happened even sooner. Which is why I spent the entire journey trying to come up with a proper way to thank you."

"Thank me?" My voice lifts with surprise. That's pretty much the last thing I was expecting.

"Gratitude is the Upperworld currency, you know."

"What exactly are you?" I say. "My guide or my fairy god-mother?"

"Today, I guess I'm a little of both." She lifts her shoulders and grins in a way that curls her lips, widens her cheeks, and makes her eyes gleam a glorious silvery/pink.

"You're serious?"

The nod that follows confirms that she is.

So I take a moment to ponder the long list of things I could ask for, then I turn to her and say, "Bring me Chay's body so I can give him a proper burial."

She shakes her head. Her tone as final as her gaze, she says, "No. Absolutely not. My intention is to grant a wish that serves *you*—not someone else."

"But that's the thing. It *is* for me. Chay was my mentor, my friend. In a lot of ways, he was like a father to me, and I let him down. If you'll just see it within you to grant me this wish, I'd feel a lot better, which would benefit me immeasurably."

"First of all, you didn't let him down. Chay died doing what he's always done best, which is helping others. While I admit, when things got hectic up here, we lost sight of all of you down there. But eventually Eagle managed to get through and alert us, and it wasn't long after when Chay's guide went down to greet him. He's in a good place now, I promise you that. They buried his body near that spring you like so much down in the Lowerworld."

"The Enchanted Spring?"

She grins. "I know it's one of your favorites. Which is one of the reasons we chose it. That way you can visit him whenever you want. Though, as I know you already know, you don't have to go there to find him . . ."

"He's a part of everything now." I allow myself a ghost of a smile. Another one of Paloma's lessons. "Though, as I recently discovered, you don't have to die in order to achieve that—we are all of us connected to everything around us."

"You're a good student," Zahra says. "And an even better Seeker. Still, there's one last thing still left to do."

I squint, having no idea what she means. The Richters are gone. The three worlds are in order. What could possibly be left undone?

She points to the tourmaline ring on my finger. "Use it to release the residents of Enchantment. We guided them home, but they're lost, confused, running on empty. As the Seeker, it's up to you to restore them to their former selves and help them find their way."

"How?"

"You'll figure it out." When she smiles, her entire being illuminates. "In the meantime, please consider my offer. And when you've decided on a wish that's entirely for you, ask Lita for the eagle feather and I promise to see that it's done. Actually, in light of all you've accomplished, I'm feeling generous. So, how about I offer a wish for each of your friends as well. But for now . . ." I look at her. "I don't mean to be rude, but it's time for you to go back to your worlds. The portals will close soon, and if you stay here much longer, you'll be staying for good. You know how to return?"

"Follow the same trail I arrived on?"

"Yes. Only now you won't find the journey nearly as treacherous."

When she turns to leave, I'm overcome with the strange sensation of loss. And before I can stop myself, I say, "Will I see you again?"

"I'll see you every day. I'm always with you, Daire. But if you can manage to stay out of trouble, I don't expect to see you in these parts again for a very long while."

I have so many things to ask her, so many puzzles to solve, but before I can get to the words, she walks a few feet away and disappears into a wondrous burst of white light.

forty-eight

Daire

It's not until we stop in the Lowerworld to pay our respects to Chay, when I decide on a wish just for me.

The thing about being a Seeker is my gifts of healing and insight are mostly geared toward helping others. When it comes to my own stuff, I'm as clueless as anyone, left to rely on a gut I'm still learning to trust.

Still, it's the only thing I can think of, and if I place the right parameters around it, it might prove to be fun.

But first I'll let my friends have a go. So after asking Lita for the feather, I hold it before me and relay everything Zahra told me.

"Trust me," Lita says, happily nestled in the shelter of Axel's arms. "This is an opportunity you won't want to waste. That feather is magick."

In a sign of respect for the elders, who have given so much, I offer it first to Leftfoot, but he's quick to decline. Claiming he has everything he could every possibly want now that he's lived long enough to see Enchantment liberated from the Richters' hold, he passes it to Chepi, who clutches it in both hands, closes her eyes, and says, "I wish for my son to find peace and forgiveness for what he's done." Her gaze centers on Dace as he squeezes my hand.

Jennika's next, wishing to never lose sight of the things Django taught her. Then she hands it to Axel, who turns to Lita and says, "My wish is standing right here beside me."

Xotichl is next, and we watch as she pinches the quill between her fingers and takes a moment to settle her gaze on each of us, pausing as though trying to memorize our individual features. "I wish to be returned to the way I was before I first came to the Lowerworld," she says.

"Xotichl!" Lita gasps. "You only get one shot—how could you—"

"It's okay." Xotichl shrugs. "Really. Most of you have known me forever, which means you should know that I don't need my sight in order to *see*. Especially when I see far better without it. True vision doesn't depend on the eyes. I guess I always knew that in theory, but now I know it for real."

She leans into Auden, and he slips an arm around her, whispers into her ear. So visibly moved by her wish, he needs a moment before he can voice his. "With the Richters dead, we're probably in the clear, but just in case, I'm asking for Xotichl and me to be released from that contract Luther had me sign. I want to go back to playing local clubs with Epitaph and become successful the old-fashioned way—because we earn it and our music merits it—not because I traded my soul for fortune and fame."

Xotichl squints at him, her eyes filled with tears, as Auden pulls her tightly to his chest and drops a kiss onto her forehead, and we all turn away, allowing them a moment of privacy.

When it's Dace's turn, he simply says, "I want the same thing I've wanted since the day Daire Lyons Santos stepped into my life."

And when he returns the feather to me, I hold it tightly and say, "I want a glimpse into the future. I want to see one good thing I can cling to if things should ever turn bad again."

Dace squeezes my shoulder as I close my eyes and wait, trusting the vision will appear in my head, but it's Valentina's laughter I hear instead.

Open your eyes, she urges, so I do.

I snap my eyes open, and suddenly I'm looking at an image of me, but I'm no longer in the Lowerworld. I'm in . . . *a sick bed?*

But I said one good thing!

Keep looking, she tells me.

I'm sweaty.

Clammy.

Pale in some places, flushed in others.

My hair much shorter than it is now, barely reaching my shoulders.

There are faint traces of lines fanning my eyes, a slim gold band on my left ring finger, and I seem to be in some sort of distress. Or maybe I'm just exhausted, it's hard to tell.

One thing's for sure—I should've known better.

Should've never asked for a peek into the future.

I never allowed myself that kind of indulgence before, so why risk it now? Just because the Richters are dead doesn't mean this will end any better.

I mean, what's next? A vision of the Bone Keeper and her sinister skirt of snakes flaying my flesh and collecting their bounty?

Daire, please, Valentina says. *Have I ever let you down?*

Well, there were times you failed to show . . . but now I realize you were always standing by, letting me find my own way.

Which is what I'm doing now. Keep watching . . .

I switch from doubt and anxiety to the scene unfolding before me, and that's when I see it.

That's when I begin to understand what's really occurring.

And before I can do anything to stop it, my face is streaming with tears at the sight of Dace standing before me, his hair cropped short, his body lean and muscular, his features a bit more angular than they are now, but he's still as devastatingly handsome as ever, if not more so for all that we've been through together. And standing right beside him is a young woman I instinctively recognize as a midwife I trained, placing a newborn baby in each of his arms.

Twins!

And they're ours?

You're a doctor of holistic health. Dace is the mayor of Enchantment. And this is your family—a boy and a girl.

Enjoy your "something to cling to." Valentina laughs, circling her arms around me and embracing me with such an abundance of unconditional love I nearly fold under the weight of it. The two of us watching the future fade. And when it's no more than a memory, she vanishes with it, leaving me sobbing before my family and friends.

"I really hope those are tears of joy," Lita says.

I nod. Swipe the back of my hand across my cheeks and confirm that they are.

"Are you going to tell us what you saw?" Xotichl asks.

"And spoil the surprise?" I sniff, shake my head, still captured by the wonder of it. "No way." I grin. "But someday, I promise, you'll see for yourself." I wrap my arms around my waist, hardly able to contain the surge of happiness and joy streaming within. Unable to recall a time when I've felt so content, I return to the present, the life that I've made, the wonderful people gathered around me, and place the feather on top of Chay's grave.

When it's done, Leftfoot looks at us and says, "I think it's time we head home."

Everyone mumbles their agreement and starts to follow his lead, except for Dace and me, who continue to linger.

"Aren't you coming?" Jennika peers at me with red-rimmed eyes, her hair falling in soft messy waves around her dirt-smudged features. Her filthy, torn clothes a testament to all that she risked to support me.

"Go home. Get some rest." I move in for a hug. Hoping to

convey just how much I appreciate all that she's sacrificed on my behalf, not just today but pretty much every day since she brought me into the world. "Dace and I are going to stick around for a bit. We'll catch up later."

She nods. Traces a finger over each cheek and tucks my hair back behind my ears. "Be safe." She lifts the buckskin pouch from her neck and loops it around mine.

"Django's Bear." I finger the drawstring, about to retrieve it and give it to her. "Do you want it? As a way to remember?"

"I don't need it." She grins. "I made my wish. It's as good as done."

Dace and I stand together, watching as Leftfoot leads them away. Then Dace pulls me into his arms, kisses the very tip of my nose, and says, "So, now that they're gone, will you tell me?"

"Tell you what?" I tilt my head, lift my gaze to meet his, knowing exactly what he's referring to but enjoying the tease.

"C'mon, just a hint?" He presses a kiss on my forehead, my cheek, before settling onto my lips.

"And wreck the surprise? No way!" My lips merge with his in a kiss that's soft and affectionate at first, though it's not long before it deepens into an urgent need for more.

Despite my exhaustion, despite knowing firsthand what they mean when they say *bone tired*, here, in Dace's arms, I'm teeming with an overwhelming sense of triumph and aliveness. Finally realizing—really, truly realizing—the enormity of what we pulled off.

The full extent of our victory so much bigger than putting a stop to Coyote.

By working together, we thwarted a prophecy.

Only this time in a way that undeniably eradicates evil and celebrates good.

The world spared because of our capacity to love, even when it wasn't easy to do.

Dace pulls away, leaving my lips cold in his absence. "Shall we?" He motions toward the spring. Its misty bubbling waters seeming to beckon.

"I think we've earned it, don't you?"

He grins, his icy-blue eyes finding mine, reflecting my image thousands of times. "You look exactly as I envisioned you that day at the cave."

I cock my head, at first not sure what he's getting at.

"When I came to you in your vision quest and described the beautiful, radiant woman you would someday become if you could just hang in there."

"I remember," I say, voice thick with the memory.

"You made it, Daire."

"We both made it," I say.

"It's like coming full circle. This is where it all began in the dream we both shared. Only this time, with the Richters gone, the ending is ours to determine."

We shed our clothes quickly and step in. The waters rising to our waists until we grasp each other's hand and immerse ourselves completely, only to emerge newly healed and refreshed.

I move toward him, clasp my hands at the back of his neck, and pull him down to me. My fingers stroking the soft spot at the nape of his neck, my tongue seeking his. At first wondering what it is that makes this kiss so different from all the others that came before, but when he cups his hands to either side of my face and gazes deeply into my eyes, I instantly realize that the one ingredient that was always lacking until now is the certainty that Dace and I have a future together.

A future far lovelier than I ever allowed myself to imagine.

"Are we happy?"

I angle my face toward his, not quite sure what he means.

"In the future. In the vision you saw. Are we happy?"

I nod.

"As happy as we are now?"

I grin, snaking my fingers over the curve of his shoulders,

across the tautness of his chest, where I pause on the key before moving down the valley of his abdomen, and then lower still. "That depends," I grin. "How happy would you say you are now?"

His features soften. His gaze grows blunted. "Very," he breathes. "Extremely happy. And you?" His fingers do their own exploring as he leads me out of the water and onto the soft bed of grass, where we lie side by side staring contentedly at the glorious, turquoise-blue sky draped overhead.

"You know, I never believed you until now." I turn, prop myself onto my elbow, and rest my head on my hand. "The first time you told me, I thought for sure it was just another one of Leftfoot's stories. But as it turns out, I never should've doubted you. It wasn't a fable at all."

"What're you talking about?" He trails a finger across the ledge of my collarbone, then toys with the small golden key that hangs between my breasts.

"That." I watch as he lifts his chin, follows the tip of my pointing finger to the blazing ball of sun overhead. "There really is a sun in the Lowerworld. Who knew?"

He throws his head back and laughs, the sound deep and true. "I knew," he says, anchoring his leg over mine and pulling me close. "I never doubted any of Leftfoot's stories, no matter how crazy they might've seemed at the time."

He runs a palm down my side, tracing the curves and valleys of my torso. His touch so intoxicating I instantly melt, though it's nothing compared to the sensation of his lips following the very same path set by his hands.

I cup my hands to his cheeks and pull him back to me. The look we share saying more than any words could. The past is behind us, the future sprawling ahead. But what matters most is this very moment. So we immerse ourselves in the present and the absolute wonder of being together.

"So what should we do about our gifts?" Dace asks, the two of us catching our breath after another round of loving. Fielding my look of confusion, he says, "You know, our magick? Seems wrong to let it slide just because we accomplished what we set out to do. And yet it seems kind of lazy to use it for mundane tasks like tidying up the house and locating the remote."

I cock my head, feign a look of deep contemplation. "That's exactly how I planned to use mine. Do you have any idea how many people wish they could manage a household so easily?"

He plants a kiss on the top of my head, gets to his feet, and helps me to stand. Raising an open palm before him, he says, "Well, if you insist . . ." Summoning my tattered red gown, as I collect what remains of his tux, which, at this point is reduced to a pair of fancy black cutoffs and a torn and stained undershirt.

"Don't we look ravishing." I shake my head at the spectacle as I pull a nearly shredded strap over my shoulder.

"You always look ravishing to me," he says. "Question is, do you look ravishing in the future?"

I playfully swat him on the rear. "You'll just have to stick around long enough to find out."

I adjust the plunging neckline of my dress, feeling overly exposed under the brightly shining sun, when the blue tourmaline ring falls from the pocket and I'm instantly reminded of Zahra's instructions.

"What do we do with it?" Dace stoops to retrieve it and places it in the center of my outstretched palm.

"Zahra told me to use it to release all of the others, though what she failed to say was how I'm supposed to go about that."

Dace shoots me a worried look, and at first I start to feel worried too. But then I remember how I used the ring earlier to accidentally start the fire that ultimately saved me from being mauled by Coyote. And thinking it might work again, I angle it high toward the sun, centering the stone until it's absorbing the light.

"You might want to shield your eyes," I warn. "Just in case. It's only a hunch, but it's all I've got."

A moment later, the stone and the band surrounding it become so hot I'm about to drop it when it bursts into a million shards of glitter and dust that spill at our feet.

"Well, I guess it's safe to say that stone's obliterated," I say, the two of us staring at the mess. "Still, we won't know what became of the others until we return to Enchantment."

"Maybe sooner . . ." Dace scoops a hand into his pocket, coming away with a palm filled with tourmaline shards and dripping blue ink. "This is what remains of the pen Luther gave Auden after signing the contract. Auden gave it to me, asked me to try to find a way to dispose of it. Guess I just did."

"So, it stands to reason that the other tourmalines are destroyed as well? I mean, there were a lot of tourmalines out there . . ."

"It's the logical conclusion," Dace says. "And, for now, it's all we've got to go on."

"Since when has anything in Enchantment ever been even remotely logical?" I watch as he tries to wipe the ink onto his pant leg, but, for the most part, it's too late. His palm will be blue for a week.

"It's a new day." He abandons the task and grasps my hand with his clean one. "Which means there's a whole new town for us to discover."

"You make it sound so exciting." I lean against him, overcome by an inexplicable reluctance to leave.

"That's because it *is* exciting. Except maybe for you." He tips his finger under my chin, tilts my face toward his. "What gives? You nervous about heading back?"

"A little." I shrug. "Guess I've gotten so used to the evil Enchantment, I'm not sure I'm ready for the new and improved version. Not to mention how the only real challenge I now face is getting through senior year. How can that ever compare to saving three worlds? Do you think I might've peaked too soon?"

"I think you've only just begun." He drops a kiss on my cheek, helps me onto Horse's back, and we begin the journey back to the portal, with Horse intuitively leading the way and Raven riding high on my shoulder.

It's a ride we've made countless times in a similar fashion but never with quite so much fanfare as now.

All around us animals pop out of shrubs, caves, and elaborate tunnels they've carved deep into the earth, calling to us in their various ways, as we make our way to the vortex.

"You ready?" Dace slides free of Horse's back and I do the same.

Stopping just shy of the place where the vibration is higher, the energy moving quicker, I take a long moment to look all around, knowing I'll be back many times, but still wanting to memorize this place the way it looks now. Then after bidding good-bye to Raven and Horse, Dace clasps my hand in his and we step through together. The two of us spiraling up through the earth, side by side, only to find this particular portal leads to the Rabbit Hole—though the formerly bleak desert landscape is gone.

"It's weird to see it so empty." It's the first thing I say as we enter the deserted club. "With the instruments still on the stage and the tables full of bottles and glasses, it looks eerie, almost like it's been evacuated."

"In a way, it was," Dace says. "But surely this is not the first time you've seen it that way?" His lips curl at the corner, his eyes flash on mine, and it takes a moment to get the reference.

"So you did know?"

He nods.

"And still you let me go?"

He squints, swipes a hand over his chin. "Wasn't easy. It took every bit of my strength not to go after you. Luckily, there was still a small a part of me that managed to cling. And it was that part that insisted on sparing you. Besides, it was fun watching Raven breach the Coyote lair right under Leandro's clueless nose."

We walk past the plush banquettes, the extra-long bar with the gleaming countertop and sparkly snake suspended overhead. Its glass mosaic tiles flashing, blinking, appearing as though the serpent is slithering, which instantly reminds me of Marliz's tattoo.

She's finally free. Free of Gabe—free of the Richters' hold—free to live her own life, her own way. Perhaps she'll even make it out of Enchantment, find a place to settle and rebuild her life. Or at least that's what I hope.

"What will become of all this?" I turn to Dace, steering my thoughts away from Marliz and back to more practical matters. "You're the last remaining Richter, which makes you the sole heir. What will you do if it all becomes yours?"

Dace looks all around. "I can't even wrap my head around the prospect of owning all this."

"But what if you do end up with it?" I study him closely, my eyes roaming his smooth brow, his perfectly chiseled cheekbones, the sheen of stubble that covers his jaw.

"Seems a shame to waste it. A lot of money was spent on the rebuild, and you have to admit they did a nice job . . ." There's a sheepish look in his eye, as though seeking permission to claim what's rightfully his. Both of us knowing this has always been a place of bad energy and worse deeds, and the black onyx they used guarantees that the energy stays. Though what if we can turn that around? While it's true that energy never dies, it can be transformed. "Besides," he says, "Enchantment is sorely in need of a place to hang out."

"Fine," I say. "Keep it. I won't try to stop you. But only on one condition . . ." I narrow my gaze on his. "You have to promise you'll get rid of all the Coyote insignia."

"And replace it with Raven?" His brow quirks, his lip tugs at the side.

"Works for me!" I grin, leaning into him as he wraps his arms around me and hugs me tightly to him.

"Ready?" He pauses before the door.

"As ready as I'll ever be." I take a deep breath and shield my eyes as he leads me into the daylight, where the sun is already noon-high. And while it's definitely warm out, it's not nearly as hot as it was before all this started. Hopefully, this marks the start of a cooling trend.

We take a quick detour to check on the chain-link fence where I placed the small golden lock as a symbol of our love last Christmas Eve—both of us amazed and relieved to see it still there. With everything that happened, with everything working against us, our love managed to survive.

And when he leads me to his newly restored Mustang, I can't help but gasp. "Wow. Lita and Xotichl told me about it, but it's a whole other thing to see it in person. It looks amazing!"

"A gift from Leandro," Dace says, helping me into my seat before sliding behind the wheel. "I should probably get rid of it. You know, bad energy and all . . ."

I shrug. "I think you should keep it. And not just because it's gorgeous, which it is, but because if we set our sights on trying to erase every trace of Leandro and Coyote in general, well, then we won't have time for anything else. For better or worse, they founded this town. Now it's our job to make something of it so it truly lives up to its name."

The engine roars to life with a single turn of the key, as opposed to the three to four turns it required before, and I settle into the ride and stare out the passenger window. Taking in deeply rutted dirt roads, the scraggly line of run-down adobes, the majestic Sangre de Cristo mountain range rising beyond. Musing at how it all looks a little better, a little sunnier, or maybe that's just the way it looks to me, knowing what I now know.

"It's funny." I swivel toward Dace. "I guess I never really noticed until now, but the horizon in Enchantment appears just as inaccessible as it does in the Upper- and Lowerworlds."

Dace looks at me, places a hand on my knee, and gives it a squeeze. "That's the thing about the horizon. Every step leads you toward it, but you can never quite reach it. But maybe that's a good thing? Maybe it's nature's way of reminding us to never give up—to always keep striving."

kindred

epilogue

six months later

Daire

I wake to the sound of banging in the kitchen and the scent of something burning seeping under the door.

All the signs indicating it's Sunday.

Lita is at it again.

"Is that what I think?" Dace rolls toward me, grabs me at the waist, and pulls me tightly to his chest as he nestles his chin at the nape of my neck. His body so warm and inviting, I'm just rolling over to face him, when the banging stops, the oven door slams, and a long string of curses begins.

I try to stifle my laughter, but it's no use. My giggling is so contagious it's not long before Dace joins in and we're forced to laugh into the pillows until we quiet down.

"She's determined to perfect those muffins," Dace says. "And I don't know about you, but my stomach can't survive another go of pretending to enjoy them. I'm pretty sure muffins aren't supposed to be charred on the outside and soggy in the middle."

"Tell it to Axel. He claims to love them. Says they're the best he's ever had."

"And just how many muffins do you think Axel had up there in the Upperworld? While I didn't really get the chance to explore,

I seem to remember there being a distinct lack of bakeries in those parts."

"You make a good point." I strive for a sober expression and the tone to match, but the sounds of Lita cussing out the muffin pan is impossible to ignore, and it's all I can do to not burst out laughing again.

"Besides, what Axel loves is Lita, not muffins. And that's just one of the side effects of love." Dace's lips find mine.

"So, what you're saying is that love makes you delusional?" I kiss him back. A real kiss. Not one of those playful nips meant to tease.

He grins, moving my lips along with his. "In Axel's case, definitely." His finger slips down the length of my neck and onto my chest where it settles at the small golden key that lies between my breasts. "What do you say we get out of town and go out to breakfast?" He pinches the metal between his finger and thumb. "My treat."

With the way his body moves against mine, I was positive he was about to instigate another kind of treat. But now that he's mentioned it, I realize I really am famished. "Well, if it's your treat . . . how can I resist?"

"Went over the numbers last night. Looks like the Rabbit Hole's making a pretty nice profit. Funny how people are even freer with their time and money when you pay them a fair wage and allow them to live their own brand of happy." He shoots me a sardonic smile, runs a hand along the dip of my waist, the curve of my hip.

"Who would've thought?" I kiss him on the cheek, untangle myself from the sheets, and slip out of bed. Pulling on some jeans and a sweater as Dace does the same, I reach for the soft buckskin pouch I left on the nightstand and loop it around my neck, as I study the framed picture of Jennika and Harlan's Malibu wedding, which I've placed beside the photos of Django, Paloma, and Chay.

"I thought Lita would never leave L.A." Dace moves to my side.

"I thought she'd wear that bridesmaid dress every day." I smile at the memory. What a fun day that was, and I'm thankful we were all able to make the trip together.

"What do you say we make this a group thing?" Dace slips an arm around my waist, hugs me tightly to him. "It's been a while since we all got together."

"Not counting last Friday, at school?" I lift my gaze to meet his—still gorgeous, still icy-blue banded by flecks of bronze, still reflecting my image thousands of times. Funny how I still find myself checking, even though the dark days are well behind us. I never have to worry about the beast resurfacing again.

"What happens in the Milagro High cafeteria doesn't count. Besides, Auden wasn't there. And now that he's back in town I was thinking we could head over to our favorite blue-corn pancake place. Been ages since we were last there. Might be nice to go some-place where nobody knows us."

"Sounds good to me," I say. "Between juggling school, home-work, and a full load of clients in need of healings, I'm starting to feel a little hemmed in. Can't even remember our last visit to the Lowerworld."

"It was last week." Dace grins. "And I'm more than happy to give you a replay of exactly what occurred there." He takes me in his arms and walks me backward toward the bed, until I place my hands on his chest and push him away.

"Rain check. And trust me, I will hold you to it. But first you have to make good on your promise to feed me."

We head for the kitchen, finding Lita leaning against the coun-ter, arms folded before her, scowling at the muffin pan as though it's the enemy, as Axel attempts to eat one.

"Stop—put the muffin down and back away!" I say, using my magick to propel the offending pastry from Axel's hand and straight into the garbage disposal, where it belongs. "Turns out, we're taking a field trip. And the best part is, Dace is picking up the tab."

After a short wait, the hostess leads us to a table big enough to accommodate a party of six. And since we already know what we want, we're quick to place our orders, which allows Dace and Auden to fall back into the same conversation they've been having for weeks. The never-ending negotiation over which days Epitaph is free to book a gig at the Rabbit Hole.

"I truly believe I should get an exclusive," Dace says.

"I know you do." Auden laughs. "Never thought I'd have to apologize for the way Epitaph is taking off." He looks at Xotichl and smiles, and the way she returns the grin I know she can *see* it as well as she could when she had her sight.

"But you are still playing the Christmas party, right?" Lita looks between them. "You do know the Christmas party has always been a big thing for me. And since it's our last year of high school and all, and possibly my last Christmas party—"

"Your last Christmas party? Seriously?" Xotichl laughs. "Wow, this is a much bigger milestone than I realized. Secret Santa just won't be the same without you rigging it to make sure you get yourself."

"Xotichl!" Lita nods toward Axel, slides a warning finger across her throat, knowing Xotichl can sense it. "Like I would ever do such a thing." She shakes her head, does her best to look offended.

"Oh, you definitely would," Axel says. "But don't worry, it's just one more thing I love about you."

"Gross." I roll my eyes, take a sip of my water.

"Ew." Xotichl frowns.

As Auden groans into his napkin and says, "I think I'm speaking for all of us when I ask: Is there an expiration date on your love-fest?"

"I certainly hope not." Lita leans into Axel, making exaggerated smacking sounds and kissing his cheek until we're all laughing and begging her to stop.

"So as I was saying . . ." Auden clears his throat loudly, attempting to divert their attention away from each other. "To answer your question, yes. It's tradition. Epitaph wouldn't dream of missing your Christmas party."

Lita grins, and pulling away from Axel, she says, "Did you see what I did there? I made you uncomfortable with an exaggerated public display of affection just so you'd agree to play the Christmas party. Works every time!" She claps her hands and turns to Dace and me. "Speaking of the holidays, are you guys staying here or heading to L.A. to visit Jennika and Harlan?"

"Haven't decided." I shrug. "Honestly, I'm just trying to get through the semester. Not to mention that big, fat pile of college applications that need my attention."

"Sing it," Xotichl says, fingering the rim of her juice glass.

"Oh, please," Lita huffs. "What could you possibly know about our angst and suffering? You've already been granted early acceptance into your first school of choice."

Xotichl shrugs, not nearly as impressed with her accomplishment as the rest of us.

"She's sad about leaving Enchantment just when things finally got good." Auden squeezes her hand.

"Well, you're not leaving yet," Lita says. "And it's not like it won't always be here for you to come visit. And let's not forget, we have Daire to thank for that. So, here's to eradicating evil and saving our town!" She raises her orange juice high, and we all follow suit. Our assorted glasses and coffee mugs clinking together. "Though, I have to say it just won't feel like Christmas without all the evil and demons and creepy Coyotes and the sky burning fire." Lita laughs. And we're all so happy and giddy from being together with a long and promising future sprawling before us, we toast to that as well.

Going through a whole series of toasts that grow sillier by the minute, until the server drops off our plates, and Xotichl squeals, "They look even better than I remember. They glow purple! It's a shame you guys can't see it in the way I do because they are truly glorious. This is clearly a chef who loves her job."

"And what color are Lita's muffins?" Dace asks, getting us all laughing again.

"Last I saw they were a deep charcoal black," Auden quips.

"Maybe to you guys, but to me they glow the color of sincere effort."

"Aw, thanks, flower." Lita grins.

"But that doesn't mean I'm willing to eat them," Xotichl quips.

"And thank you for that as well." Lita stabs her fork into her stack, and we all follow suit.

The six of us eating in a happy, contented silence, when Dace calls for the waitress to refill his coffee, and I follow his gaze to see a bleached-blond ponytail with half-inch dark roots swinging over a shoulder.

The move oddly familiar, and yet I can't place it.

Can't make sense of the overwhelming dread it elicits.

It's not until she wipes a hand over the front of her apron and tightens her grip on the coffeepot she wields in her hand that I'm able to place her. The elaborate snake tattoo that winds up her arm serves to confirm it.

"Marliz," I whisper her name, as she turns on me with a frosty gaze. Not nearly as surprised to see us as we are to see her. "I haven't seen you since . . ."

"Since you killed my fiancé."

She lifts her free hand to her hair, pushes her bangs from her face. Revealing eyes that look tired, rimmed with fatigue. Though her cheeks appear fuller, her complexion flushed and radiant. And while I'm tempted to explain that, technically, it was Dace who killed her fiancé, not me, the hateful glare in her gaze tells me there's no point in quibbling.

"With Gabe gone, I had no reason to stick around, so I left. Didn't get very far, not like that time I went to L.A. with your mom. Still, I managed to make it out of Enchantment for a whole five months and counting." Her lips lift a bit, but the grin is as tight, perfunctory, and frigid as her delivery.

"You could still go back to L.A.," I tell her. "Jennika's there. She's living in Malibu now. Married to Harlan. I'm sure they'd be willing to help you get settled."

She does an exaggerated shake of her head, causing her ponytail to sway from side to side. "No thanks. I did my time in LaLa Land. Turns out New Mexico's a much better match. Besides, it's not just me anymore. I have my son to consider." She lowers a hand to her belly, and that's when I see it.

That's when we all see it.

The unmistakable bulge straining the seams of her apron.

"Seven months," she says with a triumphant grin, as though she's been waiting for this very day. "Looks like a part of Gabe lives on." She reaches into the neck of her apron and reveals a long gold chain she arranges to hang down her front. The tourmaline engagement ring Gabe gave her now worn like a pendant, resting precisely at the place where her belly begins to swell with his child.

"So, coffee?" She waves her pot as her gaze moves among us, but we're so shocked by the sight of her, Dace can barely eke out a *no*, while I can hardly manage a shake of my head.

My pulse pounding, mind reeling, vision blurring, until my entire world shrinks down to one chilling fact: Another Richter is about to enter the world.

It's the kind of blow I never considered.

I was so sure we got every last one of them—and yet the evidence is right there before me in the form of Marliz's protruding belly, along with the only tourmaline that managed to survive.

I struggle to keep my breath even. Fight to steady myself. Only vaguely aware of Dace fumbling under the table in search of my hand, as I lift my gaze to meet Marliz's. The gleam in her eyes signaling just how much she's enjoyed the reveal—taking great pleasure in upending our world.

She turns on her heel, starts to move away. Then glancing over her shoulder as though it's an afterthought, she says, "Be sure to give my regards to Enchantment." Her lips tilt in a sardonic grin. "Funny how often I find myself missing it. As soon as Gabe Junior's old enough to truly appreciate it, I plan to return. And don't worry, I'll be sure to look you up when I do."

meet alyson noël's *the soul seekers*

and step into an intoxicating new love story that will steal your heart away

alyson noël
#1 *New York Times* Bestselling
Author of the immortals

fated
the soul seekers

BOOK 1

alyson noël
#1 *New York Times* Bestselling
Author of the immortals

echo
the soul seekers

BOOK 2

mystic
the soul seekers

alyson noël
#1 *New York Times* Bestselling
Author of the immortals

BOOK 3

horizon
the soul seekers

alyson noël
#1 *New York Times* Bestselling
Author of the immortals

Available
Fall 2013

BOOK 4

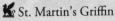